The Fall of America

Book 2 – Fatal Encounters

WR Benton

LOOSE CANNON ENTERPRISES
Paradise, CA

Ingram Edition
ISBN 978-1-944476-56-4

Edited by: Daniel Williams &Bobbie La Cour

Author photos, © 2012 Melanie C. Benton
Cover design and layout © 2014 by DancingFoxPublishing.com
all rights reserved.
Cover Photo: Shutterstock.com used with permission
Logo fonts [*Shortcut, Dirty Ego*] by Eduardo Recife, misprintedtype.com

www.loose-cannon.com

Books by W.R. Benton

War Paint

Fur Seekers (Co-authored with Grady Clark)

Red Runs the Plain

The Fall of America, Book 1, Premonition of Death

Jake Masters, Bounty Hunter

Nate Grisham, Black Mountain Man (Co-authored with Grady Clark)

Nate Grisham, Renegade Trapper (Co-authored with Grady Clark)

The Youngest Mountain Man

Missouri in Flames

War Paint

James McKay, U. S. Army Scout

Blood Money

Hell Comes To Dixie

Alive and Alone (Young Adult)

Simple Survival, a Family Outdoors Guide (Non-Fiction)

Impending Disasters (Non-Fiction)

Bubba's Dawg Might be a Redneck (Southern Humor)

Adrift

W.R. Benton
The Best in Post-Apocalyptic

DEDICATION

To Gunny MzTrouble Stitch, James Smithson, Bob Allen, Chick Jones, Zilka M Bodon, Tom Croswell, and MaryAnn Hall, good friends on Facebook and good people.

A special dedication to Jo Ella Baker Glenn, Gayle Medders Hadaway, and Susie Walton, three caring women who are always there when I need someone to listen.

A Note from the Author

Many folks who read *"Fall of America: Premonition of Death"* asked why I had shotguns as the primary weapons used by the main characters. There are a number of reasons, but the principal one is the cost of assault rifles versus shoguns. Additionally, the most commonly found long gun in American homes today is a shotgun. Shotgun empties can easily be reloaded quickly and at a much cheaper cost and ease than rifle shells. The shotgun has choke and every single time you pull the trigger, you create a cone of fire filled with lead, with different types of chokes controlling your spread. Anyone hit within the pattern of fire will feel the shot, although it may not kill your adversary, depending on shot placement and distance, along with other factors. Shotguns can also fire lead slugs, which many folks have used historically to hunt deer. Slugs have fair accuracy, but nothing like a rifle. Additionally, since I prep for survival, it just makes good horse sense to me to stick to the more commonly found weapons, because if push comes to shove, the most common ammo found following a collapse will be for these weapons. Also, a shotgun can be sawed off, which is hard to beat in clearing rooms or in close contact with an enemy.

If a fall or collapse does happen in the future, most of us will be stuck with what we have on hand, so we'll either die or survive with what we own, can steal, or take from the dead hands of our enemies. I suspect military weapons will quickly make an appearance, but only after folks have gathered together and organized to fight for freedom. I suspect, little by little, weapons will change as they're taken along with ammunition, following raids, killings, and hijacked truck convoys.

There were also some doubts a man would cry over the death of his dog and then viciously maim a man for life during an interrogation. I happen to be a man that loves my dogs dearly, which I cannot say about many people I've met. I strongly suspect, when the end comes, folks will love their pets even more than now, because animals give us unconditional love and ask nothing in return and love will be hard to find. Actually, simple kindness will disappear. Interrogations will be crude and bloody affairs and don't think they won't be. When lives may depend on information gathered, and quickly, the means will justify the end. Human life will be of little value, but knowledge of what a potential enemy may have planned will be great wealth. I, for one, will do what it takes to get information needed to protect myself and family.

WR Benton
Jackson, Mississippi

Table of Contents

"The government is merely a servant – merely a temporary
servant; it cannot be its prerogative to determine what is right
and what is wrong, and decide who is a patriot and who isn't.
Its function is to obey orders, not originate them."

—Mark Twain

BOOK 2

FATAL ENCOUNTERS

CHAPTER 1

John was glad the prisoner exchange had gone fairly well, but they'd lost Colonel Parker, and picked up a large group of civilians, which would hinder the group more than help in most cases. It meant more mouths to feed, and it's harder to hide a large group in the woods or their movements on a trail. Both feeding and hiding them were serious problems now. If Willy assumed command, which John was sure he would, then he'd release the people they'd saved. He just hoped they'd be smart enough not to return to the same location the Russians had originally captured them in. They'd weed through them and keep those with prior military training and those with medical experience. The rest would be released and sadly, have to fend for themselves.

John had a few wounded with him; most were still bleeding, because they'd not stopped to properly treat their wounds. The most serious were left behind for the medical folks and the ones with him were walking wounded. They treated themselves as they walked. John prayed the med techs would find the injured before the Russians did, or they'd be murdered in cold blood.

No one was sure of the number of dead, but he was heartbroken by the thought his wife, Sandra, might have been killed. Tom had been an old buddy of his for years too, and his death would bother John more than just a little. *Slow down*, he thought, *you have no idea if they've been killed or not. If they've not been injured severely, they'll return if they're not captured. We'll know something in a couple of days, if not sooner.*

Kate dropped back beside him and said, "I don't know what you're thinking about, and really don't care, but pull your head out of your ass. You're to be watching the right side of the path and you're not doing your job worth a damn. Your dog is doing a better job than you."

"I was wondering if my wife survived the chopper attack is all."

Her eyes narrowed as she said, "Do it after we get back."

He nodded and then said, "Listen. Do you hear that?"

Kate suddenly commanded in a loud voice, "Off the trail and into the woods, now!"

As they ran for the relative safety of the trees John said, "It's a chopper and I suspect they're looking for us."

"Once in the trees, spread out and lay flat. No movement at all." She yelled once more, and all could hear the "*wop-wop*" of the chopper blades growing louder.

John moved into the trees and lay flat on the short grasses that covered the area, Dolly lay beside him and her even breathing was comforting. He hoped the tree limbs would hide them. Then his mind switched quickly to Kate and her earlier comments. *She's right, and I should be paying more attention. These folks have never been soldiers, so I need to keep a clear mind*, he thought. John switched the safety off on his AK-47 and waited. He'd picked the weapon up after attacking an air base some months back.

The chopper twisted and turned as it flew in a lazy box pattern, looking for any movement on the ground below them. John grew anxious and tense, but there was nothing he could do but wait. When he glanced at Kate, she smiled and winked; he felt it was done to give him confidence, not as a flirt. She'd been flirting with him for months.

Suddenly, one of the rescued men on the right stood and started running through the trees. John suspected the stress of hiding was too much for him to bare any longer. When he'd traveled about fifty yards, a machine gun in the chopper gave a loud *tat, tat, tat,* and dirt flew high all around the man.

The man turned and opened fire with his pistol, which was really a wasted gesture as the machine gun coughed a few times and the man screamed, as his body flew apart. When his head separated from his torso, John suspected the crew would not land to check him over. He was a confirmed kill for the crew and hopefully they'd move on, looking for other easy targets.

Everyone could hear a woman crying from near where the man had been hidden, but John was absolutely sure the man was blown to pieces. Knowing the chopper crew couldn't hear him, he yelled out, "Stop the crying. Remain as quiet as you can." Crying, regardless if it came from a wounded person, or a wife full of grief, got on the nerves of others. If others lost their nerve and ran, they'd not get far either.

The crew didn't land, and after about ten minutes they flew on. John stood, flipped the safety back on, and hung his weapon over his shoulder. "Kate," he called out, "check the man and let me know his condition."

She moved forward cautiously, as if she expected the chopper to return. Ten minutes later she neared and said with a flat voice, "He's dead. I stripped him of his weapon, ammo, and anything else he had on him of importance, which wasn't much."

"Get us moving again and pick up the pace. As you move, listen for aircraft." He turned to his dog, "Come, Dolly."

As she turned Kate replied, "Will do."

The remainder of the trip to the base camp was uneventful, yet stressful for all. They'd expected the chopper to return any minute, but the one attack was all they experienced. John heard some gunfire off in the distance but let it go, because he had too many inexperienced folks with him to even think of attempting to help someone else.

Just a short distance from base camp, he stopped the group and sent Kate forward to check the place out. John wanted to make sure it was safe, because they'd stirred up a complete hornets nest by returning the mutilated Russian officers, and revenge would be swift. While he'd not agreed with Parker's decision to remove a body part each time Russian troops killed Americans, he'd been the commander and his decision was law. John had hardened over the last few years and honestly couldn't say what he would've done in Parker's shoes.

Kate quickly returned and said, "Looks fine. Our guards are still in place, people are coming and going from the main building, so I think things are safe enough."

"I'll enter alone, just to make sure. If it's clear, I'll wave you in. Willy wants us to break up into small numbers, no larger than ten people, because he's expecting the hunt to get hotter. We'll wait here for him to return and then find out if he still wants to do that."

"Okay, sounds good to me. I'll hold these people back and wait for you to wave. What about the dog?"

"Dolly, stay with Kate." He commanded and the big German Shepherd sat, looking at Kate.

He moved forward slowly, searching for anything out of place. It was very possible the Russians may have taken the place over and then dressed their folks to look like part of the resistance. He'd know as soon as he could speak with one. *There's a guard on the left, about fifty feet*, he thought, and slipped his safety off.

He neared the man and when he turned to see John, he smiled and asked, "Ya the last of the bunch? We have few of y'all already, but from the stories we heard, we lost a lot of folks."

Obviously he'd seen the two inch yellow material still tied around John's sleeve. He knew the guard was American by his Southern accent. He was thin, like most of them, which was a good sign. John still approached him carefully, because his trust in others wasn't what it once was. It could be he was a redneck working for the Russians, so he'd take no chances until he checked the whole place and satisfied his concerns.

"Y'all have any problems while we were gone?" John asked.

"None, but did have a chopper fly over, oh, 'bout an hour ago."

"Do you think the bird saw anything?"

"No, we were well hidden and if they'd seen anything, I think we'd have taken a few rockets from 'em, to tell ya the truth."

"I need to enter, any problem with that?"

"None, have at 'er. You'll find the same folks ya left here and nothin' has changed, but yer a cautious man and I respect that."

He walked across the compound and into the building. Things were just as he'd last seen them and he recognized many faces. John walked back to the guard, waved his hand, and then said, "Small group coming in, so relax when you see them."

"Yer an army man, because of the way ya checked this place out. I'm James, but called Bubba, and spent a few years in the army myself, but it was a long time ago."

"I was airborne."

"Me too, until I got out. I started to stay in, but got out and went to school on the G.I. Bill."

John glanced at Bubba and guessed him on the high side of his fifties, lean, dressed in a mix of different kinds of clothing, and carrying a 12 gauge pump, with a 9 mm at his waist. He looked to be an easy enough going man, but it remained to be seen if he had any sand in his craw.

The group followed Kate past Bubba and into the building, but Dolly walked to John's side.

"Is Colonel Williams back yet?"

"Yep, but the last I saw he was calling some of the brass into a room for a meeting. It's the same meeting room Colonel Parker used."

"I need to get there, then."

"Good luck in the coming days; it's goin' to turn ugly, real ugly."

When he neared the room, a guard outside the door said, "Go on in, John, the meeting hasn't started yet."

"Thanks, Fred."

Dolly and John entered, he took a chair, while she laid beside him on the hardwood floor.

Willy was standing in front and when John entered, he'd nodded at him, and then waited. Once seated the Colonel said, "Our mission was a success and our losses low; well, lower than expected. Since Colonel Parker was killed, I've taken command. The Russian's will increase the tempo now and we can expect retribution to be brutal, fast, and with few prisoners taken. We have embarrassed the great Russian bear and he's pissed."

"Are we to still break into small squad sizes and move into the countryside?" A man we all called Lew asked. Lew was short for his given name, Lewis.

"Yep, but we're going to assign folks based on skills to individual units. That means your current teams may be changed a great deal or maybe not at all. I've made an effort to get a medic and sniper assigned to each group, but that may not be possible."

"What about Tom and Sandra?" John asked, and then continued, "Any word on them?"

Willy grinned and said, "The last word I had, which was on the trail moving this way, is both survived, but sustained injuries. Neither was injured severely, so relax. Over the next few days, we'll have more and more folks returning. Some are with injured folks, so they'll naturally move slowly, and others are making a few surprises for our Russian friends."

Thank God she's safe, John thought, and then smiled.

"Surprises?" Hudson asked. Hudson was a big man, well over six feet tall, 200 pounds, and wore his brown hair long, both on his face and head. John imagined during peaceful times he'd been well over 300 pounds, but food was scarce these days.

Willy smiled and replied, "Prior to the prisoner exchange some of our ammo folks removed the powder from some Russian bullets and replaced it with C-4, which will kill anyone who fires the round. I'm not sure how powerful a blast we'll get from one cartridge, but the brass was filled to the top. If we happen to injure or kill more than the shooter, so much the better. Additionally, cases of Russian grenades had the delay settings changed. Instead of the typical 3.8 second delay they use, they will now detonate instantly. This stuff has been placed on or near dead, and severely wounded Russians."

John said, "So, you think they'll do like all military units and collect all the gear from the dead and wounded, that still looks serviceable, for future use, huh?"

"That's what we hope, because that was the idea behind the modified equipment. It has to be rough for the Russians to support their combat units this far from home, so anything that can be picked up from a battlefield that looks good will likely be kept.

But, let me continue. See, the special units that remained behind will do this and are to booby-trap areas outside the fighting area, too. And in all directions, not just the direction we fled. I'm hoping that'll confuse them a might when they try to figure out where we've moved. That confusion will, maybe, give us some time to move."

"What kind of traps?" A small man John had seen often, but didn't know, asked.

"Toe-poppers[1], pits with sharpened stakes smeared with human waste[2], and some trip wires running across trails tied to grenades with zero delay fuses. There are more, but that gives you an idea of the measures we've taken."

"Shit," Laura Jones said, "the folks we brought back here left a trail a blind man could follow."

"Agreed, so we're moving the command center today, after we break into smaller groups. We will operate as small units, hundreds of small units, and hopefully frustrate the living hell out of the Russians."

"Do these small units have any backup if shit hits the stump?" John asked.

Shaking his head, Willy said, "No, John, you'll be on your own. We don't have a way to transport forces to a hot location in time to help anyone. We'll be scattered all over the place and it'd take too much time to gather response folks and then move to the location."

"So, we're to booby-trap when we can, hit the enemy at every chance, and then run like hell, right?" Laura asked.

"As much as possible, cause confusion, and inflict pain and death on them." Willy replied and then asked, "Any other questions?"

Silence.

---

1 *Shotgun shells or rifle bullets resting with the primers setting on nails. Pressure from body weight pushes the primer onto the nail and discharges the bullet or buckshot. It usually causes injury to legs or groin area.*

2 *Human waste matter on sharpened stakes causes severe infections and, untreated, can lead to death.*

"Okay, when you leave the compound today, make damned sure you pick up gas masks for each of your team members. We found a shit load of them when we attacked the base a while back, so they're Russian masks. Filters are limited to four per person."

Lew blinked rapidly and then asked, "Do you honestly think the Russians will turn to using poison gas?"

Willy grimaced and said, "They already have, Lew. G-2 reports poison gas being used in Newton, Mississippi, last week, with hundreds of deaths. I don't understand, not fully, why the attack occurred, but it did. Hell, there's nothing in Newton that would warrant the use of gas, unless the Russians wanted to simply run a test."

"What kind of agent was used in Newton?" Laura asked.

"Samples show a nerve agent of some type. We have some technicians working on it right now to break it down. Keep your masks available at all times." Willy looked around the room and then asked, "Anything else?"

"When do you expect our injured to return?" John asked, anxious to see Sandra and Tom.

"Our injured are expected here within the hour and your team can wait to leave if you want." He gave John a big smile, knowing he wanted to wait. He continued, "Reports indicate Tom and Sandra had injuries to their arms, but that's all I can tell you at this time, John. It was reported their wounds are minor, so relax a little. Oh, and by the way, both of them will remain on your team. Since there are no more questions, all team leaders need to take a look on the wall just outside the door, to see if you'll lose or gain members. Dismissed."

Leaving the room, John noticed his team was unchanged, with the exception Kate was now officially his sniper. Sandra was their medic, so they were good to go in his view, and they'd picked up two new people. He walked to the community bathroom and scrubbed the camouflage paint from his face, ears, and arms. He'd wait to shower or bathe once relocated. More than likely, he'd end up washing in a stream, but that was fine with him.

He sat in the sun and watched the teams leaving, wondering how many of them would be alive a month from now. Few, if any, would be taken prisoner, especially if the Russians suspected them of being involved in the prisoner exchange goat roping. As Willy had pointed out months back, the Russians are brutal and vicious in war so we'd give no quarter and expect none in return. He looked down at the gas masks and filters thinking, *I hope we never run into gas. It's some nasty shit and it's very likely folks will start dropping and dying before we even realize it's around us.*

He heard a noise and glancing toward the sound, saw a group entering the compound packing a number of litters and injured. He spotted Tom first and then Sandra, who were walking and looking exhausted, so he stood and called out to them. Sandra ran into his arms and after smothering him in kisses she said, "Took some shrapnel in the fleshy part of my upper left arm."

"And, you?" He asked looking at Tom.

"Bullet burned a line almost the whole length of my right arm. We lost the machine gun, but we're both here to talk about it, so all is well." Tom said and extended his right hand.

As they shook, John said, "We've broken into teams or cells. We keep Kate, and have two new members, John Carr and Margie Lawder. John and Margie are getting us some supplies and ammo. I have a gas mask here for each of us and four filters. Seems the Russians gassed the town of Newton, so we can expect them to keep using the gas if they feel they can gain something using it."

It was then he noticed Margie and John returning with their hands full of boxes, so he said, "We need to give them a hand."

They soon had the boxes on the ground and Carr said, "Most of it's ammo, but we've a little of everything from C-4 to Claymore mines. The rations are mostly Russian, but there are a few MRE's in the box, too."

"What did you do in the army?" John asked.

"Infantry for a while, then communications. Call me Jay, as I don't answer to John much these days."

"Jay it is then." John then introduced everyone.

Margie said, "I was able to get my hands on some brass wire, a spool of parachute cord, and some fish hooks. I'm retired Air Force, E-6, and taught survival for a few years. I also have some chemical warfare suits, but they're all large sizes."

At that point, Kate walked to the group with yet more boxes. Placing them on top of the others, she said, "One set of BDU's for each of us, all large sizes, and grenades. They're giving stuff out so they don't have to hide it later. I already have my ammo, so I'm ready to go when you are."

"Okay, let's go through this stuff, divide it up and be on our way. For those of you who do not know her, this is Kate, our sniper." John said.

John saw Jay's right eyebrow raise in surprise.

Twenty minutes later, they were moving away from the compound with Kate on point and Tom on drag. The weather was clear, with a few cotton balls of clouds to the west, but nothing that concerned them. John noticed no wind and the temperature was warm, but wasn't hot. Dolly walked at his side, as if on a casual stroll.

They were to move west, toward the Mississippi River and it was up to John, as the cell leader, to select a base camp. He was happy leaving a large group and joining a small one, because it's much easier to hide a small group and they'd be a hell of lot easier to feed. All of them had field experience, so he actually felt safer. *How long will we stay in these small cells?* he wondered, as he scanned the countryside.

He'd pulled Kate aside before they left and told her to move cross country and to avoid roads and trails. She had enough sense not to cross any open fields, so they stayed in the high brush and woods. It was slow going, but a lot safer. In his mind, safety was more important than speed.

Almost two hours before dark they stopped in some trees for the night, mainly because John liked the position and they needed some food. Sandra changed the dressing on Tom's arm, then Tom changed her bandage. Both injuries were clean and healthy looking, with no sign of infection. Sandra's wound had a bad bruise surrounding it. Pulling out two aspirin she handed them to Tom, who washed them down with tepid water from his canteen. Sandra then popped two in her mouth and pulled her canteen.

John left two guards out, Jay and Kate, and relaxed a little as he said, "Reduce all rations by half until we get to the stage we know where our next meal is coming from. And, tonight no fires to cook with, because we have no idea who we share these woods with right now. ”

Margie nodded, looked as if she was going to speak, but didn't.

“Where,” Tom asked, “do you have in mind for a camp?”

“Maybe ten miles south of Edwards. What do ya think?” He sat in the dirt and leaned back against an ancient oak. Dolly put her head in his lap and he scratched her ears.

“Hell, that's as good as any other spot. We'll just need to find a good clump of trees and make a home.”

“Are you healing okay?” John asked, and Tom knew he meant from the death of his wife, not his current injury.

“I'm healing, but it's going to take me some time. The deep pain is gone, but I still dream of her.”

John nodded, but didn't reply.

“John, does it matter which MRE you get?” Sandra asked.

He gave a low chuckle and replied, “Not in the least. They're all nasty cold.”

“Why don't these have a flame-less heater with them?” She asked.

“Old is why. I'm sure the shelf-life of these expired years ago, but they're all we have. I've heard some folks are eating the old C and K rations from the Second World War.”

Suddenly Jay appeared and said, “I have movement on our back trail moving in our direction.”

As everyone moved into position John said, “Jay, go get the other guard and come back here, and do the job quickly.”

CHAPTER 2

Colonel Georgy Vetrov was in the middle of a staff meeting with his officers and senior non-commissioned officers. He was speaking as he paced at the head of a table. A huge map of Mississippi was on the wall behind him. As the senior Russian officer in charge of Mississippi, he was pissed at the poor performance of his troops against a bunch of civilians and worn-out prior military members. Vetrov was short, only five inches above five feet, not an ounce of fat on his muscular frame, and on the high side of his forties. His salt and pepper hair was worn short and he wore no facial hair at all. It was his cold gray eyes that most people noticed first, because he didn't just look at others, his eyes penetrated to their very soul. He had a reputation as a man who accomplished anything with nothing, but for some reason his promotions had been slow.

"I cannot tolerate our miserable performance and changes must happen, and now!" He yelled as he thought, *if I can squash resistance in this sector, I am sure for the star I deserve. I will not be kept from my promotion to general due to pathetic actions by my men.*

"Sir, we need more men, more supplies, and, of course, more aircraft." Major Victor Abdulov said as he glanced at the papers in his hands.

The men were seated at a well worn table in a Capital building in Jackson, Mississippi, and it was cool in the room, because there was no natural gas, propane or fuel for heating. Each wore a coat and in a couple of cases, thin gloves were seen.

"Major Abdulov, is that all you can say, more, more, and more? We will work with what Moscow gives us to work with and no more. Our supply lines are stretched thin as it is now, yet you cry for more."

Abdulov said, "Sir, with all due respect—"

Slamming his open hand down on the table hard, Vetrov said, "Enough. I want to know how we can more efficiently use the men, material and supplies we have now. Work with what you have, but work smarter. There will be no more talk about getting more of anything."

Abdulov, angry, but not stupid, replied, "Yes, sir."

"Now, I want to know more about the ambush that killed some members of the resistance and the murdering of ten of our men in a convoy. Lieutenant Colonel Pankov, update me on this."

Pankov walked to the map, and using his finger, pointed to the spot where the short fight with the partisans had taken place. He cleared his throat and said, "One of our choppers caught a large group of Americans crossing a river yesterday at approximately 1400 hours. We killed fifteen and captured two. Of the dead, ten looked to be between the ages of twenty and thirty-five, while the remainder were older. None carried any identification, but the leader of the group had about a dozen cards in his pocket; all were the Ace of Spades. As you all know, the card is used by the resistance to mark their kills."

"Have the captured been turned over for interrogation?" Vetrov asked.

"One woman has; the other, a man, managed to roll from the helicopter while in flight, falling to his death. The woman is resisting, as is to be expected, but we will break her eventually."

Vetrov said, "Keep working on her. It is not likely she knows much, but every little bit of information we can gather gives us a better idea of what we are up against. Now, about the murders of my men."

"Yes, sir. Late last night, near 0200, an eight truck convoy was moving near the small town of Edwards, when it came under heavy fire delivered by Americans. Witnesses say they counted at least three heavy machine guns, detonation of two American Claymore mines, and estimated enemy strength at forty or more men. Most of our dead were killed by mines."

"Did our men keep possession of the trucks and cargo?"

Lowering his head, Pankov replied, "No, sir, they backed off to regroup and then moved into defensive positions."

"You really mean they ran, right? What was our loss in cargo?"

"The Lieutenant in charge said he lacked the manpower to retake the trucks and our loss was total. Three of the trucks were carrying drums of aviation gas and all was lost, as were all the trucks. I flew over the area this morning and all that remained were blackened frames of the vehicles. It was in a fairly open area, with the only shelter being some old buildings to the north of the highway."

Vetrov placed his hands behind his back and walked around the room thinking, *I must do something to show the Americans I will not allow attacks on my men and supplies. I need something that will shock them and make them quiver at the mere mention of my name. Fear will make them docile and more controllable. Of course, the ambush may be in retaliation of my recent poison gas attack on the small village of Newton.*

He walked to the room's only window, his hands still behind his back, and looked out. After a few minutes he said, "Lieutenant Colonel Pankov, order the lieutenant that was ambushed last night to gather up one hundred Americans. Once they are collected, I want the lieutenant to personally see that all are executed in front of the state capital building. From this day forward, for every Russian soldier that dies by the hands of an American, ten of them will be executed."

Major Abdulov said, "Sir, think about what this will do for the cause of the resistance. I think it will hurt us in the long run, because we want to win their hearts and minds. This will—"

Vetrov laughed and said, "Major, I find it funny you bring up the American motto for winning the Vietnam War, which they lost by the way, 'Win their hearts and minds.' It is all bullshit. All these people, all any people fully understand is pure terror. My order was not a question and I expect it to be carried out without comment. We must smash all armed resistance and force the people to do our will. If you cannot do your duty for mother Russia, then I will find a major that will, but only after I personally shoot you. Do you understand me, Abdulov?"

"My apologies, sir. I meant no disrespect and will faithfully carry out your orders. However, as a member of your staff, I felt it my duty to express concern."

"Your duty, as you called it, has been noted. I want no one, not a man in this room, to ever question my motives again—ever. Remember your place, Major, or you will soon discover my warning about relieving you of duty and shooting you is no idle threat."

"Yes, sir."

"Lieutenant Colonel Pankov, remain after the meeting so we may talk of another subject. The rest of you, return to your units and straighten the men up. Tell the men I want no drinking while on duty, all guards alert and awake, and any mistakes and I will have the man shot. Now, dismissed."

The men stood at attention, Vetrov waved them off, and then moved to a chair beside his intelligence officer. The colonel still stood at attention, so the commander said, "Be seated, Vlad, and let us speak about the American resistance movement a little more."

"I will answer any questions you may have, sir." Pankov said as he thought, *Watch out, he is using your first name, so the sonofabitch is going to screw you over.* He then sat in his chair.

"What do you think happened to all the men and woman who fought us at the prisoner exchange? I mean, all of the Americans have disappeared."

"No, they have not disappeared, sir, they have broken into small cells and are scattered all over the state, or returned to their home states. It's a basic tactic used by guerrillas in this type of war."

"I am well aware of the tactics used by guerrillas. At your last estimate, how many do you think belong to the resistance?" Vetrov scratched his cheek.

"The number of members in their resistance varies from a few thousand, say four or so, to most of the state population. It seems those that are not active members support them, except for a few we have bought with money or supplies. I do not trust those working for us either, because they may be gathering intelligence for the other side."

"So, they have broken into small groups, have most of the population behind them, and are creating a nightmare for my troops. What do you think would be the best method of hurting them the most? I must get control of this sector immediately."

"Do you wish an honest answer, sir?"

"But of course I do." He said, and then smiled.

No, you want the book answer, so that is what you will get from me. Killing innocent men, women and children will not stop the resistance. Unnecessary killing will only strengthen the determination of the people, he thought. Then, returning the colonel's smile, Pankov said, "The executions may work, but if it does, it will be the first time. However, we have to try something and what are a few more deaths in this hell hole of a place? Perhaps reducing the amount of food we provide the general population will help, because, how much of it goes to the men and women fighting us? Placing stricter control on all food and water may be the real answer. A hungry people are easier to control, sir."

"Perhaps by executing the people you think me cold and cruel. The executions are required, if for nothing more than to show our enemies we will make them pay dearly for every small victory they achieve."

"Fully understood, Colonel."

"Now, get Lieutenant Ivanov to start gathering up hostages. By no later than the day after tomorrow, I want them, all one hundred of them, dead. I want the front of their capital building littered with bodies and blood to run like rivers down the hill."

Knowing the conversation with his commander was finished, Pankov stood and snapped to attention.

"Dismissed Colonel; now carry out my orders."

Master Sergeant Dmitry Belonev jumped from the back of the big truck and landed on the wet pavement with a grunt. His back was hurting him again and he thought, *I will be a happy man when I retire next year and move back to the country. I grow tired of moving around the world and living out of my backpack. I miss my Alena, and a man should have a good woman at his side as he grows older.*

"Senior Sergeant, have the men break down into squads and start gathering people. If we get all one hundred here, we can return to camp quickly. But, be warned, if all are not gathered here, we will go elsewhere to look for more." The Master Sergeant ordered. He found gathering hostages distasteful, but his job was to follow orders.

"Why are we collecting people in the middle of the night?" A private asked the Senior Sergeant.

"I do not know, and it does not matter. Our orders are to collect people, and we will do as we have been told to do."

"Senior Sergeant, move the men!" Belonev yelled. The Master Sergeant was older than his men, on the high side of his forties, and had entered the Russian army at the tender age of seventeen. While he had little education, he wasn't an ignorant man, and most of his knowledge was self taught. For his age he was an excellent example of a Russian NCO, but it was his lack of formal education that prevented him from earning a warrant officer promotion. His hair was brown, with a slight suggestion of red, easily seen in sunlight, and cropped close to his skull. He was thin, except for a slight trace of a potbelly starting to form over his belt, and his uniform was always spotless. Not a short man, his frame was close to six feet; his uniform gave the impression he was much taller.

Warrant Officer Titov walked to the Master Sergeant's side and asked, "You have been in the army many years, so why do you think we are out gathering up civilians in the middle of the night?'

Titov and Belonev often shared a bottle of vodka and were friends, except when in performance of their duties, then it was all by the book. "Sir, I suspect we are gathering up hostages for a camp or execution."

"I think killing civilians would be rather stupid, do not you think?"

"When I wear this uniform, I do no thinking on my own. I simply follow orders like a good little boy. I suggest, sir, you do the same. It will keep your ass out of hot water."

Laughing Titov said, "Hell, I know you better than you realize. You are walking around thinking of your wife, Alena, and your farm. Once you are drawing a pension, your army days will be over."

"You are right, those were my thoughts, but first I have to live long enough to retire, my friend. Nonetheless, I fully intend to survive and to retire, no matter how many Americans I must gather for the commander. However, once I am home, I will make love to my wife for a solid week, eat like a starving pig, and drink myself self silly for a month. But before my dream can come true, I have to serve this last tour in this God awful country. A year is a long time to survive in combat."

"This was once the land of milk and honey, or do you not know? Just a few short years ago, Americans were the richest people on earth, with all owning big expensive cars, new homes, and making more money in a day than we earn in a month."

"That may be so, but I am still earning my money while their whole country has fallen. I just hope I am able to retire before the damned Chinese start warring with us. There are too many of them to fight in this place."

"I have heard the Chinese were warned to leave us alone or we will use tactical nuclear weapons against them."

Belonev laughed and once quiet again, he said, "So, we use a nuc and kill, let's say a million Chinese; that will not put a dent in their population. The Chinese fear no country and as Asians, I feel they cannot be trusted."

Titov said, "I had an uncle who served as a military adviser in the Korean war against the Americans. It was a long time ago, 1952, and he's dead now, but as a young boy he told me the Chinese only have one tactic in war—overrun the enemy by numbers. He claimed he once saw a thousand Koreans and Chinese attack a small American outpost, and while they won the battle, the Americans killed almost ten of them for each man they lost. It is not the smart way to fight a war."

The Master Sergeant shrugged and said, "I am tired of the army and of war. I just want a chair in my home, a bottle at my side, and my wife cooking in her kitchen."

Suddenly shots were heard, followed by an explosion. Screams for help were heard in Russian, and both men moved toward their troops.

Three Americans, one a woman, broke from the front door of a house, each tossed a grenade, and the resulting blast knocked Russian soldiers over like a huge hand slapping toys. More screams were heard, in both languages, and automatic fire was heard from across the street. The three Americans fell, one screeching and jerking, but the other two unmoving. Titov moved to the injured man screaming, pulled his pistol, and shot the him in the head.

"Men, bang on the front doors to the homes and order people out. If they do not come out, toss in a grenade. Then enter the home after the explosion and remove those still alive." Belonev ordered, hoping to control the confusion among his men. *I should be back at the base sipping on a bottle of vodka*, he thought.

Titov was walking toward the Master Sergeant when the front of his head exploded, sending brains, blood and gore in all directions. The warrant officer's body fell like a limp rag doll, jerking and twitching as his central nervous system shutdown.

"Sniper!" someone screamed.

Then at an even rate, four shots were fired and four soldiers fell, each fatally injured.

"Senior Sergeant, the sniper is in the church tower. Gather your squad and flank the position, while we keep him pinned down. Now, damn you, move!" The Master Sergeant screamed.

The Senior Sergeant took about ten steps running, then he was struck in the chest, which sprayed the ground behind him with bone and blood. He fell to the pavement, unmoving. His men continued to run.

The Master Sergeant noticed his men made it to the relative safety of the buildings across the street and then disappeared down the alleys. "Fire at the church steeple! Cover our men!" Belonev screamed.

An explosion was heard near the church and then it grew quiet. Five minutes later three soldiers started toward the sergeant.

Suspecting the sniper was long gone, or dead, the Sergeant stood and ordered, "Start collecting people and do it now!"

Minutes later the three men walked to him. A husky looking Junior Sergeant said, "The sniper was gone before we got there, and we lost six men to a mine as we entered the church. The door opened easily enough, but once the lead man was moving across the main floor it exploded. I think it was an American Claymore mine. It tore our men to pieces."

"Good job, all of you. You, Junior Sergeant Arsov, are now a Senior Sergeant and will be running a squad as soon as I can get you some replacements. I will make sure your bravery is known to the commander and have an extra ration of drink sent to you after we return. I suspect you will receive a medal for your actions."

It took the Russians almost three hours to round up the one hundred captives they wanted and it cost them ten more men in the process. Unlike when the Germans had gathered the Jews in the Second World War, the Americans did not go willingly into captivity. They resisted with tooth and nail, when they lacked guns or explosives. Most of the civilians were beaten and a few were near death when the trucks started moving once more.

At dawn, in a drizzling rain, one hundred and twenty people were pushed onto the lawn of the Mississippi Capital Building. Colonel Vetrov was discussing the round up of the hostages and the number of soldiers lost the night before. He was furious, and asked, "What in the hell can be so hard about gathering civilians?"

"Our intelligence indicated the part of town we raided was fairly passive, but we were wrong, and our men were actually dealing with part of the resistance." Pankov stated, knowing his words would bring immediate anger.

His eyes narrowed and his face grew red as Vetrov turned to his chief of intelligence and said, "I suggest you do a better job of gathering information, Colonel, or the next time I might just add you to the condemned group. I will no longer accept failure in my command. Do you understand me?"

"I understand, sir." The Colonel replied. *You arrogant sonofabitch, my father may be retired, but he has many connections still in the army. I will write him tonight.*

"Good. Lieutenant Ivanov, come to me, please."

A young officer, barely old enough to shave, neared and saluted.

"I understand you had a number of men killed while near a small town west of here, is that correct?"

"Yes, sir, ten men."

"In a few minutes the Russian army will have it's revenge, Lieutenant, and I would like to give you the honor of being in command as we do so."

Looking around, the lieutenant saw no one to command. There was a company of men surrounding the hostages, under the leadership of a Captain, a score of high ranking officers and few American civilians. Confused, he asked, "What am I to take command of, sir?"

"The execution of the Americans. I want all of them killed."

"Y . . . yes, sir." Lieutenant Ivanov said, but his mind was going a thousand miles an hour. *These people are unarmed and this is murder, but I have my orders and cannot refuse. If I refuse, I will shame my family, and there must be a reason for their deaths. I will do this, because a lieutenant does not know all reasons and cannot question an order.*

"There are three machine guns in position, so all you have to do is give the command. The gunners have already been informed."

Lieutenant Ivanov hesitated, so Vetrov added, "Simply move your men a safe distance away from the civilians and start shooting. Once the guns grow silent, have a couple of squads move through the Americans and shoot any still alive."

Knowing he had no choice, Ivanov moved to the front of the mass of people and called out, "I want all soldiers to move away from the Americans, now." He watched as his soldiers moved and once well out of danger, he stood looking at his enemy. He saw old men, children, and women. Looking closer, he spotted a small American flag held in the hand of a pregnant woman near the center front.

It was deathly quiet, except for those about to die, and he heard them praying. He didn't understand English, except for a few words, but if he had, he would have noticed they were not praying for themselves. They were praying for the preservation of their country, for unity, and that their deaths, like thousands of others, be avenged by the resistance.

They'd already made their peace with God, and were ready to die.

Vetrov said, "Lieutenant, give the order when you are ready."

Pulling his pistol from his holster, the young soldier shouted, "Fire!"

The three machine guns opened up at the same time and the gunners were excellent, firing short bursts that knocked the doomed from their feet. Bullets went through five or more bodies before striking the wall behind the people and ricocheting into the air with a loud *zing*. Ivanov saw body parts flying through the air and heard the screams of the seriously injured and dying. He closed his eyes and attempted to shut out the noise. Finally, it grew quiet.

An occasional moan or groan was heard as Lieutenant Ivanov yelled, "You men on the left, move into the people and put them out of their misery. I want none left alive. Now, move!"

Turning to Pankov, Vetrov said, "Colonel, that is the way a Russian officer obeys orders. I suspect you could learn a great deal from our young lieutenant."

"Yes, sir, I have noticed." Pankov replied as he thought, *This will eventually take you down, Colonel, and it has never work in any country I have studied. The people will now rise up in a mass to crush you, you dumb bastard. Unfortunately, it will take all of us down with you.*

CHAPTER 3

Moving forward, Jay rigged two claymore mines and placed the clackers close at hand. As a man who'd survived more than one ambush and numerous attempts on his life, it was hard to believe ten years ago he was an English high school teacher. He removed the tape holding the spoons down on his grenades and placed two at his side. Then, picking up his rifle, he flipped the safety off. He was ready, but he already felt the sharp teeth of anticipation gnawing on his stomach. Once a battle started, his anxiety always disappeared with the sound of the first shot. *It could be another cell of ours or Russians*, he thought, *and it's better to be prepared if things turn to shit.*

Dolly gave a low growl, so John said, "Easy, girl. Quiet."

The approaching group was closer now, less than a two hundred feet, and all saw they were wearing a mixture of BDU's, jeans, and other civilian clothing, which meant they were likely their own troops. Then, John spotted Lieutenant Joshua Holland in the center of the group. His point man was nearing so he called out, "That's close enough. Who are you, and why are you on our asses?"

The man froze, looked around as if he was unsure of John's position, and then replied, "We're a cell from Colonel Parker's group. I'm Sergeant Macon Brown, but who are you?"

"Who I am isn't important right now. Is that ugly man in the middle of your group Lieutenant Joshua Holland?"

The man relaxed, smiled, and then replied, "Uh-huh, that's him."

"I'm going to stand, but keep your finger away from the trigger. Right now, there are five rifles and shotguns aimed at you. Do you understand?"

"Stand, you're safe enough."

He stood, gave a big grin, and asked, "How have you been, Brown?"

Dolly sat up beside John, but remained quiet and didn't move.

"I'm livin', so I guess I'm doin' fine. The Lieutenant will be here in a few minutes."

"Son, ya need to start payin' more attention to where you're walkin'. Didn't you see any sign of our passing?"

"No, very little sign that I could tell."

Either we're good, or this boy had his head up his ass as he moved, John thought, but asked, "Why are you following us?"

Scratching his cheek, Brown said, "I was given a compass headin', and I've been followin' it the whole time." He was of average size, thin, with long brown hair and beard.

John guessed his age to be mid-twenties and he had a reputation as being sharp. *Well, somewhere along the way today he screwed up, if he didn't know we were in front of him*, he thought.

Holland was close now and the man smiled in recognition. He was tall, just over six feet, wore a nicely trimmed beard of black, and sported a crew-cut. This day he was wearing a camouflage ball cap, BDU blouse, and jeans.

"John, excuse me for not saluting, but what are ya doin' out this way?" He asked, his teeth white and even. His smile was contagious, so John smiled in return.

"Movin' to our area after the break up, and you?"

"Same. Are you headin' straight north?"

"Nope, so why don't you pass through us and go about your business? We'll be behind you for a while, then change directions."

"We can do that."

"Joshua, your point man Brown never knew we were in front of him, so either we're good or he's got his head up his ass. Usually he's pretty sharp, so I feel the need to warn you." John said in a voice just above a whisper.

Shaking his head, Holland replied, "He lost his wife during our prisoner exchange, and when I asked him about it, he said he could still do the job."

"Well, I suspect he can't do the job. You do as you wish, but I'd replace him with somebody else for a week or so."

Turning, Joshua spotted a man and said, "Hart, take our point. Brown, you slip back and walk drag a while." The Lieutenant then winked at me.

"Jay, pull the claymores and the rest of you saddle up; we'll leave after these folks pass."

Shaking John's hand, Joshua said, "Best of luck to you, John. I suspect we're in for some really hard times. Not sure, but I might move down about two miles and call it a day. We'll be gone at first light."

John nodded and said, "Watch your ass, buddy."

He turned, motioned his group forward and in a few short minutes, they were gone.

"We'll give 'em fifteen minutes, then I want Jay on point, and Margie on drag. Jay, keep your eyes open and stop if you feel something out of place. Just because they're in front of us, doesn't make us any safer." He said and then scratched Dolly's head.

"What direction?" Jay asked.

"West for a mile or so. I want to be in position before darkness catches us unprepared."

"I hear ya." Jay replied, and then stuck the mines back in his backpack.

Two hours later, they were in their night position, Claymores were in place, and John established a guard schedule. The weather was warm, but not hot, and the overhead sky was clear. Those who'd not eaten before, now had chow. He opened an entree` and placed it in front of Dolly, watching it disappear in seconds. He smiled when she turned and stuck her big head in his lap.

Sandra, who was sitting beside him grinned as she said, "She's always been a daddy's girl, but you know that, huh?"

"She loves you too, but she knows she's special to me. At times, I really miss the other dogs, especially Newt and Skillet."

"I do too, but we'd better stop the chatter, because it's hard to say who we share these woods with tonight."

She made sense, so he didn't reply. *Newt, you were such a lovable and fun dog,* he thought and then remembered Skillet. *He was huge, well over 150 pounds, and a big baby. I don't think he ever realized just how big he was, but then I remembered the day I put him down. Enough of this, you need to get some sleep.*

He pulled a blanket from his pack and was asleep in seconds.

He had no idea how long he'd been sleep, when he felt a gentle tap to his left boot. He opened his eyes and saw Jay. He leaned close, cupped his hands around John's ear and whispered, "I just heard one hell of a fight north of us. Gunfire and explosions. It was too far away to estimate distance."

His mind shifted to Holland and his group. He whispered back, "Wake another person and two on guard for the rest of the night. We can't help whoever stepped in the shit, so keep your eyes open."

John saw him nod in the moonlight, so he went back to sleep.

Dawn arrived with gray clouds moving fast overhead and it brought a threat of rain. He donned his poncho, took a sip of water from his canteen and then said, "We'll move back on our original course this morning. Now, according to Jay, a firefight took place far enough away that he heard it, but not close enough to wake any of us. If we come to the place where the fight occurred, do not touch anything and keep moving. It is very likely the bodies will have booby-traps, and keep your eyes open for mines or lines running across the trail. I don't know what we'll find, so stay alert this morning."

"Why don't we just move off a bit when we come to it?" Sandra asked.

"We may do that, but a lot depends on what I feel and see when we're there. Now, let's move. I want Tom on point and Jay on drag."

Less than an hour later, Tom stopped and motioned John forward. They could see bodies and the dead looked to be Americans, but who John couldn't tell. He pointed at Tom and drew a circle in the air. The man nodded and moved away, to return about ten minutes later.

"It looks like it's clear. As near as I can tell, they were ambushed while moving."

"Any idea who they are?"

"It was Holland's group, but the only body I got close enough to see was Brown's, the man they had on point yesterday. I spotted other bodies in the brush, but didn't want to do more than just look right now."

"Jay?"

"Yo."

"You and I will enter the kill zone and check to see what happened. We might find someone wounded, so go easy with your trigger finger. Tom, I want you and the rest to provide us security. I'm sure the killers are long gone, but they may have left some wounded that are determined to take an American to hell with 'em."

"I hear you." Tom replied, and then began positioning folks so they could cover them. Of the folks providing protection, John liked Kate the best. He'd actually seen her nail a dime at two hundred yards with her scoped rifle.

Both men immediately saw where the Russians had used a NON-50, their copy of the Claymore and many of the bodies were riddled badly. John looked around and quickly spotted where they'd been placed in trees, pointing downward, to give them a better dispersion of fragments when exploded. The dead had been walking one minute and dead the next, and it was a better death than most.

Dolly, who was walking beside him froze and was looking at something in front of her. John strained his eyes and eventually spotted a thin line stretched across the trail. He suspected, but damn sure wasn't going to check, it was a NON-100 anti-personnel mine. *I need to warn Jay not to touch anything, and to keep his eyes open for wires*, He thought.

John turned and was looking at the man, about to speak, when a loud explosion filled the air and the man flew apart from the blast. John fell to the ground and heard a loud ringing in his ears. Dust, blood and bits of flesh rained down on him as he covered his head with both hands. He knew the danger was over, but survival was his only thought. John was lucky the mine had been positioned toward Jay, so he'd missed the main force of the blast.

"Tom, keep everyone where they are!" John commanded and then stood on shaky legs. *I don't need a bunch of folks running in here and triggering more mines*, he thought.

"I hear ya."

He glanced at Jay's body, or what little remained, and from the knees up, he was blown away. He must have been close to the mine, because his jeans were smoking. He looked in the direction he'd been moving and saw two dead bodies. He moved around the trip wire in front of him, and walked forward, slowly. He encountered no more wires or pressure activated mines, and didn't find Lieutenant Holland's body. John didn't think he'd been taken prisoner, but he may have. *It's more likely he was unhurt or maybe injured and got away. It all depends on where he was when the blasts went off*, he thought as he called Dolly and moved back to his people.

Tom neared and asked, "And, Jay?"

"He triggered a NON-100 mine and we've lost him. I'm not sure, but it looks like they mined every other body or groups of bodies. The good news, maybe, is I didn't find Holland."

"I think if you circle the ambush site, Dolly will pick up his scent."

"I'd thought of that." John replied and then looking at his dog said, "Come on Dolly, we're going for a walk."

Dolly and John took their time and were about half way around the site, when she pulled him toward the right. "Tom, over here. But look for tripwires as you come, because I saw a couple behind me."

When the group arrived, Tom asked, "Any sign of blood?"

"Nope, but I'm going to take the point and have Margie pull drag. It's possible we'll find him alive and if we do, he may be a tad trigger happy. No shooting, and if you see him, call out in English."

Sandra moved to his side and said, "You be careful and don't be a hero. It's very possible the Russians know where he is and are using him as bait."

"I've considered that, too, but find it unlikely, since the ambush happened in the middle of the night. Now, I know they've got night vision goggles, but for one reason or the other, I suspect he made a clean getaway."

Tom gave him a crooked grin and said, "Assume nothing when you get near him."

"If they mine the dead, use extra caution if Joshua is seriously wounded. They may have him mined as well. None of us are explosives experts, so use some common sense, if you find him."

"Let's move and do the job now." He said, knowing there were many variables in a given situation and a man needed to consider all of them, and quickly. He'd deal with Holland, if and when they found him.

They'd covered about a quarter of a mile, when he heard Kate say, "John, look, blood on a leaf."

He stopped and he walked to her position. A fallen leaf had a slight blood stain, but it was impossible to tell if the injury was serious or not. It was dry and about the size of a dime.

"He's bleeding some." Tom said.

"Okay, we keep moving." John said and moved back into position. He suddenly heard a sharp crack of thunder and when he looked up, noticed rain clouds moving overhead. The clouds were dark gray on the outside and almost black in the center. He ignored the weather and followed Dolly.

It was almost another quarter mile before he heard her give him a low warning growl. He looked in the direction she was looking, but saw nothing. He raised a balled fist and everyone stopped moving.

John led Dolly toward the spot she'd been looking and saw the shape of a man wearing camouflage under a large pine tree. He was sitting on his butt, chin down, and knees up. He spotted a small patch of blood on his left arm and it'd been crudely bandaged. He held an M-16 in his hands and the barrel was pointing up. On Holland's black face, he noticed his eyes were open, and actually watched him blink a few times.

"Joshua, this is John, are you okay?"

"John?" He asked, and appeared confused.

"I'm a cell leader, like you, remember?"

Joshua gave a low chuckle and said, "My arm hurts, not my head. I'm in some serious pain and a bit messed up from blood loss."

"Blood loss? We didn't see but one drop of blood on the way here. By the way, Dolly saved your ass."

He gave a weak grin and then said, "I always did like her. I have three or four used bandages in the cargo pockets of my BDU's, because I didn't want to just toss them away. Ain't no need to make it easy for anyone trailing me."

"Josh, is it safe around you? I need to know before I allow anyone forward to treat you. We found mines back at the ambush site."

"Yep, it's safe, and no one followed me. I've been here for hours and ain't even heard a fly fart."

John turned and said, "Sandra, I need your help."

She neared and asked, "Safe?"

"He claims it's safe and he should know."

Sandra moved forward and squatted at Joshua's side. Opening her medical bag, she then turned her attention to the injured arm. As she worked him over, John checked out his folks and they were all alert and watching the woods. *Good bunch I have, and I hated to lose Jay,* he thought and turned to see Sandra cutting the shirt sleeve. The bullet, from what John could see, was small caliber and had passed through the meaty part of his arm. While it'd bleed like hell and hurt, it wasn't normally a killing wound, not if kept clean.

"I need to get him to a safer spot and clean the wound." She said a few minutes later, "It's got debris from his shirt and the soiled cloth bandages he used."

"I used what I had and that was my tee-shirt." Joshua said.

"I'm not complaining, just telling John what needs to be done." Sandra said.

"Tom?" John asked.

"Uh-huh?"

"Set up a perimeter as Sandra works on Holland. Keep all alert and awake."

"Not a problem." He turned and walked away.

Less than an hour later, Holland was wrapped up nice and pretty, and Sandra said, "I can't give you anything for pain yet, because we're on the move. Once we're where we'll spend the night, I'll

take care of your pain. Right now, swallow these." She handed him two pills, which John suspected were aspirin or some sort of over the counter pain reliever.

He nodded and then looking at John, smiled and said, "If you'll help me up, I'll join your group."

John moved to his side, helped him to his feet and then said, "Pull 'em in, Tom, we're moving again."

As soon as Tom neared, he took Holland from John and slipped the man's uninjured arm around his shoulder. John heard Holland say, "Damn, Tom, I had no idea ya cared so much for me."

"Try to kiss me and I'll beat your ass." Tom replied with a big grin.

"Oh, never on a first date, I'm a man of honor." Holland said and then gave a low chuckle.

It cheered John up a bit, hearing the two of them clowning around, and when he glanced at Sandra she was wearing a big smile. Gazing into his eyes, she winked.

John's mind drifted to the days just after the fall of America and the wonderful life he'd had. His first wife was a good woman, who was raped and killed while he was away from home one day. He'd gone out after the fall to horse trade some items and when he returned, discovered her bloody body. In the weeks that followed, he'd almost blown his brains out. Tom had helped him, a lot, but when someone you love deeply dies, you have to get your shit together on your own. He'd known Sandra for a while, they'd met in college, so one thing led to another, and eventually they'd gotten married. He quickly discovered a wonderful woman.

Sandra was beautiful, intelligent, hard working and a passionate lover. They'd grown very close and he missed their home and time alone. He'd often heard men say their wives were their best friends and always thought, "*bullshit*," only that was the case with the two of them. He hid nothing from her, could speak his mind openly, and neither of them had a spark of jealousy. John had lady friends, as she had men friends.

John's long dead cousin had been a clinical psychologist and he'd told him years ago, "John, jealousy comes from a man or woman who is insecure or a person who is abusive, thus controlling. Or, maybe both. It's healthy for men and women to have friends of different genders. However, once trust is broken, it's impossible to regain. Always remember that and remain faithful to your wife."

Thomas, his cousin, died when a gang of rednecks busted into his home, shot him to death with a couple of shotguns, and took his wife and daughters with them for sport. He'd heard nothing about the women since.

John missed the simple things; like cuddling up on the sofa with Sandra, glasses of wine in their hands, while relaxing and watching a good movie. Those days were long gone and he might never see them again. Alcohol, while available, was expensive, and few places still had electricity, so movies were long gone. Their lives would never be what they once were, just as the country, hopefully, would never be the same.

The insane bickering from both political parties over this bill or that bill they attempted to pass, knowing we didn't have the money to fund an outhouse, was over. America was no longer a superpower and all government was gone. Some politicians had died swinging in the wind, tied to the short end of a long rope, while others had been shot down in cold blood. A few escaped to Europe with their money, but their numbers were small, and the average American didn't care. Today people were scattered all over, formed into small tribes or quasi military units like John's, attempting simply to stay alive.

An hour before dusk they moved deep into the trees, away from the path. Tom rigged some grenades to tripwires on our trail and then placed Claymores around them. All hunkered down for the night, but John expected it to be quiet.

Holland had moved most of the day and while his pain must have been bad, John finally had to ask, "Josh, what in the hell happened?"

He looked at John, blinked back tears, and said, "We'd heard a chopper not long after we left you, after it turned dark. Since it seemed to be off in the distance, we kept moving. Brown warned me the bird might have infrared technology, but I didn't listen."

"Why not?"

"I don't really know, but guess I didn't think the Russians had developed a thermal imaging system to the point I needed to worry about it. But, I was wrong, dead wrong. I suspect they flew in a circle, picking us out by body heat, then they simply watched us, plotted out our course on a map, and then placed troops on the ground ahead of us. I'm prior service, kind of; I spent three years on active duty, as an enlisted administration puke, and maybe my ignorance got my folks killed."

"Want to tell me what happened?" John asked, knowing it would be hard for the man, but they needed the information.

CHAPTER 4

Colonel Georgy Vetrov was so mad his veins were bulging in his neck, his face was red, and he had a difficult time speaking. He glanced at the four dead men who'd been left behind, as a convoy moved on, to repair a broken down truck. All that remained were the smoking shells of two vehicles.

Seeing something in a dead man's mouth, Vetrov walked to the body and removed a playing card, the ace of spades. He grew white as he held the card and threatened to execute thousands of Americans. Pankov shook his head, while safely on the other side of a burnt truck, and thought, *You can kill as many as you wish, fool, only you will never kill their spirit. These Americans are proving to be much more than we bargained for and if we were smart, which we are not, we would leave today.*

"Major Abdulov, gather some men and track those that committed this crime. I want their heads for this, do you understand?"

The major snapped to attention and replied, "Yes, sir. How long should we look for them?"

"Until you find them, fool. I want them caught, so we can make an example of them."

"And, if we cannot find them, sir?"

"You keep looking until you find them. Do not return without the guilty ones! Stay out as long as it takes, but if you come back without them, I will have you executed along with some other fools I have in mind."

"Lieutenant Ivanov and Master Sergeant Belonev, prepare the men to leave. Sergeant, do you have a dog on this trip?"

"No, sir, they were turned over to the guards at the new internment camp."

"Go without the damned dogs, Major," Vetrov roared in anger as he walked in circles. Finally, after the major walked away, he glanced at the card in his hand and said, "They taunt me, like a child. They think they can toy with a Russian Colonel like a small baby. I will show them." He turned and yelled, "Pankov, collect forty Americans for me and do the it today. Tomorrow I want them executed at the Capital Building, just like the last ones. But, these I want decapitated. Do you hear me?"

"I hear you, sir, and will have them gathered up."

"Now, let's get back to the base and I want a staff meeting within an hour of returning. This murdering of my men must be stopped." He said, and then moved toward his staff car.

The Russians moved through the woods cautiously as they looked for tripwires, mines, or checked out sites for potential ambush. Major Abdulov suspected they'd run into something eventually, because it was the way the resistance always fought. *Colonel Vetrov is doing this all wrong. Killing the hostages will not reduce the attacks on us and even a private soldier knows this. We should be helping the people, feeding them, building medical centers and schools, not shooting them. Violence breeds violence, it is just common sense,* he thought.

"Sir, I have some tracks here, but they are not clear." A private said as he squatted in the grass.

Abdulov looked closely but saw nothing out of place. "Show me the sign."

"Sir, see where this rock has been knocked over? The soil is different texture than the other dirt beside it and if," he pointed to a limb about chest high, "you look here, you'll see a broken twig. That tells me it was done by something big, like a man or woman, not a rabbit or squirrel. They have moved this way."

"Is it enough to follow?"

"For now it is all we have to follow. I think after a few meters, the sign will become easier to read, sir."

Confused, Abdulov asked, "Why will it become easier?"

"Following most ambushes the attackers make every effort to hide their trail at first, sir. If we have no idea where they have gone, we cannot follow. Then, after a short distance, it becomes more important to them to increase their speed to get out of the kill zone. They do not want to be discovered anywhere near where the attack happened."

"Then follow the tracks, and I hope this was not done by a deer or other large animal."

The Russians had fifteen men, which included one on point and one bringing up the rear. Keeping the tracker as the second man in line, Abdulov hoped to keep the man semi-safe, but he had to be near the front to keep them on course. The Major was in the middle and the lieutenant was near the front of the group. This was done so if ambushed both leaders would not be killed, hopefully. The soldiers were well trained to follow orders, but they were not strong independent thinkers, and required strong leadership. Master Sergeant Belonev could run the men if needed, but he lacked, in Abdulov's mind, the refinement and knowledge of an officer.

There suddenly sounded a loud explosion and the man on point disappeared in a cloud of dust, smoke and fire. The noise was still echoing in the trees when Sergeant Belonev ran forward, passing the men in the group. As he ran by the tracker, he tapped the man on the shoulder, and said, "Come."

Five minutes later, they returned and Belonev said, "Mine with a tripwire across the trail, so they expected to be followed. As near as I can tell, it was one of our mines, but our point man is dead."

"Are you sure?" Abdulov asked.

"Major, you could bury what is left of the man in a shoebox, if you took the time to gather up the pieces."

Turning to a private beside him, the Major said, "Take the point, and watch for tripwires."

A few minutes later, the group began to move once more, but too slowly.

About an hour later, the major said, "We move too damned slowly. Sergeant, move forward and instruct the man to double his speed. We will never catch them at this rate."

As the Master Sergeant moved forward he thought, *You may catch something you will want to let go of quickly. I just want to live through this assignment and retire. I miss my Alena and my farm, and I'm am getting too old to run around in the woods of America looking for people. Home is all I think about these days, but I grow close to retirement, so what else is important?*

When the point man heard the sergeant nearing, he swung around, his weapon ready. He saw the NCO and lowered the barrel of his weapon. He suspected he was about to receive an ass chewing, but like most soldiers, he wanted to survive.

"Private, the Major said for you to double your speed." Belonev said.

"That is crazy. It takes time to look for mines, tripwires and ambushes. If I speed up, I cannot do the job properly."

"You have your orders, now move, or I think he will have you shot."

"All officers are fools. You do not see his ass out here, do you?"

"That is enough! Double your speed or I will arrest you for failing to follow lawful orders."

The man moved off at a faster rate and the Sergeant could hear him cursing officers, the Russian army, and America. *He is right, and I suspect if the American's left other surprises on their trail, he will soon discover one. But, he forgets he is a soldier in the best army in the world, and like all soldiers, from the beginning of time, we must follow orders. An army cannot function if orders are always questioned, he thought, and then turned to wait for the main group to move up to him.*

Close to noon they took a short break in the middle of a small open area. Rations were opened and the men tore at their food like hungry wolves. The sunshine felt good on the Sergeant's face as he checked the guards he'd posted.

The Major had just opened his beef stew and hard biscuits, when a man beside him screamed, grabbed his bloody head, and fell jerking to the grass. The echo of a single gunshot was heard.

"Medic!" Abdulov yelled.

"Sniper!" Screamed the men as they scurried for cover.

"Medic, see to the private!"

A thin man, wearing no identification ran to the downed man's side and lay down beside him.

"Did anyone see where that shot came from?" Lieutenant Ivanov asked.

"No one saw it, sir," The Sergeant replied, "because they were busy eating. Everyone stay down or you will be the next one hit."

One of the guards posted earlier by Belonev, who was laying beside a huge pine log said, "I saw movement just before the shot was fired. Look to the west and look at the largest pine, maybe fifty meters from me. The movement was about eight meters from the very top."

"Spray that tree with fire, now." The major ordered.

AK-47's spat flames and shots filled the air as pieces of the pine were seen flying in the air. The Sergeant suspected the sniper had moved right after firing the shot, but kept his mouth shut. A minute or so later Abdulov yelled, "Cease firing!"

The injured man continued to scream and kick wildly at the grasses. He was flat on his back, bleeding profusely from his head, and screaming for his mother. The man giving first aid, pulled a needle from his pack, and inserted it into a vial of medicine. Abdulov was watching as the medics head exploded, sending skin, bone, and blood high in the air. His lifeless body fell over the injured man and lay unmoving. The Major knew the medic was dead, because the top of his skull from the eyebrows up was missing.

"That shot came from the same tree, Major!" Belonev yelled.

Scared and confused, Abdulov ordered, "Lieutenant Ivanov, take three men and attempt to circle the tree. If possible, come in behind the sniper. I want that man dead!"

Ivanov pointed at three privates and said, "You three, come with me. Back into the brush slow and crawl into the trees. Once in the trees, we will kill a Yankee."

"Fire to cover the men, but single shots, now," the Sergeant commanded, knowing the Major was unable to think clearly.

AK-47 fire was sent into the tree and the sergeant knew the bullets would completely penetrate the soft wood of the pine. But snipers, he knew from experience, would kill one or two men and then run. It was very likely Ivanov and his men would find nothing.

"Cease fire!" The Major yelled after a few minutes. He wanted to move, but didn't dare stand or reveal himself in the least. The sniper was an exceptional shot, shooting twice and hitting heads both times. The first victim was now moaning and groaning; his screaming ceased.

"Watch the tree, but no firing unless you have a clear target!" the Sergeant shouted.

They heard four sharp cracks, followed by a pistol shot, saw no movement in the tree, and then a horrible scream. The gunfire had come from a distance and on the other side of the pine.

"No one move. We wait." The Major said, and then scanned the area.

A few minutes later, Ivanov walked around the tree and approached the team.

Where are the rest of his men? The Major wondered and then stood, realizing the lieutenant wouldn't be walking in the open if the threat was still around.

Ivanov appeared to be in shock as he neared and his eyes were staring off into space. The Sergeant, having more combat experience than the other men, moved forward and said, "Sir, take a drink from my canteen. It is vodka and will help." He held his drink to the young officer.

Taking a long drink from the offered canteen, Ivanov said, "The sniper is gone. When we neared the tree someone was laying in the grasses. Then, with three quick shots, I lost all my men. I shot at her as she ran into the woods."

"She?" The Major asked.

"A young girl of maybe, sixteen, sir. Each of my men was shot in the chest and dead in an instant."

"A woman did this? A woman killed five of my men?"

"Sir, I'd like to remind you," the Sergeant said, "during the Great War, many of our women snipers were credited with over three hundred kills. All women can be lethal at the right time."

"Give me the radio!"

As the major called, the lieutenant listened to part of the conversation as he sipped the strong drink.

"Reinforce me with an additional squad, a medic, and ammo." Abdulov was almost shouting into the headset as he spoke. "Now, damn it. I have orders from the Colonel to find these partisans, and I intend to complete my mission."

The voice back at base must have ended the conversation, because the major handed the radio back to the private.

"Well, sir?" Sergeant Belonev asked.

"Retrieve the bodies of the Lieutenant's men and place them near the other two. A helicopter will bring us additional men and supplies within the hour."

"You four men, come with me." The Sergeant said and then thought, *How many fights have I survived in the past? How lucky can one man stay? One day, my luck will run out.*

The rest of the day was quiet and uneventful, but slow. The new troops, brought in by helicopter, heard the story of how the men in the unit had been killed and no one wanted to be the next one. Frustration at fighting an enemy who wouldn't stay and do an open battle was making tempers short. The Sergeant had seen it all before, in many smaller nations, and his father had even told him stories of the same thing in Afghanistan. His grandfather, a survivor of the Great War, had told him of the French resistance and others who'd battled the Germans.

"Sergeant, get a defense ring placed around us. I want all guards using NVG's[3] and I am to be awakened, time permitting, and warned of any danger prior to any shooting. Send our tracker and another man to circle us, maybe a hundred meters out." Major Abdulov said.

"Yes, sir."

Once the men were in position and the scouts gone, the Sergeant took a drink of his vodka and opened a ration. He removed the chocolate and hazelnut paste, along with two biscuits. He smeared the paste on his biscuit and started eating. Supper was his only meal and he rarely ate breakfast at all, because his stomach often rejected food early in the day. Most of the time his duties caused him to miss lunch, but when available, he could eat then.

Removing a serving of beef goulash he quickly ate and then placed the empty wrappers in his backpack. He'd leave nothing behind for the Americans to find of his passing. He wanted a smoke, but knew the thought was stupid. The uncontrollable desire for tobacco, which showed a red burning tip on a cigarette, had killed more than one man or woman in wars. Besides the glowing red tip, the smoke could be smelled a long distance. *I will do without, for now, but will surly enjoy my pipe after I retire.*

The two scouts soon returned and reported of a house off in the distance. According the tracker, it could very well be where those that ambushed the trucks were hiding.

"Any lights seen at the building?" The Major asked.

"One light, which I suspect was a lamp of some sort."

"Any movement spotted inside or outside?"

"None."

The Major gave the finding some thought and then said, "Sergeant, bring our men and come with me. We will pay a visit to this house and see what we can find. I want all troops wearing NVG's."

As the tracker led the group back to the house, some of the newer men were heard complaining about the need to be out at night looking for the partisans, but Belonev silenced them with a

---

3 *Night Vision Goggles*

low verbal warning. The house sat in a clearing with what looked to have been open fields of crops, at one time, surrounding the place on three sides. A single lamp of some sort burned in one room.

The Major quickly explained his plan to the men and then said, "Let us finish quickly, so we can return to our night camp for some sleep." He then stood and started for the small farm house.

The Sergeant laughed at the Major's words in his mind, as he followed the man. Most of the men were new, on their first or second year of service, so they were wound up tighter than a cheap watch. After a fight, if there was one, they'd have a hard time going to sleep.

The men moved silently to the front door, then two moved around to cover the back door. After giving all the men enough time to move into position, the Major stood and kicked the front door in. He entered, ready to start shooting, but saw a family of four siting unmoving at a kitchen table. Their eyes were huge in surprise and he noticed a young boy with his hands together, as if they'd interrupted a prayer.

"No one move!" A private who'd been sent as a translator yelled. The family remained still.

Walking to the table, the Sergeant saw what looked like a typical family to him. There was a man, woman, two school-aged children, and an infant in the mothers arms.

As the Major spoke, the translator gave orders to the Americans, "Stand, but slowly."

"What do you want?" The man asked as he stood.

"You are not to speak, unless asked a question by the commander."

"Ivanov, check the house and do a thorough job."

As the Russian troops began to ransack the house, the man protested, "Why are you destroying my home? I have done nothing to you. I demand you stop and right now."

The Sergeant spoke very little English, except a few words he'd picked up watching American movies, but he knew by the man's tone he was protesting.

The Major slapped the American and said, "Where are the ones who attacked us?"

The translator repeated the question in English.

Giving a shrug, the American said, "I know nothing of an attack on anyone. We live here alone and manage to survive by our small garden."

"You are a liar."

"No, it is the truth. We have seen no one."

It was then a private entered the kitchen with a .22 rifle and said, "There are three boxes of ammunition for it in the bedroom."

Holding the rifle under the man's nose, the Major screamed, "What is this? Why would a farmer have need of a rifle?"

"I use it to hunt squirrels and rabbits to feed my family. I'm no partisan. I'm a farmer."

The Major raised his pistol and the shot was loud in the small structure. The bullet took the man in the face, slightly below his nose and a long string of blood flew from the back of his head, spattering crimson on the wall behind him. He fell to the floor, dead before he struck the rough wood.

Turning to the woman, who was screaming, the Major slapped her hard and asked, "Where are the rest of your members? I know your husband was involved because he had a rifle."

"H . . . he hunted, that's all. He was part of no resistance and didn't attack you. You must believe me!"

"Sergeant!"

"Sir?"

"Take all of them outside and line them up in front of the house."

The translator said, "You are to go with the sergeant."

After all had left, Lieutenant Ivanov said, "With all due respect, sir, but I think the family is telling the truth. I have read that all American's have guns in their homes. That is the main reason the Japanese did want to go to war with them during the Great War. I think this family is no threat to us."

"Guilty or not, these people will be an example to those that resist us."

Knowing if he spoke again it would lead to problems once they returned, the lieutenant wisely kept his mouth shut. He walked beside the Major as they left the house.

Abdulov heard a Russian voice scream, "The boy, stop him! Stop the boy!"

Shots filled the night air and Russian curses were heard.

Nearing the men, the Major asked, "What happened? Did one of the boys get away from us?"

Snapping to attention, a Senior Sergeant replied, "Yes, sir. As the civilians moved along the wall, the boy in front kept moving, slipped around the corner and then disappeared, running into the darkness."

Slapping the Senior Sergeant hard, the Major screamed, "Why are your night vision goggles perched on the top of your heads like fools? Did you not lower them after we left the room?"

Lowering his head, the Senior Sergeant said, "No sir, we forgot to lower them."

"Enough of your stupidity! I want these people shot and this house burned to the ground. Can you do that much without help, Senior Sergeant? If so, do it right now."

The woman, knowing death was coming to visit, was happy her son Aaron had gotten free, but she could do nothing to save herself or the other children. She began to pray aloud, "Lord, I ask you to welcome my family into your loving arms in a few minutes. It is you, Lord, our Father, that adds meaning to our lives."

"Yes, sir." The Senior Sergeant forced five privates in a line, as the woman prayed, and then said, "Ready, aim, —fire!"

The shots were loud and all victims fell to the grass—dead. It was then the infant boy began to cry. The Major, boiling in anger that the young boy got away, walked to the child, picked him up by the ankles and swung his small head against the side the house, splattering the wall with brain, bone, and blood. As the baby's body shutdown, it's small frame quivering and shaking, the Russian dropped the child to the grasses and screamed, "Why is this place not burning yet?"

CHAPTER 5

"The mines were command detonated at the perfect time, and I lost all but two people right then. I only heard one scream following the explosions and it didn't last long. Then Brown opened up with his rifle, only he didn't last but a minute or so. I heard him grunt, at least I think it was him, and a piercing scream followed. I moved into the brush, concealed myself and waited. I had two Russians walk right by me and both were wearing NVG's."

John suspected the unit would have night vision goggles and that opened his eyes to the fact they weren't as safe at night as he'd thought. He thought for a few minutes and then asked, "So when did you get wounded?"

"I gave the Russians enough time to start laying mines and such, then broke through the brush like a bull was on my ass. I heard all kinds of fire directed toward me, but it was a pistol round that put me on my ass. I got up, changed directions, and ran again. After I grew winded, I slowed and eventually stopped. I sat under the tree, and you know the rest of the story."

A light rain began to fall and everyone started removing ponchos and rain gear from their packs. While it wasn't cold, being wet would bring a chill, and even with moderate temperatures, hypothermia was a consideration. While removing his poncho, John pulled a ration and tossed it to Holland.

Catching it easily, he said, "Thanks. I lost my pack and most of my gear at the ambush site. When I thought about running, I dumped anything with any weight."

Tom, who'd remained silent asked, "What now? You're the leader of a cell, but no troops."

"Stay with you, I guess. There is no way to contact Willy Williams, so it's up to us to make a decision."

"Okay, I would be proud to add you to the team, but you'll be number four in the pecking order around here. Me, Tom, and Kate outrank you, but if you don't have a problem with that, welcome." John said.

Lowering his head, Holland replied, "I don't think I'm good enough to be a leader."

"That's bullshit, Joshua, and deep down inside you know it." John said and then added, "Ain't a leader alive today that hasn't lost people. I'd follow you and I know things happened out here we have no control over. The Russians are good soldiers and they have a technological advantage on us. Learn from it and move forward."

Tom added, "John's right, you know?"

Raising his head, Josh said, "Maybe, but I need to think on this a spell."

John said, "Tom, establish guards for the night, and I want us up and moving an hour before daylight."

The night passed uneventfully and John was well rested when he awoke. While the rain had stopped, drops still fell from the limbs of trees and the area was covered in a dense fog.

"A warm front must have collided with a cooler one." Tom said as he sharpened his knife.

"I want Kate on point this morning, because her eyes are the sharpest of the bunch. Have Margie bring up our rear."

"What about Joshua?"

"He's useless for a week, most likely. I think he'll be preoccupied most of the time, reliving the ambush."

Tom nodded.

Near noon, Kate returned, met John's eyes and whispered, "I have two Russian supply trucks and a smaller maintenance truck on a narrow macadam road, oh, maybe two hundred yards from here."

"How many men did you see?"

"I counted an even half-dozen, which means a driver and guard per truck and two mechanics."

"That's it?"

"Because of the road, I didn't circle them, but that's all I saw on this side and near the trucks. I didn't want them to see me if I crossed the road. I got a good look inside both trucks and they're carrying supplies."

"Tom?"

"Yo?"

"Take Sandra and check it out. If there are only six of them, rig a claymore to blow into the largest number of men. If they're like most soldiers, they'll be gathered near the mechanics as they work, shooting the shit. Then, once you're ready, send Sandra back and we'll move forward."

"Got it. Sandra, come with me." Tom said then started moving.

While they were gone, John pulled out a map and looked the area over closely. The road eventually met another, and continued into Jackson. It was a county road, isolated, and from the marks on my map, not near any known Russian base or outpost.

A little later, Sandra returned, smiled and said, "Tom said for you to move forward. The mine is in position and he's ready."

Turning to his folks, who were all near, he said, "Spread out and slowly move forward. Once in position, I'll give us a few minutes to get ready. If you have to toss a grenade, try like hell to avoid the trucks. We have no idea what's inside and we might need the gear. Once we shoot, run forward and overwhelm them. Any questions?" Most shook there heads, but he saw anger in Joshua's eyes. *I hope he doesn't do something stupid*, John thought, and then moved toward Tom.

When he neared Tom, he could see four of the Russians sitting on an open tailgate of a camouflaged Russian wrecker. They were drinking something from a bottle and he suspected it was vodka or alcohol of some sort. The remaining two men were standing on the front bumper of what an American soldier would call a deuce and a half truck. The hood was up and they had tools in their hands, obviously working on some part of the engine.

John gave everyone about three or four minutes to get ready. He knew some would pull extra magazines and others would remove tape holding the spoons down on their grenades. He grinned when he saw Margie attach a bayonet to her M-16. Rarely was the knife used, but if she felt a need for it, it didn't matter to him. He glanced up at the sky, saw no threat of bad weather, and meeting Tom's eyes, nodded.

Tom picked up a clacker, squeezed, and then heard a loud explosion as the Claymore fired. The Russians on the tailgate were suddenly surrounded by a red mist —their blood. Screams were heard and the men on the tailgate fell to the ground, with two jerking and twisting. The remaining two were unmoving. Screams filled the air.

At the truck, both men looked around confused, and then the sounds of rifle fire were heard. The head of the man on the left exploded, sending blood and gore in all directions. The other man dropped to the ground, went prone, and fired one round before his body suddenly went limp.

"Cease fire and move forward, now!" John yelled.

Margie moved to a Russian near the wrecker and all heard him scream as her bayonet entered his stomach. Removing the blade, she stabbed again, again, and again. Finally, she ran toward the prone man, near the trucks, her bayonet dripping crimson. John heard a shot, and Tom had fired into the other injured man near the wrecker. The Russian jerked once and then lay still.

"Tom, check the cargo in the first truck!" John yelled, as he moved for the second vehicle. He then added, "Kate, I want you about a hundred yards in front of these trucks and Sandra, you move about the same distance behind us. If you see or hear anything, let me know."

John then moved to the supplies, climbing up and into the truck. He found a case of AK-47's, rations, some winter clothing, gasoline and fresh produce. He pulled the weapons, rations, winter clothing, and produce. Once the supplies were on the side of the road, he poked holes in the cans of gas and left it leaking on the gear they didn't take.

"Joshua, crawl under each truck and poke holes in the gas tanks, slash the tires, and fill the carburetors with dirt. Margie, gather up all the weapons and gear we can use from the dead and check the inside of each truck."

Tom neared and said, "Other than Russian packs and some ponchos, with liners, most of the load in the first truck was plywood and gasoline."

"We need both the packs and ponchos. Make sure we take two extra ponchos for each person and a pack each, if our folks need a new one. Get two liners a piece for us, because when the weather turns nasty, and it will in a month, we'll be happy to have them."

John walked to the senior man, who was a sergeant, and placed an ace of spades card in his mouth. He noticed Margie had turned the pockets of each of the dead inside-out, looking for anything of use for intelligence, but it was a wasted effort. They no longer had an intelligence branch, but it was good to know she was thinking.

When Tom neared he said, "I want you to gather up our folks and these supplies. Start moving west, but I'll remain behind. Once you've been gone for about thirty minutes, I'll set these trucks on fire. Expect choppers shortly after you see the smoke. I want you to keep moving, and I'll catch up as soon as possible. Tell the drag not to shoot my ass, too."

He grinned and asked, "Are you doing this job alone?"

"I'd thought I would, why?"

Turning serious, he said, "Keep a person with you. I don't like the idea of leaving you by yourself." Then turning, he said, "Margie, get Kate and Sandra."

"Leave Joshua then. I think he did a good job during the attack, and we need to get him back in the saddle as soon as we can."

"Josh!" Tom called out.

"Here!" He replied from near the supplies.

"Stay behind with John and cover him as he torches the trucks."

"Sure." He said, and then stuffed a half dozen camouflaged Russian rations in his pack.

"Let's pick up the supplies and move, people." Tom ordered. "Margie, you take point and Kate cover our rear. Be aware that John and Joshua will join us at some point today."

Kate gave a thumb up and moved across the road, with the rest following her after a minute or so. John turned to Joshua and said, "Go across the road and try to cover all sign of their passing for fifty yards or so. It won't throw off a dog, but it might some lazy troopers."

As he left, John glanced at his watch, scanned the countryside, and then the sky. He knew eventually the dead Russians would be missed, but seriously suspected once the trucks were in flames, they'd respond. He took two grenades, pulled the pins, and held the spoons as he positioned one under the dead men by the wrecker and the other under one of the men near the trucks bumper.

When Joshua returned, he glanced at his watch again and saw it was time to start the fires. Gas covered the road and he double checked the grenades, so any explosions from the vehicles wouldn't trigger his surprises.

Turning to Joshua, he said, "Move across the road with me, in a minute. Once the flames are burning, let's move opposite of our group's heading fast. After we cover a mile or so, we'll swing north and then finally west. I know it won't throw a good tracker off for long, but it's the best we can do."

He then pulled a lighter from his pocket, ignited a Russian map he'd found in the wrecker, and then asked, "Are you ready to move?"

"Uh-huh, so have at it."

The burning map struck the pavement and a second later they heard a swoosh. Already moving, John glanced over his shoulder to see the whole road engulfed in flames. Joshua was in front of him and moving at a fast jog. They heard a loud explosion, quickly followed by two more, and glancing back, he saw a fireball rolling toward the sky. John knew once the tires and oils were burning well, thick black smoke would pinpoint the location.

For over a mile they kept the jog up, but after turning west at a small stream, John said, "Stay in the water as long as the stream is moving west. Once we leave the water, I'll stay in the rear and try to cover our trail."

Right then, they heard a jet flying low, almost right over their heads, and he'd appeared out of nowhere. John suspected at his speed they'd be almost impossible to see, unless in an open field, and they'd cross no open spaces this day. A few minutes later, they left the stream.

Keep your wits and cover your trail, John thought as he straightened bent grasses and small sticks, from where they'd stepped from the water. He could do nothing about the water dripping from their boots, and hoped if anyone got on their trail they were far enough behind the water would dry before discovery of their tracks.

After about three miles, they moved slightly south and soon came to a blacktop road.

"Jog about a mile or so down this road, crossover, and then enter the woods. Keep moving straight west. Stay under the trees and in the shadows as much as possible."

They'd covered about half the distance, when John heard a vehicle approaching from the rear. They were in a slight valley, so anyone coming from either direction would have to top a rise to see them below.

"Off the road and into the brush, now!"

Less than two minutes later a motorcycle passed, and when he glanced at Joshua, he knew not to move. *Rarely is a bike out alone and my partner knows this, too. I suspect a convoy will be right behind him,* he thought and then glanced the way the motorcycle had come.

Two motorcycles approached and behind them the two men saw a long line of big trucks. *Supplies,* John thought, *or men.* As the vehicles passed, he started counting and when he was at ten, an empty bottle flew from the rear of one truck and landed six feet away. He saw it was an empty vodka bottle. At twenty, John ran out of trucks, and saw another motorcycle riding the bumper of the last truck.

Joshua started to move when John whispered, "Wait, I'm sure they have a bike guarding their rear."

Five minutes later a couple of bikes passed and as soon as they went over a slight hill, they ran across the road. Covering their tracks was fairly easy, since it was mainly long grasses, so once the job was done John said, "Follow me. Dead west."

The convoy got John thinking about mining roads, snipers, and all kinds of things they could do to piss the Russians off. *Once we reach our location, that's what we'll start doing. If we can find small camps of the bastards, we can use Kate to take out a few of the officers. Maybe stretch some wire across the roads to knock some bikers on their asses or de-capitate one or two. Lay some mines on dirt roads and some Claymores beside the macadam ones. We can stir the pot well, with just a few of us*, he thought.

An hour before dark they'd seen no sign of the others and John was growing concerned. He'd checked the map over and over again, but was on the right path. By his guess, they should have met the others two hours back. Leaning close to Joshua, he said, "Move into the deep brush and we'll spend the night back-to-back, in the trees, for safety. Once in place, place a Claymore to-ward our trail, another in the opposite direction and lay out two grenades. We'll eat one-at-a-time after that and then sleep. One of us will be awake at all times."

"Understood."

It was about fifteen minutes before the two men were situated and moving into the trees. Finding a small clearing, well camou-flaged by trees and brush, the two men sat back-to-back. Joshua was eating when John heard a noise. He flipped the safety on his weapon to off.

Joshua dropped his meal and whispered, "Sound like jeans rubbing jeans."

Both men could hear brush being moved and the sound of feet moving over the forest floor.

"Clear your target." John whispered, unsure if Joshua heard him or not.

Sobs were heard and then someone asked, "Why? Why did they do that to us?"

Sounds like a kid, John thought, but he waited to call out. He could hear someone sniffling and crying. Finally, hoping it was a child, John asked, "We are near, and friends. Are you alone?"

"W . . . who are you?" The voice was thick with fear.

"Americans, and you?"

"The Russians killed my family."

"What is your name? I'm John, and the man with me is Joshua."

"I'm Aaron Hart."

"Are you hungry, Aaron?"

"No; my family is dead. I heard them shoot them after I ran."

"Aaron, can you be brave for me? I need you to move straight ahead for about twenty feet. Once there stop and I'll come to you."

"Y . . . you won't hurt me, will you?"

"No, son, we're your friends. I think you need friends right now, don't you?"

"I'm walkin' toward you mister, but I don't trust you."

"That's good, it means you're a smart lad. I see you now, so I'm going to stand."

John stood, moved to the boy and squatted. He asked, "How old are you Aaron?"

"I'm fourteen. Why is your face green and black?"

"I'm an American soldier, I guess."

"What am I goin' to do now? I don't have a home or family."

"John, look to the South." Joshua said from the darkness.

A flickering light that grew in size was seen, and pulsed and moved like a living thing. All knew it was Aaron's home and his family was dead.

"What now, John? Do we check the house in the morning?"

John gave the idea some thought, but said, "No, we have to meet the others. Aaron, are you hungry?"

"Not really, but I was before the Russians came to visit us."

Placing his hand on the young boy's shoulder, John said, "Come with me and you can sit with us. I have some food, so if you get hungry later let me know, okay?"

"Uh-huh." Aaron replied as he followed John.

After a few minutes, John said, "To hell with it, we'll check the house out tomorrow. I doubt we'll find any survivors, but it's possible and Aaron here, he needs to know what happened to his family."

CHAPTER 6

Major Abdulov used the radio to contact the Russian base camp and reported the death of four resistance members, without the loss of a single man. As far as he was concerned, his mission was complete, or close enough in his view. Moscow and Vetrov only lived for body counts, so numbers he could deliver. He knew no one in the unit he commanded would say a word, because like him, they wanted to return to the safety of camp. He cursed, handed the radio headset back, and said, "We have to spend the night here. So, we will sleep in the barn."

Lieutenant Ivanov didn't like the idea, but said nothing. He realized the Major didn't like suggestions, even ones that might save his ass.

"You," the Major said pointing at a private, "bring the rest of the men here. We will sleep in the barn. Sergeant Belonev!"

"Sir?"

"Throw the bodies in the fire. We must have it tidy when the helicopter arrives in the morning. I want one guard at the door to the barn, one in the loft with the door open, and another at the back at all times while we sleep, understood?"

"Yes, sir."

As he moved toward the barn, he said, "See to it now."

The Master Sergeant had the bodies thrown to the fire, except for the baby. He picked the child up, muttered a prayer under his breath, and then tossed the small body into the crackling flames. *There was no reason to kill these people. The Major is not following orders, he is trying to get on Vetrov's good side by calling in a body count. Hell, he might even be awarded a medal, all for killing a damned farmer and his family. I grow sick of this, because I've seen so much of it.*

"You feeling okay, Sergeant?" Lieutenant Ivanov asked and then continued, "We had better get to the barn before the Major comes out looking for us."

"I am fine, sir, just looking forward to my retirement."

"I would guess so, but that is a long way off for me, if I can stay alive long enough. Now, let us get to the barn." As they walked a bright line of lightning lit the sky, a loud clap of thunder sounded and looking up, the Lieutenant saw black clouds rolling. They were just a few feet from the entrance to the barn when the rains came.

Inside the barn, the men were scattered into little pockets, with the Major beside the radio operator. Belonev had passed a guard by the door on the way in and now climbed to the loft to check on the other guard. He found a private sitting on a bale of hay, back in the darkness, looking out the loft door. The man was experienced, using the shadows to help hide him.

The farm house was still in flames, clearly seen from the loft, but if the rains remained long enough, the fire would go out. Nodding to the guard, Master Sergeant Belonev left the loft, and putting on his poncho, went outside to check the guard at the rear. He discovered the man standing under a slight overhang out of the rain.

"Wet night." The guard said.

"It usually is when it rains. Keep your eyes and ears alert to anything. It is possible the men in the resistance have noticed the fire and they might come to investigate. If so, daydreaming will get your throat cut."

"I am awake and plan to stay that way all of my shift. Sergeant, I do not really understand why we are in this country."

"We are in this country because Mother Russia told us to come here. We are soldiers and as such, we do what we are told, when we are told to do it, and without question. Just do your duty, try to stay alive, and leave the politics to the politicians."

"I understand, Sergeant," the guard replied, but really didn't. Like soldiers all over the world, he was lonely, tired, hungry, sleepy and confused about why he was stationed in America. He didn't hate Americans, but didn't like them either, because he'd never spoken to one. He knew little about them and the family they'd killed were the first ones he'd seen up close. He'd seen movies about America, also read some westerns and science fiction books, but as a people, he knew little about them. He was a farm boy, just turned eighteen, and wanted to be back on the farm with his cows and chickens. The smell of the barn brought many fond memories to the forefront of his mind.

Belonev said, "Stay alert, and I will be out at odd times over night checking on all guards. If I catch you asleep, if I do not kill you, you will wish I had. I will have you working in the kitchen so long your hands will start to crack from being wet."

Snapping to attention, the guard said, "I will be awake when you visit my post, Master Sergeant."

The Sergeant grunted loudly and then returned to the barn. He moved to a dark corner, opened his pack and pulled out a ra-tion. He ate a meat with peas and carrots meal, washing it down with a concentrated tonic drink. He would save the jam, biscuit, and coffee for his breakfast. Opening his canteen, he placed a mul-tivitamin in his mouth, and swallowed a large gulp of vodka. He leaned against the wall of the barn and promptly fell sleep.

It was later, well after midnight, when Belonvev awoke to pounding and banging sounds on the tin roof of the barn. He sat up, rubbed the crusted sleep from his eyes, and then stood. Like most of the men, he walked to the rear of the structure to relieve himself. As urine flowed he groaned in satisfaction as the pressure in his bladder was reduced. *Nothing like a much needed pee to make a man feel better.*

Donning his poncho, he opened the barn door and saw the ground littered with hailstones. Some were as large as a walnut and the ground was covered with them. Between flashes of light-ning he saw the black clouds churning and twisting, but gave it lit-tle thought. The hail stopped, so he moved to the rear of the barn to check the guard. He discovered the man alert; it was not the same guard, and he was standing as close as he could to the wall of the barn, still under the overhang. It was obvious to the Sergeant, the guard was trying to avoiding the hail. *It had to be rough out here just a few minutes ago*, he thought.

"Rough night?" The Sergeant asked.

"Rough enough. I do not mind the rain, but the hail almost beat me to death."

Belonev chuckled and after he grew quiet he asked, "Seen anything at all moving?"

"No, I think anything with half a brain is in a shelter someplace, do not you?"

"Maybe, but anytime we spend the night, no matter the weather, guards will be used. That is how I lived long enough to become an old Master Sergeant, so remember my words." He then turned and returned to the shelter of the barn.

Returning to his sleeping spot, he'd just gotten comfortable when the guard at the door said, "Sergeant, come here. I see something I have never seen before."

At your age, that could be anything, the old Sergeant thought as he stood and walked for the door. When he opened the door wider, there came a bright flash of lightning, and he saw the tail of a tornado on the ground. He watched a second or so longer, and then yelled, "Everyone out of the barn and now! Now, move, we have a tornado heading right for this place!"

Confused, one young man asked, "Tornado? What is that?"

"Move, dumb-ass, or you may soon be killed by one. Ask questions later, if you are still alive." An unknown voice replied.

Remaining by the door, Belonev screamed to be heard above the roaring winds, "Move to the lowest spot you can find! Move!"

The Major ran past him and the Sergeant Major thought, *You self-centered sonofabitch, you should have been a real leader and been the last man out of this place. Typical officer, worried about his own ass first.*

A huge part of the destroyed house was picked up and thrown into three men moving toward the trees, exactly where they should not have been running for safety. In the wind, the Sergeant didn't hear the impact of the debris or screams of the men, but he knew the Major's claim of no man lost, was now a lie. He watched as one man was suddenly raised in the air while still running, his legs still pumping wildly to avoid the twister. In a few seconds the man was sucked into the black funnel and disappeared.

Master Sergeant Belonev saw all of the men were out, so moving at right angles, he moved toward a stream bank. Knowing the creek would be swollen from recent rains, it was the lowest spot he could see in the darkness. Now running as fast as he could, he prayed over and over that God would allow him to survive. He was a member of the Russian Orthodox Church and while now he rarely attended church service, as a child he had gone on a regular basis. Seeing the bank of the stream during a long flash of lightning, he jumped high and landed roughly in the water—on top of someone.

"Sorry!" He screamed to be heard but didn't get a reply.

Looking at the barn, he saw the roof wobble and then fly high into the air, and then the walls began to fly away piece by piece as well. *This sounds like a train going full speed over me*, he thought, and then pushed his forehead firmly against the muddy bank of the stream.

From beside him he heard a shriek of pain and the sound wobbled for a minute, but then turned to what sounded like choking. Scared for his own safety and knowing it would be suicidal to move toward the man, the Sergeant stayed where he was for the time being. The wind threw stones, branches and pieces of lumber from the house and barn into the air. Rain pelted them hard and the water level in the stream was quickly rising.

Then, suddenly, it was so quiet the lack of noise was loud to his ears. He knew he was in shock, but slowly he raised his head, and waited for the next flash of lightning. When it flashed, he saw four men in the stream with him, one obviously dead with a long sliver of wood in the middle of his chest. He stood and called out, "Everyone meet near where the barn used to be, now!"

After he left the water, he helped his men up the muddy bank one-by-one and then as a group, they moved for what remained of the barn. From flashes of light, all Belonev could see was a slab of concrete, and even some of it was missing, blown to where, only God knew.

As men gathered around, Lieutenant Ivanov approached and asked, "Have you seen the Major?"

"I just got here a few minutes ago, and I do not think most of the men are here yet." Lightning flashed, and the Sergeant saw blood streaming down the young officers arm, so he asked, "Are you okay, sir? I see blood."

"I took a piece of something through my arm, but have no idea what hit me. I know it hit with the force of a bullet, but that is all I know."

The radio man neared and said, "Base contacted me and said due to the weather, our pickup is on hold. Weather reports a long storm front just passed, but three more heavy lines are coming in about an hour."

Glancing at his watch, Ivanov said, "It is about an hour before dawn. We should have more men here than I see. Have half of the men break into small teams and use flashlights to see if any of our men are injured and unable to move. We must hurry, Sergeant, because we have more bad weather coming."

"Yes, sir."

A rough night was spent by John, Joshua and Aaron as the storm battered them to the point they had to crawl under trees to keep from being injured by hailstones. Joshua had an extra poncho he'd taken from the convoy ambush and gave it to the boy. When dawn arrived, water dripped from limbs and leaves, and the ground was muddy. After a quick breakfast, where the three of them shared a Russian Ration, they began moving toward the main group.

Rain fell, off and on, most of the early morning but near 10 hundred, Joshua suddenly stopped, just as a voice called out, "It took you two long enough."

"Sandra," John said, "the Russians were all over the place. No choppers were heard, but they were on the road in large numbers."

"Come with me, my dear, Tom is about to have a conniption fit worried about you two. Who is the new man?"

"Aaron, and the Russians murdered his family. They had a farm a few miles from here and I saw it burning last night."

"Well, unless they unassed the area by foot, they're still at the farm. We had a twister last night and scared the hell out of all of us. It missed us, but by less than a mile, but that was as close as I ever want to see one."

Entering the camp, John said, "We're back, did ya miss us?"

Tom chuckled and said, "By God, I did. I thought the Russians caught you."

Shrugging he replied, "No, but it grew dark early and we had to dodge a convoy of twenty trucks. Our new man is Aaron and while he's young, he's tough enough. Let me explain how we ended up with the young man."

When John finished, Tom said, "It's likely the Russians are still there."

"Aaron said he saw about twenty men, give or take a few."

Tom asked, "Aaron, did your farm have a barn or other out buildings on it?"

"We have a big barn, but it's old with an old rusted tin roof and it was made by my grandpa, or so my daddy said."

"Any animals?" Tom asked hoping for horses.

"We ate 'em a couple of years back and our pets, too."

"Are you thinking what I'm thinking?" John asked with a grin.

"Uh-huh. Aaron, if we got you back to where you met John, could you find your way home from there?"

Confused, the young man replied, "I know where I am right now and know a shortcut."

"We'll plan our attack once we see the place." John said and then added, "Saddle up, we're moving."

The walk to the farm was short, just under two hours. As Kate glassed the area, John did the same with his Russian binoculars. He said, "Looks like the tornado hit the place and I can see where the barn used to be, but it's gone. Most of the rubble from the fire is gone as well. I count ten men." He then handed the binoculars to Tom and added, "Take a close look."

The Russians, were all in a group near a fire and eating. Kate counted ten men and two were pulling guard.

Tom noticed the area around the barn, except on the south side, was bare of any cover, so they'd have to take 'em out there. One man, who he recognized as an officer, was strutting around like a big rooster and yelling orders. The man's left arm was in a sling. A man walked to him, wearing a radio on his back, and handed him a headset. He couldn't near the conversation, but that didn't matter, because Tom couldn't speak Russian anyway.

"I count seven bodies wrapped in ponchos and three more walking wounded. I'll bet they're waiting for an evacuation chopper."

John glanced at the dark sky and said, "It won't be anytime soon, because more rain is on the way. We need to move to the South and enter the woods. We'll try to take the group out by the fire with a Claymore, and Kate, you take out the guards. Once the Claymore fires, move in among them shooting. Then, if we get lucky, maybe we can snag a chopper later. Let's do this job first and see what happens."

It took them almost an hour to loop around and approach from the woods. All the while they kept listening for a chopper and John knew if a window in the weather opened, a bird would show. He leaned close to Kate and said, "If things turn to hell and a chopper appears, wait until it almost touches the ground and then take out both pilots."

She didn't reply, but gave him a big grin. He knew the idea of downing a chopper appealed to her.

The Russians, when John parted some bushes to see, were still gathered around the fire. Tom positioned the Claymore and the soldiers were less that fifty feet away. He looked at John and nodded. Taking once last look around, he check the positions of his people, saw they were spread out well and then looked at Tom. He then pointed at the man and nodded.

The explosion was loud and quickly followed by two sharp rifle shots. John knew Kate had taken the guards out as expected. They rose from the wet grasses and charged the downed Russians. Many of the downed men were dead, but three were screaming in pain. Margie ran to a major and the long sharp blade of her bayonet entered the man's soft stomach. A scream erupted, so she stabbed him again, but this time in the chest. The knife stuck, either in the ribs or the major's back, which she quickly fixed by firing a round from her rifle. His screaming instantly stopped. She pulled the bloody blade from his body, looked around and saw the other soldiers were dead.

"Tom, you and Margie check the guards. I'm sure Kate killed them, but make sure."

"You bet." Tom said as he walked toward the downed men with his rifle held at the ready.

Kate walked to him and said, "They're dead; both were head shots. I saw movement in the woods off your left side, but never found out what it was."

"It might have been a deer or rabbit." John replied.

"I don't know, because right after that, the Claymore exploded and I dropped the two men."

John walked around, looking at the dead Russians and pulled an Ace of Spades from his pocket. He squatted beside Major Abdulov and placed the card in this open mouth. He started to close the man's eyes, but then remembered the killing of Aaron's family and stood instead. Aaron had stayed back in the grasses and John figured the boy had seen enough blood in his young life anyway. There was no need to expose him to more.

Tom approached and said, "Both are dead, now what?"

"We move back in the trees and see if we can catch us a chopper. The first shot you fire, Kate, has to put the door-gunner out, or we're all dead. Then, pop pop, take out the pilot and copilot. Do you think you can do the job?" John asked.

"Honestly?"

"Uh-huh, honestly."

Kate nodded and replied, "Yes, I can fire three shots in the time it takes your heart to beat three times. Is that fast enough?"

He grinned and said, "Everyone back to the trees."

"What about the radio?"

"Take it. None of us speak the language, but we'll know when the chopper gets close, if nothing else by the background noise."

Tom stripped the radio from the back of the dead man and carrying it by the straps, moved for the trees and brush. As he waited, John shared part of his rations with Sandra.

Lieutenant Ivanov and Master Sergeant Belonev had both gone into the woods to answer the call of nature. Neither man knew of John and his group until the Claymore exploded. The wise old sergeant shook his head as he thought, *I warned the Major the men should be spread out and in holes, not sitting on their asses by a fire eating. He has paid for not listening to his senior NCO with his life and the lives of our men.*

"Did you hear that?" Ivanov whispered.

"Yes. Follow me, sir."

Moving away from the farm and toward a road he knew was south of the farm, the same road where the ambush had happened, he knew there were no survivors. His expert ears had heard the two shots immediately following the exploding mine and knew the two guards were dead. *If we can make it safely to the road, all we have to do is wait for a convoy.*

Glancing behind him, he noticed the lieutenant was too close, so he whispered, "We have to take it slowly, sir."

"Let me lead. Usually around noon a convoy drives the road and if we get there before then, we can ride home."

"Go slowly or we will never get there."

"Off to the left is a narrow trail, we can move faster on it."

"Sir, I think—"

"You heard my decision, so move to the trail."

All went well until they'd covered most of the distance and then the lieutenant walked into a tripwire John had stretched across the trail as they moved away from the ambush. There came an explosion and the young officer was blown into thousands of small pieces in the blink of an eye. Pellets were heard hitting the trees on the other side of the dead man and all that lingered in the air was a cherry-red mist. His boots were all that remained and they still contained parts of his legs and feet.

The Sergeant was too terrified to take another step forward, deep in his mind he knew the officer had moved too quickly and foolishly. He glanced in the direction he had to cover to the road and estimated it was less than a hundred meters. Slowly, he gathered his courage and moved forward, constantly searching the trail for any sign of mines.

CHAPTER 7

John listened to the Russian radio, but heard nothing. Finally, he sent Margie and Joshua out to collect weapons, ammo, other needed items. He should have done that earlier, but he was tired and not thinking clearly. They were to drag the dead into the rubble of the burned house. He wanted little seen if the Russians sent a chopper to the scene, which he suspected they would.

Joshua was the first to return to the brush and then Margie, who looked preoccupied to John. He neared her and asked, "What's on your mind?"

"As I was moving the Russian bodies, I had a thought. Why don't we put their clothing over ours, lure the chopper in and destroy it? I mean, if one of us can get close enough to the door of the bird, we can toss a grenade inside."

Tom met John's eyes, grinned and said, "I do like the thought. But, if they capture one of us in a Russian uniform, they'll kill us."

John laughed and replied, "Hell, if they catch us period, they'll kill us, so how we're dressed doesn't come into play here."

"Well?" He asked.

"What of the radio? If they call and we don't answer, they'll know something is wrong, right?"

"Look, we both know radios go out; either the batteries die or they just go kaput. We stand out in the open, let the chopper see us and when they near, I'll send a sign that the radio is out. If we're dressed as Russians, they'll have no reason to doubt us. We've both had it happen enough in the past. You guide the chopper to the ground and the rest of us will act."

John turned to Kate and said, "Hold off on your shot, until one of us get's close to the door before you take the gunner out. If we can get a grenade or two in the bird, we'll do some serious damage."

She nodded.

"Sandra, Joshua and Margie, I need the three of you to strip the dead Russians. Some of us need to stay in the trees in case the bad guys show. Then, try to hide the bodies so they can't been seen from the air. Be sure to get their boots, too."

John grew apprehensive as the small group moved forward, knowing from the air their actions would be clearly seen. The idea was sound, but he knew from past battles something could go wrong and if it did, folks would die.

"Be sure to leave the card in the Major's mouth. I want them to know who was behind this today." John yelled.

Less than an hour later, they were dressed as Russians and standing around the fire.

Tom said, "It looks to me as if the twister hit this place dead on and blew it to hell and back. Many of the bodies out there under ponchos were killed by flying debris." He threw another log on the flames.

John said, "A tornado will do that and we both have seen the damage they can do. I don't know of anything as—"

"Quiet. Do you hear that?" Tom asked.

The radio suddenly came alive with Russian chatter. None of them spoke the language and John wished Willy Williams was with them, because he spoke the language fluently.

Joshua said, "I have a chopper at the three o'clock position and it looks to be some sort of gunship. Slightly to the left, is a second bird."

"Ignore the second aircraft, but Sandra, since you're wearing the radio, come to me and I'll act as if I am talking. Maybe, if we work this right, all will go well." Tom said, and he was dressed in the dead major's uniform. He then turned the radio off.

Pointing to the north, Margie said, "The other chopper is now at our twelve o'clock position. We'll be hearing it in a few seconds."

Seconds later the *wop-wop* sound of blades beating the air to death were heard and Tom said, "John, you move into the wind and prepare to lower the chopper with your rifle. The rest of you line up beside me. Look sharp and keep your eyes open. Any movement by the door gunner and Kate will smoke his ass. Margie, since this idea is yours, you have the honor of tossing the first grenade. Joshua, you'll be next, so toss a grenade, too. Now, don't put too much muscle behind the toss or the damned thing will go out the other side, if both doors are open or removed. Once the grenades are tossed, move your asses, because when they explode I suspect the whole bird will go up."

Aaron, who'd refused to not play a part, was dressed in the smallest Russian uniform they could find. John didn't like using him, but as Tom said, "The boy has an ax to grind with the Russians, so let him participate, too."

The chopper made a straight approach, flying about fifty feet over the ground and all the partisans waved. The bird then circled a few times and the small group kept waving. Finally, Tom began to point at the radio and shrug, with his hands held out palms up, so the helicopter pilot would suspect the radio was not working. When the chopper went into a hover, about fifty feet up and a hundred feet away, Tom pointed at the radio and shook his head. The other aircraft was flying circles off in the distance.

John raise his rifle over his head using both hands, unsure how Russian troops lowered a bird, but it was the only way he'd been taught. The pilot met his eyes and nodded. As John slowly lowered his rifle in front of him, the chopper started to descend.

Tom noticed only one door was open and the door gunner was watching every move, ready to open fire any second. When the aircraft touched the grass, the gunner motioned for them to board, so the line moved forward. The barrel of the machine gun swung away from the group and the gunners attention was focused to the trees on the south side.

Margie, who'd already pulled the pin on her grenade, as had Joshua, moved forward. When she was about three feet from the door, the gunner must have noticed something out of place, because the barrel on the machine gun began to move. Suddenly, as

Margie watched the man, his head exploded, sending gore in all directions. Margie tossed her grenade inside the helicopter, turned to the right and started running. The second grenade landed a split second after hers and the whole line scattered and began to shoot at the aircraft as they fled to the trees. The plexiglass windshield exploded as a shot from Kate killed the pilot flying in the left seat. The bird wobbled a few times as the co-pilot took over the controls. John, moving toward the trees was blown off his feet as the aircraft exploded into a ball of flames.

"Move people!" Tom screamed as the helicopter fell in a huge ball of fire to the ground.

Secondary explosions were immediately heard.

John stood and ran for the trees, where his dog waited, but glanced over his shoulder to see the second aircraft lining up to attack. "Spread out, spread out!" he yelled, knowing the gunship would be looking for blood.

The attacking aircraft flew a straight approach, with it's guns spitting flames. The ground in the trees erupted into mini-explosions as the rounds struck, sending dirt, dust and clumps of soil six feet into the air. The noise was loud, from both the engines of the chopper and the cannons firing.

No sooner had the aircraft passed overhead than John yelled, "Move deeper into the trees! Missiles will be next! Move and scatter!"

On the next pass, the aircraft lined up and two puffs of smoke were seen as missiles were fired. The area they'd just left exploded, but the small group kept running. As the chopper passed off to the side, John saw two bullet holes suddenly appear near the cockpit. Kate is shooting. *She needs to lead the bird a little more*, he thought as he increased his speed.

As the Russian aircraft suddenly broke left and broke off the attack, Tom said, "It's smokin' a little. I think Kate may have hit an engine or something."

All eyes were on the chopper as the smoke grew from light gray to a dark gray.

"Keep moving!" Tom commanded.

"What about Kate?" Sandra asked.

"She'll catch up with us."

John, his eyes on the sky as he ran said, "The chopper is leaving."

"Don't stop, and I'll explain later." Tom said, "Keep running."

They'd covered maybe a hundred yards when Joshua yelled, "Airplane!"

"Run!" Tom yelled in fear, because he knew what would happen next.

The aircraft, obviously not concerned about small arms fire, made a straight approach toward the woods. If anyone running had looked over their shoulder, they would have seen a container fall from the jet, spinning as it fell. It hit the ground with a loud *swoosh* and flames filled the edge of the treeline.

Tom, running faster now, called out, "Move at right angles behind me! **Now!**"

Margie's lungs were about to explode and then she realized the napalm had sucked a lot of air into the exploding flames. She ran in a mechanical fashion now, knowing to slow down meant to burn to death or suffocate.

It was well over a half mile before Tom quit running and said, "Five . . . minute . . . rest."

Gasping and wheezing, the small group came to a complete stop. John smiled when he noticed all of them turned to guard their flanks as they rested.

A couple of minutes later, John said, "This line of trees will turn north in a few minutes and so will we. Before we stop for the day, I want to be twenty miles or more away from this farm."

John was on drag when he spotted movement behind them. He stepped behind a tree and waited. A couple of minutes later, Kate walked up the back trail. He waited until she was almost in front of him and then said, "Welcome back, Kate."

She swung the rifle in his direction, but immediately lowered the barrel. "John, you just scared ten years off my life."

He gave a low chuckle and said, "Move forward and join the others."

As she moved forward, he scanned the rear, but saw no one. He turned and started after the others.

The day was long and just before dusk, a light rain started falling and the temperature dropped fast. John, who was now in the middle of the group said, "Off to the right, maybe a hundred feet, is where we'll make camp. If you want hot chow, eat it now, because once dark, no fires."

Soon two sheets of tarp made crude lean-to shelters and everyone was eating, except John, who was standing guard near the trail, with Dolly. He saw and heard nothing, but that meant little. *The Russians must be pissed, with a chopper and crew dead. Then there are the soldiers we've killed. They'll come, but hopefully they'll not find us. I wonder if that heat sensing chopper they have is the only one or do they have more? I know some of our gunships in Vietnam had the same technology, because dad talked once about how the heat from the North Vietnamese trucks glowed red to the sensor operators on the aircraft. I'm sure the technology has been perfected, but Lord, keep them away from us.*

His shift passed quietly and then he moved back to the rest to eat. All but Joshua were asleep. He pulled out a ration bag, cut it open with his pocketknife and since it was dark, tried to select his supper by feel. Locating the entree`, he tore it open and discovered vegetable stew. Feeling for the biscuits, he opened the pouch and removed one. He's just given a biscuit to Dolly, when he heard a chopper off in the distance and a few minutes later, he picked up the sound of another.

He moved to Tom and whispered, "Choppers."

His eyes flew open, he sat up and listened. After a while he said, "One of three things is happening. They're hunting us with heat sensors, dropping teams off to look for us, or they're scouting and looking for campfires. Let's hope it's fires they're looking for. Any difference in the pitch of the birds?"

"Nope, continuous so far."

"I think they're looking for campfires, because it's cold and good hypothermia weather. I think we're safe enough, for now anyway."

"What do you want to do?"

"Nothing, and we'll stay where we are. They may not catch our heat but if we move, all it would take is one Russian wearing night vision goggles to see us, especially if we're out in the open. Listen and let me know if the pitch changes."

"Will do." John said and then went back to eating his meal.

The night was uneventful, but wet. At dawn, John allowed a modest fire, about the size of a coffee cup, so they could have some hot drinks and food, if they wanted to take the time. Margie was guarding near the road and all were huddled close to the fire, when they heard a laugh.

Everyone scattered into the trees, so John used the toe of his boot to push mud onto the flames of the small fire. The smoke blended well with the fog, but he worried about the smell. He knew the smell of a fire could be carried a long way by winds. He then took Dolly and moved behind a large oak log.

He heard what sounded like a question in Russian and then silence. He whispered to Dolly, "Stay and hush." John slipped the safety off his weapon and waited, his tension growing by the second. *If they smell our smoke, we're goin' to have a fight.*

Two Russian voices were heard near the trail and by the tone used, they seemed to be arguing over something. *It must be the smell of our smoke*, John thought.

A third voice, louder than the other two was heard and the talk stopped immediately. He heard the sound of metal hitting metal, but they moved south.

Ten full minutes passed before Margie appeared and Joshua went to take her place by the trail. Moving to her, John asked, "What'd you see?"

"Squad of ten Russians moving down our back trail. I'm not sure why they stopped, but I could smell the smoke from our fire, only it was faint. I suspect they picked up the smoke smell, too. They stopped, a couple argued about something, and then an officer must have told them to shut up, I guess. After that, they continued south, away from us, without another word. They had one man on point and another bringing up the rear, for a total of ten men. I'm tellin' you, it scared the living hell out of me."

Tom gazed into John's eyes and said, "I suspect the choppers we heard last night served two purposes. One, to deliver men to search for us and two, to look for campfires. I think they must have dropped teams in advance of us, hoping we'd run into them."

"If we'd left at our normal time, an hour before dawn, we'd have ran right into them." John felt a shudder go through his body.

"Well, we didn't, so don't worry about it. I suggest we stay off the trails, move west, overland, and try to find a staging area."

Joshua asked, "Near Edwards?"

"Yep, why?" John asked as he donned his pack.

"My daddy owned some land near there and we grew cotton. The roof of the house has caved in, collapsed the same year as the fall, but there is a cellar there. Not huge, but plenty big enough for us, all our gear, and then some. That is, if it's not been destroyed already."

"Close to Edwards?"

"I'd guess three miles south of the place and then east a bit, oh, maybe two more miles."

Tom pulled a map from his coat, opened it and said, "We're right here. Edwards is here, so where is this plantation of yours?"

Grinning, Joshua said, "It ain't a plantation and never was, but the place is right here." He pointed on the map.

"Maybe five hours west?" Tom asked.

"About that," Joshua agreed.

"Okay, folks," John said, "saddle up and let's move. I want Sandra on point and Margie on drag. After three hours, I want Josh on point. Once on point, Josh, try to lead us to your place. Keep the pace slow and keep an eye on the weather."

He nodded and said, "Will do." He started out at a slow walk, west.

"Weather?" Tom asked, looking confused.

John laughed and said, "This is the season for tornadoes, in case you don't remember. Spring and fall, we get 'em both times. If we spot a twister, move at right angles away from it and hunt a hole."

"Let's move." Tom said and started out after Josh.

The morning passed slowly and over time, John grew less apprehensive over the Russian patrol that passed so closely to them. That didn't mean he lowered his situational awareness, but instead his mind moved on to other things. It was late afternoon when Joshua stopped and waved John forward.

From beside the man, John asked, "Is this it?"

"Yep, off to the right, about a hundred yards, you can see the remains of the main house. The barn has fallen in and the outbuildings are in sad shape, too. The cellar is about a hundred feet from the house and a bit north."

"We'll check it in the morning, after light." John started to turn, then he heard a jet flying overhead and when he glanced up, it was maybe ten thousand feet and straight and level. He grinned when he saw Dolly looking up as well.

CHAPTER 8

At the Russian base camp, Vetrov was in another of his vicious moods. It seemed to those who served under the man, all he did was go into a rage about one thing or another, and with no other emotions shown. Some even thought the man had lost his mind, and those who'd known him the longest were the most assured of his insanity. He'd taken to drinking much more vodka than usual, and he'd always been a heavy drinker.

Lieutenant Colonel Pankov stood at attention in the room they used for staff meetings, and he'd been explaining the loss of the helicopter, when Vetrov exploded, "How in the hell do a group of peasants kill ten Russian soldiers and then blow up a helicopter, killing the whole crew? By God, I want answers! And, I want answers *now*, Pankov, or I will personally see you spend the rest of your worthless life in Siberia!"

"Sir, we have teams on the ground right this minute, searching for the killers. Our soldiers were found naked, their uniforms gone, and yet the dead from the weather were still wrapped in their ponchos. The other helicopter stated the lost aircraft told him the men on the ground were having radio problems. There were no indications anything was wrong until the aircraft exploded."

"And, the cause of the explosion?"

"Our initial reports suggest grenades, but it is being looked into very thoroughly right now."

"So, did the other aircraft do nothing? I have dozens of dead men and not a single body of a responsible American!"

Pankov, feeling the stress of briefing the commander, was sweating in the cool room as he said, "Yes, sir, he attacked with full force, using both his cannons and rockets. Once that was over, one of our jets dropped napalm on the area. Our estimates are ten members of the resistance killed."

Exploding from his chair, Vetrov screamed, "Moscow does not want estimates, but bodies! I want you and your entire staff to go out to the place we lost that helicopter this afternoon. You will stay there until your estimates turn into cold dead American bodies, or so help me, I will relieve you of command and send your ass home shamed. Do you understand me, Colonel Pankov?"

Snapping to attention, the colonel replied, "Yes, sir."

"Now, get out of my sight. Next, I want the weather briefing."

Pankov cursed as he entered his office and sat at his desk. Opening the top right drawer, he pulled out a quart of vodka and took a long drink. The rough alcohol burned a trail to his stomach and kicked him hard. Standing he said, "Sergeant, prepare the entire staff for the field. Full combat load and gear, including you."

"Yes, sir, I will get the word out."

As soon as the sergeant left, Pankov put the quart of vodka in his pack and began to gather up his gear.

The aircraft tipped a bit to the left as it touched down just a few yards from the destroyed one, and the intelligence team moved from the aircraft bent over at the waist. This was their first deployment to the field since the unit had arrived in America and all were nervous, with some more than others. The senior NCO had a lot of years behind him and he'd been a line troop before moving into intelligence. He was the least concerned, but the privates were terrified by just the thought of the American resistance. They'd heard many stories, although most were lies, about how inhumane the enemy was to those they captured.

"Sergeant!" Pankov yelled to be heard over the engine of the chopper.

"Sir?"

"Move our troops into the woods and get a tent up. Then, place guards around."

"Sir, I think one guard near the door to your tent is enough. There is a whole company of men here and guards are all around us."

"Take care of it, and do as you wish with guards." Pankov pulled a flask from his coat and took a swig. He walked to a Major who was with the infantry and asked, "Have any of the teams made contact yet?"

The Major saluted and then extending his hand, said, "I am Major Galkin, sir. Let us move to my tent, because I do not like discussing business out in the open."

A few minutes later, seated in folding chairs, the Major pulled a quart of vodka from under his pillow on his cot and asked, "Drink, sir?"

"Yes, please."

He picked up two canteen cups and poured about three fingers of the clear drink into each. He handed one cup to Pankov, and then said, "The American's have been very active. We have a Sergeant of yours named Belonev with us. As far was we can tell, he is the only survivor of this mess. We discovered him on our way here, but down by a secondary road. When we found him he was mumbling about 'all dead' and needing help. He is sleeping now, but from what little we gathered from him, he had been in the woods taking a pee when the attack happened. Along with a lieutenant, something or the other, I have it in my report, and they fled toward the road. The officer died and we discovered the Master Sergeant when he flagged us down yesterday."

"Any other attacks I should know about?"

"Well, this one was carried out by the same group that carries the ace of spades. One of our teams searching ran into a small group north of here. Our men were pretty well shot to hell, but three out of the ten lived. Our initial report shows Claymores were exploded and," Galkin walked to a map on his wall before he continued, "we have had attacks here, here, here, and here." As he spoke he pointed to circles drawn on the map.

"What's the time difference between attacks? I mean, could one unit be doing this much damage?" Pankov took a big chug of vodka, knowing Vetrov would shit when informed.

"Impossible for it to be just one unit. The distance and time involved has ruled that out. What we have here, in my opinion, is a number of small cells carrying out random attacks, with no coordination. See, two of the attacks were within a mile of each other, but happened close to five minutes apart. I suspect two different units." Galkin threw his drink back.

"Do you have any idea how many cells there may be?"

Galkin laughed and replied, "No, sir, and there is no way to know, other than just guess. We have a total of four American bodies, which were taken back to Colonel Vetrov by the same aircraft that delivered you."

"Taken back? Why?"

"The boss no longer wants a count, my good colonel, he wants to personally see the bodies. Another drink?"

"Sure, I will have one more. If he wants to see the bodies, he must not trust his commanders in the field."

"Well, just between you and I, my uncle is general officer and he told me on his last visit here that Vetrov has just one hundred and twenty days to clear this area of all resistance or they'll remove him. I was told this about a hundred days ago, so the pressure must be getting rough for the man."

Good God, that explains his behavior. Hell, if they do not shoot him, he will end up in Siberia alongside me, Pankov thought, but said, "Can he do the job?"

Galkin sat on his cot, took a drink of his vodka and replied, "I do not think anyone could do the job. My uncle told me that no one in Moscow had considered, not seriously, the number of guns the Americans had when they decided to come here. When you consider the number of hunters, military veterans, and those that just had a gun to protect their homes, damned near all of these people were armed."

"The last intelligence report I had stated there were an estimated 270 million guns registered, or 89 guns for every 100 people. That is a hell of a lot of weapons, even if some of them are small caliber or old shotguns. I think it is important to remember, some additional guns may have been passed down from father to son and many may not have even been registered. Also, what happened to all of the weapons the Americans had in gun stores after the country fell? I suspect all were stolen, but how many were taken? Who knows? Our intelligence has no idea."

"Interesting Colonel, but the resistance we are fighting has a full arsenal of weapons from pistols to automatic weapons, including Russian and American machine guns."

"Of course they do and will continue to collect weapons each time they kill our men. I am sure your men found no working weapons near our dead, right?"

"Not a one."

"Well, from now on, if you find any ammo, guns, grenades, anything, return it to base camp, because a number of troops have been killed using gear gathered after a fight."

Galkin looked confused, so Pankov continued, "The American explosive C4 was placed in cartridges which exploded when fired, our hand grenades had the delay setting changed, and some other rather deadly modifications to other gear has occurred. Use nothing after a fight."

"I understand, sir."

Standing, Pankov said, "I enjoyed our small chat, Major. As soon as my tent is erected and I am back in business, I will have a staff meeting."

Snapping his heels together with a loud click, Galkin replied, "My pleasure, sir. I look forward to the meeting."

"I must see to my men." The colonel walked from the tent and thought, *Sonofabitch, no wonder Vetrov is about insane. There is no way he can clear this area of partisans in the time given and he must know that. Hell, he is on borrowed time, but I suspect when he goes down, the top brass will allow him to take many of us with him. I cannot allow that to happen. I'm too close to full colonel and then just a short step to general officer. I must survive to be promoted.*

He was near the woods when his sergeant ran to him and said, "Sir, one of the helicopter pilots caught a large group of Americans in an open field and estimates over forty dead! He shot them to pieces with his guns."

"Contact the base and report this and have the pilot report to me immediately. Also have helicopters sent to the kill zone to pick up the bodies in nets. Then, have the nets dropped in the grass in front of base headquarters."

"Sir?"

"Do what I said, Sergeant, and do it now."

"Yes, sir."

As the sergeant hurried away to complete his tasks, Pankov thought, *If Vetrov wants bodies, I will give him bodies. I have got to make this look like I had a hand in it or I will go down with the commander. If I have forty dead delivered to him, he will have to recognize my efforts with a medal or at least in a letter to Moscow. That alone may save my ass.*

The pilot arrived at the Colonel's tent thirty minutes later, looking tired, but happy. It wasn't often a chopper pilot caught that many of the enemy out in the open. The guard at the door asked his name, told him to wait, and then went inside. A minute later he heard a voice say, "Enter. Private, wait outside by the door."

The pilot entered, saluted, and said, "Lieutenant Yevseyev reporting, sir. I was told you wanted to speak to me."

"Please, sit down, Yevseyev. Would you like a drink?"

Sit down? Drink? This man wants something, so watch him closely, Yevseyev thought and then said, "No drink, because I have to fly back to the base, sir." He then sat in the chair Pankov offered, suddenly feeling uncomfortable.

"Yevseyev, I understand you killed forty Yankees in an open field today. Is that report true?"

"Yes, sir, I did. The last I heard, other aircraft were inbound to remove the bodies."

"You must be glad I gave you the information on where to find such a large number of the enemy?"

"Sir?"

"Do I need to ask the question again, Yevseyev, or do you want to stay a lieutenant the rest of your career?"

Damn, he is wanting credit for my kills, but the last thing I need is a senior officer after my ass, Yevseyev thought and then said, "I might take one finger of vodka, sir."

Pouring the alcohol, Pankov asked, "Well?"

"Oh, I am very glad you briefed me on the mission, yes, sir. Without your assistance I would not have made a single kill today. Your intelligence section is excellent, Colonel."

"I'm glad to hear that, Captain Yevseyev, well maybe not captain yet, but you will be when the next promotions come down."

Throwing his drink back, Yevseyev said, "Is that all, sir?"

"No, I want an after action report written by you now and left with me. I will see copies are sent forward. You will make sure my name is mentioned, understand?'

"Yes, sir." *He's either covering his ass or hunting a medal. I do not care who gets credit for the kills, because I know it was pure luck. I could fly here ten years and never have the same thing happen again. I will write you a wonderful report Colonel, but not for a promotion. No, sir, I may need a favor from you one day and when I do, I will come to you to collect.*

The flying maintenance commander gave his briefing to Vetrov and waited for the response. He had close to 25% of his aircraft grounded due to maintenance updates or needed fixes and while he was doing the best he could, the Colonel was never happy, not with anyone. Vetrov lowered his head to his hands and asked, "When do you expect to be back up to full strength?"

"Ten days at the maximum."

The Colonel shot from his chair and exploded in anger, "Ten days! That is totally unacceptable, and I want the job finished in half the time!"

"We'll try our best, sir."

"You will do it in that time, or I *will* remove you and get some-one in that can do the job. I want no more excuses from any of you. I grow tired of threatening and will take action the next time."

The Major who worked for Pankov, stood and was shaking when he walked to the front of the room and said, "Sir, I am happy to report, Lieutenant Colonel Pankov contacted us a few minutes ago to inform us that forty resistance fighters have been killed."

Vetrov raised his head from his hands and said, "That's impossible, he just arrived there. Has he personally seen the bodies?"

"Well, no, sir, but the bodies should be on their way here, right now. We dispatched three helicopters to retrieve the remains and they should be here within the hour, or so."

"I do not believe a word of this. It cannot be possible. How did these forty Americans die?"

"Sir, a Lieutenant Yevseyev, working on intelligence provided by the Colonel, caught the Americans crossing an open field just after dawn. Using his guns and rockets, he was able to complete his mission successfully. A detailed after-action report is on its way here."

"I will be damned. That must be the largest kill for a single man to date."

"It is, sir, but it is yet unconfirmed. The bodies will add credi-bility to the report."

"When are these bodies to be delivered here?"

"The Colonel didn't say, sir. He just instructed me to pass the kills on to you during the staff meeting."

"Well," Vetrov said, "finally some good news. Sergeant, bring us a few bottles of vodka, this deserves a celebration!"

I hope there are at least forty dead Americans or Vetrov will have me and Pankov hanged from the highest tree, the Major thought, as he gave a false smile.

Glasses were handed out, drinks poured and then Vetrov stood, and said, "To a quick Russian victory over the Americans!"

"To Mother Russia!" A Captain responded as he held his drink high.

The drinks disappeared and then the Sergeant said, "Sir, I am to inform you of three helicopters due here in five minutes. According to the message I have, the aircraft are carrying dead Americans."

"Here? Why here?" The Colonel asked.

"I have no idea, sir. Your captain asked me to inform you."

That damned Pankov is doing this on purpose, so he can show me the dead, he thought and then said, "Gentlemen, shall we go outside and watch the delivery?"

Due to his rank, no one refused, but most didn't really want to see the blood and gore. They were members of the commanders staff, not combat troops, and few had served in combat. They left the room, went down a flight of stairs and out to the lawn.

It was a nice day, with a few clouds hanging high in the sky to the west, but otherwise clear. The air was warm, but not overly hot, so most of the staff enjoyed a light breeze that blew.

"To the west, I see three aircraft." Someone in the group said. As all looked in the direction the small points gradually grew larger. A few minutes later, three helicopters were seen, and each had a big net hanging below.

The first aircraft flew to the center of the big lawn and slowly descended until the net touched the ground. It continued to lower, until a private on the ground disconnected the net from a thick cable. The aircraft started up and in a matter of a minute or two, it was gone and another started toward the lawn. Ten minutes later, the three aircraft now gone, the staff stood in shock. Blood covered the bodies and dripped to the grass, pooling in puddles. Arms, legs, and heads had been thrown onto the net loosely, so many had rolled off once the net was released from the aircraft. The heat, while only warm, intensified the coppery smell of blood, urine, and human waste. A young lieutenant turned his head to the left and puked.

Vetrov was smiling as he walked to the first net and saw the devastating damage done by just one helicopter. He then turned and said, "I want intelligence to pull these bodies from the nets and count them. I want an estimate on ages, determine the genders and any other intelligence you can gather from the remains.

That means going through their pockets and gear. I want an exact count of the number dead. Major, you will give me a detailed briefing as soon as the information as been gathered. For the rest of you, dismissed."

CHAPTER 9

John liked the cellar, but knew if they were all caught inside they'd be easily killed. The top was covered with dirt and grass had grown high on top, along with brush. No one had walked around it in years. The trees from the forest, over the years, were slowly moving toward the cellar. From the forest proper, John guessed it was fifty feet, which was a short run, but if trapped in-side, the same run could take a lifetime. The two doors were hinged with a cross bar of metal that held the door securely against high winds, but it offered no protection at all against weapons, not even small arms fire.

As they worked, Joshua said, "Me and my daddy, God rest his soul, grew a lot of cotton here one time, way before the fall. Cot-ton paid my way through college and made me a good living for a long time. Then, one day when I was about twenty-three, I got me an idea to join the Army. Just like that, I was gone. Daddy did fine for a couple of years without me, then due to his age, he had to quit."

"Did you grow up here too? I mean in the house?" Tom asked.

"Nope, but my daddy and grandpa did, and his father before him."

"That's a lot of years in a piece of land. I'd imagine your folks put a lot sweat into this place."

"I've never given that part much thought. We made a better than average living from this land, so I think we got out of it what we put into it. We were all hard workers and I can remember many a day coming home tired and beat. Those were good days, only they're lost forever now, because this country will never be what it was before."

"By God, ya got that right, but once we clear the invaders out and get started up again, we'll need some good people. We'll need folks to represent us that really care about us and our country. Just before the fall, all the politicians were in the business for the money. Hell, it didn't make much difference if they were Democrat or Republican, money bought their votes."

"I hear ya. I was always confused about how we could give billions of dollars to other countries, but yet had to make cuts to programs that helped our veterans and old folks. We should have taken care of our own before helping anyone else. My daddy always said, 'Charity starts in the home.'"

"Actually, when you're running a government and run out of money, you can't keep spending. No money, no spending, pretty simple in my mind."

John, who'd been guarding outside stuck his head in and said, "Tom and Joshua, I want the two of you to circle this place and make sure we're alone. Start close, then slowly widen your search."

"Come on, Joshua." Tom said as he picked his rifle up and moved for the door.

Once out in the fresh air, Tom said, "John, check the air vent, because the air is stale in the hole. I suspect some critter has made a nest in the thing to keep dry. We'll be back in a couple of hours."

The two men stepped into the woods and were soon lost to view.

John found a nest of some kind in the vent and Sandra said it was rats. He removed it and then moved to the old house to see if anything could be found they might be able to use. He had Margie and Sandra on guard and when he'd looked around earlier, he'd seen no tracks or evidence to suggest others were around. Dolly had circled the place with him and she'd not alerted to anything.

Part of the roof to the house had fallen in, and the steps had rotted through in a few spots. The door was missing and he discovered it on the inside, laying flat on the floor. Old newspapers, paper cups and a few wine bottles were seen. All of the furniture, pictures and all possessions were gone, likely taken when the last occupant left. Dolly sniffed at some old stains on the floor and then looked bored.

In the kitchen an old stove stood, and on opening the oven door, he discover an oven rack, so he removed it to cook on. The roof had fallen in on the bedrooms, so he made his way back outside. He didn't expect to find much, but the rack would make cooking easier. He bent down, removed four bricks from the yard to place the rack on, and returned to the cellar. He then cleaned his weapons and checked his gear.

Tom and Joshua returned later in the day and reported they'd seen nothing. They did discover a dirt road to the north and Joshua said it led to pavement after a few miles and then went into Edwards.

John thought for a minute and then asked, "What's left of Edwards now?"

"Well, likely not much, because it wasn't a big place before the fall. The last I heard, all the towns between Jackson and the Mississippi River, on the main highway, are under Russian control now. They send supplies up the Mississippi from the port in New Orleans. From Vicksburg, they can send supplies to any part of the state, or the South; why?"

"The last briefing Colonel Parker gave involving Vicksburg was bad news, because it was heavily guarded."

"Vicksburg is out, but we might want to visit Edwards."

"Are you thinking what I'm thinking?"

"Probably not. I'm thinking we can sneak around the town, get a feel for traffic going in and out, then ambush somebody."

"Good, because I'll not enter a town without my guns. I thought for a minute there, you intended to actually go into the town and take a look."

"He can't do that, but I'll bet I could." Margie said, and then smiled.

"What makes you think you can do it, without being caught?"

"I'm a woman. If I go in there begging, dirty and looking a mess, they'll not stop me. Now, if you send Kate, they'll line up to use her. Soldiers can smell a pretty woman." Margie said, and then broke out laughing.

"Very funny. Besides, you're pretty, too." Kate said and then shook her head.

"I'm not ugly, but I'd win no beauty contests, so let's be honest here. I'm a plain looking woman."

"Damn, Margie, do you realize the risk?" John asked.

"I really haven't given it much thought, but I suspect it could be done. Most soldiers don't see a woman as a serious threat."

"Last I heard, the Russians haven't started issuing travel papers or any form of identification, so it might work." Tom said.

"We need the intelligence, but I won't tell you to go, Margie. I still think it's a big risk."

"Do we have anything I could trade that isn't military? If the Russians run the place, there are sure to be booths for trading things. Hell, I'm not even sure what they'd want to trade for anyway."

"I have my lucky silver dollar from 1886, but that's all I have." Kate said.

"Gold necklace from me, but it's not worth much." Joshua said and then pulled it from his neck.

Sandra said, "All I have is my wedding rings, but you'll never get them, so I'm sorry. I once had thousands of dollars in jewelry, only lost it all when the house was taken."

"I'm the same as Sandra. We were forced out our home by a bunch of thugs and have nothing left, except each other and that's more than most folks have these days." John replied.

Tom tossed his wedding ring to Margie and said, "I don't need this, not since my wife was killed, and to tell you the truth, wearing it brings back too many memories of her."

"I have some earrings my brother gave me. He died the first year after the fall, and I'll use them if need be, but with a silver dollar, gold necklace and wedding band, I should have plenty to trade with. I'll try to get us some veggies or meat."

"Horse trade with 'em, if you can, and talk. Get them to talk about the town and how you're passing through looking for your lost family. I suspect there are a lot of lost folks these days." Kate said.

"You know, I hope one day, if we ever get our country back, that people understand and know what we sacrificed for our freedom. Freedom is just a word, until one day you no longer have it and then it's valuable. I'm willing to die for our cause, because I believe in our future. I want our future generations to grow up free, like we did, with the American flag flying high. I want to live long enough to see that, but I'm willing to pay any price for freedom, including my life."

"Hell," Joshua said, "you should run for office, I'll vote for you." He then broke out laughing.

John was thinking about her words and realized he felt the same way. He wasn't killing to kill, but to free his country. He didn't hate the Russians, he hated occupation. All he wanted was the Russians to leave and the world to allow the American people to rebuild their country.

John thought for a minute and then said, "Okay, Margie, you can enter Edwards, but I'll go with you part way. I'll wait outside the town limits for your return. Go in, trade a little, try not to use all the jewelry you have, and learn what you can. The key is to get the trader to talking about all they know. But, for God's sake, avoid the Russians if you can."

"Do you have the clothes you'll need?" Sandra asked.

"I have most of what I need, but I could use a coat of some kind."

"I have a jean jacket I usually wear under my uniform, but that's all I have of the civilian world any longer." Sandra said and then pulled the coat from her pack. Handing it to Margie she said, "I want it back when you return."

"Okay, guys, lets go outside and let her change. Once you're a civilian again, we'll move to Edwards. Now, if things get to feeling strange or not right, get the hell out and do the job quickly. If the Russians approach you, try to talk your way out, but if not, use this." John handed her a snub-nosed .38 and then added, "It's loaded and ready to use. Carry it in the small of your back."

The walk to Edwards was nice, with the weather cloudy, but warm. Dolly enjoyed it as she sniffed and scanned the countryside as they walked. Margie was scared, but knew they needed to know what was going on inside the town, or they might not be able to plan well for any future attacks. Poor planning would lead to deaths of some, if not all, of the group.

Peeking through the brush, John said, "I see no checkpoint on the road leading to the town, so they must feel pretty secure. Now, visit one or two booths, if you can find any, and then get the hell out. Do not draw any attention to yourself if it can be avoided."

"I'm no hero, and pretty scared right now."

"Any normal person would be scared, because it's natural. Nonetheless, that fear will keep your senses sharp and might just keep you alive. Here," John said and handed the leash to her and saw the look of confusion in her eyes as he said, "take Dolly. She'll respond to commands, but take good care of her. Do not risk your life for hers, only pay attention to her head and where she's looking. She's also been trained to give you a low growl of warning if danger nears. If you say attack, she'll attack to kill, so remember this."

"Do you think I need her?"

"Uh-huh, I do. She'll be another set of eyes for you. Now, is the pistol on you?"

"In the small of my back. I'm ready."

Extending his hand, John said, "Best of luck. I'll cover this end of town, so if you have to break and run, try to come out this way."

They shook hands and then Margie stood and moved toward the small town of Edwards.

Margie moved slowly and staggered a few times to give, she hoped, the look of being tired and hungry. No one spoke to her or approached her, but she did pass a few others, who were dressed no better than she. The town was dirty now, trash on the streets, with debris rolling in the light wind. She'd no sooner entered the town than she spotted a group of booths lining the street. She moved to each one, carefully looking at what they offered. Most had old canned goods, the used before date well passed, and some had expired ten years ago.

Finally, she spotted a vegetable and a couple of meat stands sitting close together. When she neared, Margie saw most of the veggies were stunted and not well shaped, but she didn't care. While the addition of fresh food would be welcome, she'd come to talk.

Dolly walked at her side and only growled once, when a Russian mounted on a motorcycle passed heading for the main road. She picked up a cabbage and asked, "How much?"

"What do you have to trade?" A woman asked as she smiled.

Pulling Joshua's necklace out, she showed it to the woman and then asked, "What will this gold necklace get me?"

"I need to see it first."

Margie handed it to the woman and then looked her over closely. She was slightly plump, which was rare, her black hair was streaked with gray, and her eyes were a dark blue. She was short, just a tad over five feet, and had once been a beautiful woman. She was still attractive, but grime and dirt covered her face. While the woman looked sixty, if cleaned up and dressed nice, she would pass for forty.

The woman met her eyes and asked, "You're new here, aren't you?"

"I'm traveling and looking for my family. Are the Russians strict here?" Margie asked.

"There are many searching for a family, and I hope you find yours. No, they don't care much, except if you get too close to the main base."

"Main base? I don't need any trouble. Can you tell me where it is?"

"Uh-huh, on the other side of town, the north side. You're safe enough here. I can give you three cabbages, a small bag of carrots and two onions for your necklace."

Shaking her head, Margie said, "That's not enough. I want some potatoes and a stalk of celery too. Can you give that much? The necklace is the last one I have and when it's gone, I will have no more to trade for food."

"The gold on this necklace is electroplated and not of good quality, but I will give what you have requested." The woman started gathering up the produce.

"What do you do with the jewelry you get?" Margie asked to get the woman talking again.

"I trade it to the Russians. They're shrewd traders, but I make a living doing it. I think it will be better here after the prison is built."

"I don't like the Russians much, because they give me a hard time, and I want to be left alone to search from my family. I'm scared one day they might shoot me. Prison?"

"I haven't seen them on the street bothering people here. They mainly stay on their base, but I can go to them and trade. Like any army, they have those that will trade anything for gold. You may see two or three of them walking in the town, but you'll never see one alone. I haven't seen them checking anyone or rounding them up, not like they do in Jackson. Some of the guards were saying they'll soon have a prison here for people who resist them. I have no idea if it's true or not, but they're working to make something big."

"I may stay here a day or so, if you think it's safe."

"If you do, use caution, because most young women are taken to the base to entertain the troops, if you understand what I mean. The Russian's bother few people and we don't bother them. All I want is to be left alone to run my business. I thank God that most of the armed resistance is east and north of us, or they'd likely kill us like they do in Jackson. They kill ten Americans for every dead Russian, or so the posters say."

"Posters?"

"There's one across the street and they're placed throughout the town on buildings. They warn us, all Americans, not to resist them." The woman handed a tow sack with the vegetables and then added, "I won't fight them, but I pray for those that do the job."

"Thank you for the talk and the produce. I must be on my way now, after I find some meat. Is one booth here better than others?"

"Two booths down is a good meat man, Fred. Tell him you know Sally and he'll treat you well enough. I hope you have some good quality gold, because meat is costly."

"I have only one item left and I'd hoped I had enough to last until I found my brother."

"May God bless and protect you in your travels." Sally replied, and then moved to help another customer.

Margie said, "Come, Dolly, let's find us some meat."

Two booths down was the first portly man Margie had seen since the fall. He was obese with jowls hanging to his filthy tee-shirt, and he was a tall man, close to six feet. He wore a faded pair of jeans, patched in many places, and was bald. Flies were sitting on the displayed meat and flying around. They were the green blowflies she'd seen on corpses in the past.

He looked at Margie and asked, "Can I help you?"

"I'm looking for beef or venison. Do you have any of either? Sally told me to ask for Fred."

"I'm Fred, and have both, but beef will be expensive. What do you have to trade?"

Removing one of her gold earrings, she asked, "How much red meat will this get me? It has a diamond as well as being solid gold."

"It's not solid gold, because there is no such thing. However, this looks to be 24k and if so, it has a good value. Let me look it over and I will tell you in a minute or so. Are you sure you only want red meat? I can give you much more white meat for this, if it's authentic."

"Red meat only. The last time I traded for white meat, it was human."

The man chuckled and said, "How do you know that?"

"It was in Vicksburg and the Russians raided the butchers stall. They found human remains in boxes under his tables, hands and feet."

The man paled and then asked, "W . . . what did they do to him?"

"They shot him on the spot. No trial, no warning, just pulled a pistol and blew his head off. You would think they would put him in a prison." Margie hoped he would comment more.

"H . . . he deserved it, I guess. We don't have a prison here, not yet anyway. I have heard they are making one here now for the families of those who fight against them. Uh, let me check your earring."

From the reaction of Fred, Margie suspected he was offering human meat, too, so she'd stay away from white meat. Many butchers, or so she'd heard from other resistance fighters, were now selling human meat as pork and it was hard to tell the difference. Most folks were so hungry, it really didn't matter to them and they'd eat both.

"I can give you four pounds of red meat or twenty of white." Fred said a few minutes later.

"I need more. Can you add another pound? The diamond is worth much and you know it, too. Just the sparkle will catch a Russian's eye."

"Okay, I will add another pound of red meat."

"Beef, no deer meat. I paid over two thousand dollars for these earrings, so I know their value."

The fat man smiled and said, "You know what the value was once. Now days, it's worth only what someone will give you for it. I will give you five pounds of beef for the earring."

"Deal. I need the meat." She said, and then shook her head as if frustrated.

"I thought you'd say that, because times are rough."

"I must travel by the army base here; are there many soldiers there? I do not want to be bothered or shot by them."

Fred said, "Not if you passed them by in the day. If you try to get near at night, they will shoot at you, even if you are traveling on the road. There aren't many of them, maybe a hundred in the camp, so they're isolated from the rest. They are known to shoot first and then ask questions. I don't know, but I heard, they provide security for convoys traveling from Vicksburg to Jackson. They'll not bother you on this day, if you pass before darkness."

"You sound like you know them personally."

"I know a few and they don't like being here anymore than we want them here." Fred replied, and handed her another burlap bag. He then added, "I know they have no tanks, cannon, or other big equipment there, so they're scared most of the time."

His words frightened her, as if he was volunteering too much information and knew who he was giving it to as well. She shrugged and replied, "I don't know what a tank is and all I know about a cannon is it's a big gun. I hate guns and violence, which is all I've seen since the fall."

"Well, if you dislike violence, then stay the hell out of Jackson, because all the Russians do there is round folks up and shoot the shit out of them. They've executed over two hundred people there this month alone."

"I only want to find my brother. I pray he still lives, but it's not likely."

"Well, if your jewelry runs out and you grow hungry, come see me. I can always use another wife and I'll feed you well, but only white meat." Fred said and then laughed.

"Oh, and how many wives do you have now?"

"Three, but none are as fine or young as you are. Each Friday we get a bottle of rotgut and have a party."

I'd starve to death, lard-ass, before I'd go to bed with you, Margie thought, but smiled and said, "Why thank you, Fred. I'll keep you in mind if things turn much rougher. At times, I could use a real man in my life, but now I must move on. I still have hopes of finding my family, only I can't go much further alone without help."

Fred reached down, picked up two pig ears and handing them to her he said, "Take these so you know I mean what I offer you. I'll treat you well, young lady, and enjoy doing the job. It'd be a crime to let a pretty young thing like you go hungry."

Margie smiled, winked and then said, "A man who can provide food for a woman is a special man these days in my eyes. Besides, I think I could learn to like an older man like you, since you're more experienced with life. I like the thought of a man who takes good care of his women, too. Now, that was the last of my jewelry, so don't be surprised if I return in a few days and take you up on your offer. Are you serious or just joking with me?" She ran her tongue over her bottom lip in a seductive manner and gave him her most teasing look. She saw him quiver.

Fred blinked his eyes rapidly a few times, gave a loud gulp, and then said, "Hell, for you, I'd throw them other women out of the house and feed you red meat."

Knowing some men fantasied about having more than one woman at the same time, she said just above a whisper, "Let them stay. I think we could have a special party with a man like you."

It was then Dolly gave a low growl, and when Margie glanced around, she saw two Russian soldiers nearing. She lowered her head and quickly said, "I must continue on my journey, but I'll remember your invitation."

"You, woman, stop!" A Russian called out in thickly accented English.

Glancing over here shoulder, she saw them looking at her. She turned and asked, "Yes?"

"Your bag has hole. Meat will fall out," the man on the left said. Their rifles were still over their shoulders on slings.

Margie removed the meat and placed it in the bag with the produce. She'd just turned to walk away when the same solder asked, "Have you husband?"

"No."

"Come with us. We take care of you."

CHAPTER 10

Pankov was standing tall when Vetrov presented him with his medal for his participation in the killing of the forty Americans. The citation had spoken of the great risk taken to gather the intelligence and how he'd gone into the field to gather even more. It read well, but the Lieutenant Colonel wasn't surprised by the words, because he'd written them himself. Standing beside him was Major Yevseyev, who'd just been promoted to major, completely bypassing the rank of captain. The quick award of both the medal and promotion, showed how desperate Vetrov was for positive news to report to Moscow.

Vetrov saluted Major Yevseyev and said, "I want both of you to stay long enough to have a drink or two in celebration of your achievements. It is not often I have the privilege of awarding medals and promotions these days."

"Yes, sir." Both men replied.

"Please be seated with the other members of my staff. Sergeant, bring us four bottles of vodka and glasses."

Gunfire was heard just outside the window and it was loud. Pankov looked at his commander and then the Colonel said, "More executions this morning. They must learn I am a man of my word. I will keep killing ten of them until all resistance is crushed."

"How many this time, sir?" Pankov asked. *You are a fool, but I have had this thought before.*

"Fifty-one just died. We had a supply depot at another base broken into two nights ago and lost a large quantity of rations and gas masks."

"Did they get the filters, too?"

"Of course they did. They knew what they were looking for and somehow knew where it was stored, too. I suspected they had men or women on the inside passing them information, so I had all our American civilians from the base killed. We only lost a single man, the guard, but traitors I will not tolerate at all."

"True, they must be squashed." Pankov agreed.

The sergeant arrived, handed out the glasses and placed four quarts of vodka on the table. He then walked to the rear of the room, where he stood at parade rest, in case he was needed again.

Pankov was happy with his new medal and to be out of the field again. He took a long chug of his vodka, enjoying the way it burned a path to his belly, and grinned. Life was good back at the main base and he appreciated the comforts.

Vetrov took a sip of his drink and said, "Pankov, I have word from Moscow your promotion is now assured, with the killing of the forty Americans, effective immediately, once the listing is released next week. I have been told you have been placed at the very top of those being promoted." He extended his hand and as they shook, he added, "But, as a colonel, we cannot have you working in intelligence any longer."

Now I will finally be given a real command, Pankov thought.

"We currently have two openings that require a man with your new rank." The commander took a long drink, gave a light cough, and then continued, "We have need of a tank commander and an anti-terrorism commander. I suggested to Moscow the anti-terrorism position, but they are allowing you to make the choice."

Tanks are damned death traps, and burning to death as steel melts around me is not a good way to go. But, first I must have some answers. Pankov asked, "I have not heard of any anti-terrorism group."

Vetrov laughed and said, "We do not have one, but Moscow considers the acts by the partisans to be acts of terror. You will have free reign over the people and decide what to do to reduce the damage done by their attacks. I must tell you, if you do a good job, a promotion to general is very likely. However, on the other side of the coin, screw it up, and they will have you murdered, I think. They seem to think you are just the man to do this job."

I could do a better job than you, for sure. Pankov said, "Of the two positions, due to my background and experience, I think I am better qualified to do the anti-terrorism job. I know little of tanks, except they're hot and stuffy in the summertime."

"Great, then it is okay if I pass your name on to Moscow?"

"Sure, but where will I work and have an office?"

Grinning, the Commander said, "Why at any small base you want to work out of, because your position will be in the field. They want you actively involved in preventing terrorism and you cannot do that from a staff position. I expect your replacements name on my desk within the hour. Gentlemen, if you wish, you can stay and enjoy the drink, however, I have work to do. Please remain seated as I leave the room."

As Vetrov left the room with a big smile on his face, Pankov was seething. *That sonofabitch set me up, knowing I would take the job before he even offered it. He wants me in the field and out of his way, damn him. I will show him, I will take the position and work out of the quietest base we have, Edwards. Nothing has happened there since we arrived. I will stop the resistance, only he may not care for the way I do the job.*

"Sir, are you okay?" A major said from beside him. Pankov didn't know the man, except he was Abdulov's replacement.

"Why," Pankov replied, "I am fine. Just a bit overwhelmed to be awarded a medal and a promotion on the same day."

"War makes or breaks a man, and I'm happy for you. I think many men who are captains today, will soon be generals."

"Oh, why is that?"

"We all know many are in command due to their connections with Moscow. If they do not do their jobs well, some will be retired, some shot, some will go to prison camps, and others will simply disappear. I see a great future waiting for some of us."

Edwards wasn't much from the air and even less once on the ground. Pankov immediately called for a staff meeting and set his ground rules in concrete. "I will have no drunks on duty; if you want to drink, do it on your off time. The enlisted are not to have hard drink, only beer, and the only exception is Master Sergeants. I will tolerate no sleeping on duty either, so get the word out. Any questions?"

There were none.

"Also, I want to establish a registration and identification system for all Americans, and my executive officer has data we have stolen from the Americans. This data lists everyone in this country who has owned a gun or had a drivers license. Anyone we stop, you can check to see if they once owned a gun, but keep in mind about 90 percent of all homes were gun owners. If they once owned a gun it does not make them a criminal, but they may be, so use caution. If they cannot explain where the gun is now, put them in a prison camp."

"Sir, we have no prison camps."

Pankov smiled and said, "We soon will have, and the first one will be here. I want at least twenty in this state alone."

"How can we feed them?"

"I did not mention food, did I? How, or if, they eat is not my concern."

"Surely you will feed and clothe the prisoners, sir."

"Do I look like the Red Cross? Now, see to your men, I have things to do."

After the staff meeting broke up and everyone went their way, Pankov walked from the building and made his way around the small camp, looking things over. The men looked to be in good shape, physically, but lazy and not well disciplined, in the Colonel's eyes. The defenses were poor and he suspected the camp wasn't surrounded by mines, and just by looking, he wanted more wire strung along the perimeter for protection. Obviously, stuck out in the woods away from the Russian brass, the base had grown complacent and shoddy, which was always the way of troops away from commanders.

I suspect, once the prison camps start to fill, the resistance will grow, as people join the fight to avoid camps. As the groups grow and become larger, they will be harder to hide and easier to find, maybe. There is always a chance they will split into small cells to resist us. Mass killings are not good, as they simply make desperate men more determined to win, but the camps may work. I will have to feed them, only not much, say 900 calories a day per prisoner. The lack of food has broken many men and women, Pankov thought as he walked around the camp.

"Colonel!" A voice called.

"Here!"

A major walked to Pankov, saluted and said, "Sir, I'm Major Bebchuk, civil engineer, and I am to build your prison camps. Colonel Vetrov told me I am assigned to you until further notice."

"I want you to spend today finding a good spot for the camp. Later, during construction, if you need laborers, simply make a sweep through the town and gather up men or women. I want this first camp up in a week, can that be done?"

"Yes, sir, but all of the buildings cannot be completed within that schedule. I can get wire up, towers in place, and a few struc-tures completed."

"Will it be able to accept prisoners?"

"Oh, yes, sir, but they will have to sleep on the ground, until we can get barracks made for them."

"Good; so start immediately and keep me informed of any problems; and I want a daily update during our staff meetings."

"Yes, sir."

"Oh, can the outer wire be charged with electrical current?"

"You mean an electric fence? Sure, I can do that, sir."

"See that it's done. Dismissed, major."

As the major saluted and then walked away, Pankov thought, *Things are looking up, already. If the camp is completed in a week, I can start adding prisoners very soon. If we start by collecting women and families of those known to be involved with the resistance, shoot a few of them that have family members as leaders, then their motivation to fight may decline. But, all executions must serve a purpose and not be mass killings like Vetrov has done recently. The resistance must understand why people are being killed, or it serves no purpose.*

Master Sergeant Belonev exited the helicopter bent over at the waist and with ten new men he made his way to a briefing. From his years of military service, he knew he was about to be informed of the nature of his sudden reassignment. His bags were heavy, and he grunted as he moved into a room and placed his gear against the far wall. He then took a seat near the front of the room. He was no longer able to hear as well as he once did and as the senior NCO, he figured something would be said to him or he'd have to answer questions. He was still tired, but mostly from the drunk he'd gone on after surviving his last trip into the bush. The colonel had given him three days of rest and he'd spent it with a vodka bottle in his hand.

Lieutenant Colonel Pankov entered the room with a couple of junior officers and the men came to attention. "Be seated, please." The colonel said.

After the men were seated, Pankov asked, "Which of you is Belonev?" He scanned the room, expecting the Master Sergeant to be at the rear.

He was surprised when the Sergeant stood almost at his feet and said, "I'm Belonev, sir."

"Men," Pankov said, "look at this man and remember his face. When he speaks, he speaks for me, and it is as if I have given you the order. You may be seated, Master Sergeant Belonev. Now, many, if not all of you, may be wondering why you are here in this small place. We are about to open a prison here for those who re- sist our right to American soil. You men, as well as some others, will be guards. Now, before you think of what a great deal you have just landed, let me make myself clear to all of you; your jobs will be tough and I expect all orders to be carried out without question. If a prisoner escapes on your shift, I will be hard on those found responsible or lacking in the performance of their du- ties. Each of you is a soldier and I expect all of you to act like one at all times. Beer will be available for all men, when off duty, but hard drink is reserved for Senior NCO's and officers. If you re- port to duty drunk or with a hangover, I might have you shot. Many of you will leave here with a promotion, as well as a medal, if you do what is expected of you. Now, Lieutenant Glukhov, the executive officer for our civil engineers will cover a few things. Lieutenant." Pankov sat in an overstuffed leather chair.

A short portly officer stood and said, "First, your barracks have not been completed, due to our efforts to complete the prison camp first. So, you will be living in small tents for a couple of weeks. Additionally, you will be pulling guard on the construction site, night and day, starting today. More guards are due in today and tomorrow, but until then do the best you can. I would suggest five men on duty today and five tonight. Once more men are available, your Master Sergeant will make a duty roster. Sir, that is all I have for right now."

Pankov stood and said, "The town is currently off limits to all of you and will remain that way until we do our first security sweep of the place. Master Sergeant Durchenko, please stand. Sergeant Belonev, Master Sergeant Durchenko will take you on a tour of the base as soon as I conclude my briefing. He will show you the messing facility for enlisted men, location of our supply section and much more. If you have any questions, he is the man for you to see. However, if you have any problems and need my help, my door is open to you. Any questions?"

Belonev shook his head and replied, "No, sir."

As Pankov moved toward the door, Durchenko called the room to attention.

Once the colonel was gone, Durchenko walked to Master Sergeant Belonev and asked, "How are you, Dmitry?"

"I am well, Alexei, and you?" Belonev extended his right hand.

"Well, but I thought you would be retired by now." Durchenko said as they shook.

"I was told my retirement was on hold until I completed this assignment. I had less than ten months remaining. The damned involuntary extension ruined all my family plans and Alena is still mad about it."

Shaking his head, Durchenko replied, "They did the same to me. I am pissed and had just six months left to serve. Come, let me show you around as we talk of old times."

"We can do this, but what can you tell me about this town?"

"Not much to say. It's a small quiet place, where we trade for gold or other things at booths they have in a small market. Some of the gold is of excellent quality, but nothing happens around here. I am not sure how much of a change the prison camp will cause, but usually folks move away from prisons, because they fear them."

Belonev pulled out a cigarette, offered one to his friend and then said, "Hell, prisons are depressing and no one wants to end up in one. I do not blame people for moving away." He lighted his smoke, and then his friends, with a lighter he'd carried for over twenty-five years.

"We will visit the town later. Off to the right is the supply building, to the left is headquarters, and over beside supply is the mail-room. There are no enlisted entertainment facilities and each man will be issued a ration card for alcohol and tobacco. You and I are authorized ten quarts of hard liquor, while the lower enlisted can have two cases of beer, per month. Most of the hard drink is vodka, but there are cases of bourbon, if you like the taste."

"Where did the bourbon come from?"

"I heard, but don't really know, that some of the American distilleries were raided and the drink removed. I can see us doing that, but I do not like the taste much and neither do most of the officers. A quart of it counts as half a ration, so if you can develop a taste for the nasty stuff, you will do well."

"It may be my lucky day, because I love it. I have only had it a couple of times in my life, but I found it smoother than vodka and with a slightly better taste."

Durchenko shrugged and said, "I'm a soldier and as such, I can drink any damned thing that does not kill me. Come, and I'll take you to the mess facility."

"How are the meals?"

"Better than most bases, because we buy most vegetables from town, and have a small herd of goats, sheep, cows, and some chickens. The colonel wants to increase the size of our herds, and chickens, most likely to feed the prisoners. He is getting additional men who will care for the animals."

"Good, my men will be happy to hear that. Are the herds on or off base?"

"Off right now, but that will change as soon as we string some more wire. The size of the base is to be increased, almost ten times, to allow the prison camp to be inside the base and to provide additional security. A squadron of helicopters are to be assigned here any day now."

"What do you mean, additional security?"

"Pankov wants bunkers constructed, towers, sandbagged positions for heavy machine guns, and the list goes on and on. He wants mines up the ass and all around this place, plus more wire than you have ever seen before."

"Why? It almost sounds as if he is scared."

"He might be frightened, and he has reason to be. As the commander responsible for the prison camps that will soon spring up all over, he will be a wanted man. Can you imagine the anger the resistance will have when their mothers, fathers, sisters or wives are placed in a camp or killed?"

"They will eventually come and try to take this place, or so I think. If not here, it will happen someplace else, because they will want to show their people we cannot keep them as prisoners."

"I hope like hell I am gone when that fight happens." Durchenko said and then added, "It will be worth the cost in men for the propaganda they will get from freeing their people."

"The officers will just line up a group of hostages and shoot them in retaliation."

"But the damage will have been done already. My tent is here. Do you want to come in for a quick drink or two? I have some American bourbon."

CHAPTER 11

Margie almost panicked, but was able to keep her composure as she asked, "Where will you take me?"

"We take you to alley. There we will make you happy woman."

"What if I don't want to go?" She gave Dolly a stroke on the top of her head.

The soldier who spoke English said something to his partner and both men pulled their weapons from their shoulders. Pointing them at her, the soldier said, "Come, now."

They walked a block up and then down a long narrow alley. Trash, empty bottles and other debris littered the broken concrete. Margie knew she had to kill the two men, but feared using the pistol. The noise would draw attention.

One man placed his rifle against a wall and the other said, "Clothes off."

Margie decided there was no way out of the situation, except to fight, so she might as well go down fighting. If all went well, she'd survive, if not, then she'd die. *I will not be used like a whore by these two*, she thought.

She slowly removed her blouse, teasing both men as she did so, and when she reached back, as if to remove her bra, she pulled the pistol and fired one round, catching the man holding a weapon in the middle of the chest. He fell to the ground unmoving and didn't make a sound. As the second Russian moved for his gun, Margie screamed, "Dolly, attack!"

Dolly jumped for the soldier and he was pushed up against a wall, where he began yelling for help. As the dog suddenly lunged for his throat, the man made an attempt to stop her with his left hand, but missed, and Dolly clamped her strong jaws on her intended target. Blood began to spurt high into the air as the Russian fought with the dog. A few minutes later, the soldier lay still and Dolly turned away from him. The dead man's throat had been torn and ripped.

Margie quickly dressed and pulling a shirt from one of the Russians, she cleaned the dog as well as she could without water. Then, picking up the foods, she walked from the alley and walked up one block before she turned left. *This street*, she thought, *should take me out of town. Someone must have heard my shot or the screams of the last man. I have to walk slowly and not blow my cover, no matter how much I want to run. Good God, what a mess.*

All went well, until she could see the brush where John was hiding and then a truck pulled up in the road behind her and half a dozen men jumped from the rear. A loud shout was heard in Russian, but Margie only had about fifty feet to safety, so she ignored it.

"Stop! Woman! We shoot!" A voice called out in poor English.

There came a burst of automatic fire from the brush and she heard John yell, "Run, now!"

Bullets struck the road in front of her and at her sides, sending chunks of concrete high into the air as the bullets *pinged* off into space. *Just a bit more!* She thought and then glanced over her shoulder to see three men racing for her. She pulled the pistol she'd stuck in her coat pocked and squeezed off two rounds. No man slowed, but then John fired once more and the men fell, with two of them screaming. He then called for Dolly.

Just as she reached the bushes she felt something strike her left arm and the force of impact, and the fact she was off balance, knocked her to the ground. John moved to her and asked, "You okay?"

"I think so; took a hit to my arm."

She watched as John pulled tape from a grenade, pulled the pin and then tossed it toward the truck. Bullets continued to clip the brush and bushes around them until the explosion, which set off the gas tank, engulfed the truck in a fireball. As the flames rolled inside of themselves, over and over, John stood and snapped off single rounds. Other explosions followed as ammunition, grenades and spare gas cans went up in flames.

"Move, and let's do it now. We'll head east a bit and then swing north. I don't want to lead them straight back to our camp. As we move," John said, and handed her a bandage, "wrap your arm up as tight as you can. We'll stop in a couple of hours to do the job properly. I'll lead, but keep up with me, because I won't be able to come looking for you. If you feel weak or faint, let me know. Come, Dolly."

"They were going to rape me."

"Enough talk, move." John started off at a slow jog, designed to cover miles and not tire a person too quickly. *They'll come*, he thought, *but hopefully if we can make the swamps, we'll lose them there.*

They moved fast and, as they moved, Margie said, "Listen to me, I have some things I need to tell you. In case something happens to me, the information is not lost."

"Talk fast, because they'll be after us soon."

As she jogged, she handed the tow sack with the meat and vegetables to him and said, "Around a hundred men are assigned at Edwards, but they plan to make a prison for family members of those they suspect are in the resistance. Right now, the base is poorly defended, with no mines or much wire in place. During the day, we can almost walk up to it, but at night they shoot first, and then ask questions."

John met her eyes and said, "Good job. I can't believe you learned all of that in one visit. What's in the bag?"

"Five pounds of beef, 3 cabbages, bag of carrots, two onions, and one stalk of a celery. The cost was high, which is why I handed the bag to you. I don't want to lose it."

"We'll stop in a few minutes, and then I want you to tie the bag to my pack. I need both hands free as we travel, in case of trouble. I've not had fresh beef or veggies in a long time."

"Looking at Dolly you'll see some blood on her, but it's not hers. I had to shoot one man and she killed the other. She's a fine dog and saved my life, I think. I might have killed the second man but I think another shot would have made my getaway impossible."

"Enough talking."

Hour after hour they ran until they reached the edge of the swamp. At times, to slow down any pursuit, John would stop and make a booby-trap or lay a mine.

John grinned and said, "They'll never follow us far into the swamps, because it's too easy to get lost."

"Do you know this area?" Margie squatted to rest.

"I've hunted gators in this part of the swamp, but we'll not go in but a couple of miles. There is an old mansion, oh, maybe two miles from here and we'll spend the night there."

There came a loud *boom* of thunder followed by a light wind.

Standing, she said, "Let's move so the rain will wash our tracks away."

"Step where I step. There are places in here that look solid, but they're not and you fall into water. If you fall into the water, either snakes or gators will get you, understand?"

"Oh, I hear every word, because I'm scared to death of snakes."

John chuckled and said, "Let's pray the Russians are, too."

When the rains came, they were gentle and not pounding. Glancing behind them, John saw the dirt turning to mud and knew they'd be impossible to track, even with dogs. He began to hum a no name tune as he walked.

Fog began to move in and Margie said, "Damn, I don't like this. I mean this is a scene out of some horror movie. Rain, old house, lightning, fog, all we need now is for Dracula to meet us at the front door and say, 'Good evening.'"

"Relax; if it bothers you, it'll bother the Russians, too. Just keep moving, because I'm going to place a couple of anti-personnel mines in case they follow us this far. You'll notice I've pretty much stuck to the left side of the trail when it forked or branched. If something happens to me, just lean heavy to the trails to the right to return to solid land again." He squatted and began scooping mud from the center of the trail with his hands.

Hearing a small noise, Margie turned and saw a large cotton-mouth snake swimming toward the bank she was on. "Uh, John, we have a big snake heading for us."

"Flip it out of the way. I can't help you right now, I'm arming the mines. Use a stick."

She picked up a limb, broke off the branches and shivered when she saw the snake open it's mouth and it's long fangs were clearly seen. *Lawdy, I hate snakes*, she thought and then placed the limb under the snake and flicked—hard. The snake went high into the air and landed with a loud plop, right beside her.

She almost screamed as John said, "Knock him out of your way, like this." He then used the barrel of his AK-47 to flip the snake off the trail and into the water. Margie shuddered in fear.

"Come on, it's about a quarter mile to the old house."

The rain increased in volume, the trail became slippery, and lightning flashed bright lines in the black sky, which exploded into many smaller lines with a loud *crack* of thunder. It was now late afternoon and the weather brought early darkness.

Stopping, John said, "That's the place." He pointed to an old broken down building off the right side of the trail. Part of the roof had caved in, the windows were mostly missing, and the door was hanging by one hinge.

Margie chuckled and said, "When I was a kid and used to watch horror movies, when I'd see a place like this, I'd always scream, 'Don't go in there!'"

John's laughter joined hers and he said, "It's spooky looking and if you don't like it, we can stay out here, but it has a fireplace and it's mostly dry inside. The choice is yours."

"Let's go in, because we'll drown out here. I'm a big girl and while I don't like the place, I'm sensible enough to know it offers us shelter."

"The last time I was here, the floor was rotted in a few spots, so follow in my wet footsteps once we go inside. Here, use this," he said as he handed her a small flashlight.

The first step to the porch was busted and fallen in, so they moved up the other steps slowly, expecting them to collapse. Standing on the porch, Margie saw the railing that once went around the front was missing. Stepping around the hanging door, John entered.

Stairs were to the right, but there was no way she'd go to the second floor, because the structure was too old and it looked ready to fall in at any moment. John lowered his backpack to the floor, moved to the fireplace and removed his flashlight. He stuck his head in the fireplace and looked up the chimney with the light.

"It's clear this time. About a year ago, I had to clear out a nest of pack rats."

Wood was stacked up against a wall near the front windows, so in a few minutes a small fire was burning. Removing a Russian ration, which was designed for two people, he opened it and shared it with Margie.

As they ate, she asked, "Why are the Russians making a prison?"

Wiping his mouth off with his hand, John said, "They have a history of locking up those that are criminals, insane, or political enemies of the state. They'll be treated poorly, fed a starvation diet, and most will die of diseases or firing squads."

"It sounds rough to me, but how will the resistance react if their families are imprisoned?"

"Well, how do you think they'll take it?" He took a bite of biscuit and then a bite of goulash. *This stuff is better than our rations*, more variety anyway, he thought.

"Be hard on a man or woman knowing their family was being treated like that. But, if you're really asking me will it change anything, then no. If anything it'll bring more unity to those resisting the Russians."

"Willy Williams once old me, 'The Russians are a hard people and they only respect brute strength.' At the time, I thought he'd lost his mind, because he was in the process of burning a Russian to death. Now, after fighting them a few times, ambushing and being ambushed, I realize he was correct."

"Do you think we'll make an attempt to bust people out?"

Taking a sip of his instant coffee, he looked over the rim of his metal canteen cup and replied, "It all depends on the defenses they have and how it looks. We've attacked bases, supply depots, small camps and ambushed convoys before, so anything is possible."

There came a loud crash near the front door and John scooped up his AK-47. He moved behind some ancient furniture and waited. Margie moved to the other side of the room and from the firelight, her eyes were huge. Dolly was ready to lunge, but after a few minutes her ears dropped, and she sat on the floor.

Suddenly John laughed, stood and moved forward. He was lost for a minute in the darkness and then said, "The door is no longer hanging by a hinge, it's fallen to the porch."

"I almost filled my pants."

"I suspected if it had been Russian troops, we'd have known it immediately. They would have tossed a grenade in and then entered, shooting anything that moved. I've heard other noises while sleeping here, so get used to it. I think you handled it well."

Moving back to the fire, she asked, "What do you know of this place?"

He walked to her side, sat and asked, "Do you want the legend or the truth?"

"Both."

"Well, the legend is ole man Packerman went crazy one night back in 1865, took an ax and hacked his family to death. That's all a lie."

"Oh, who killed them then?"

"History tells a different story. It seems in early 1865, March is as near as I can remember, the South was losing the War of Union Aggression, and Packerman knew it, because he was a full colonel in a cavalry unit. He disbanded his troops and told them to go home; for them the war was over. His family, who'd been in Jackson for the duration of the fight, joined him here on his return. Within a month, Colonel Packerman was dead of an unknown fever and one-by-one his family died in this very house. The last living relative attempted to get rid of this place, only who wanted a home in the edge of a swamp, where a whole family died mysteriously?"

"I wonder why the house is even here."

"Packerman was wealthy and had little use for others. He was a recluse, if you will, and some say the death of his first wife, following childbirth, lead to some strange behavior. He often sat up all night, in this very room, sipping whiskey and reading his Bible."

"Did they ever determine what disease killed them?"

"No, not officially, but it could have been malaria, bad water, or a dozen other fevers that a swamp can give a person. It's important to remember, doctors in those days knew very little real medicine, when compared to today. They thought illnesses were all related to 'bad blood' so they'd bleed a patient, or blister them, and that surely didn't help. If anything, it made the patient weaker."

"How do you know all of this stuff?"

John gave a lopsided grin and said, "My great-great-great grandfather was Moses Packerman, on my momma's side. He'd sit in this room, drink whiskey and shout Bible scriptures when angered. Now, I don't want to make him sound insane, because he wasn't, but he had his ways. Momma told me after his first wife died, he mourned her death for two years. Finally, he remarried and I've seen old tintypes of his last wife and she was beautiful."

"He sounds pretty damned strange to me."

"Oh, he was at least strange, but he was rich and made his money in shipping, but his cargo was humans, not other goods. He made his fortune in the slave trade. You know, I should hate him for that, but I don't. Over the years I've come to realize his world and my world are totally different. Now, I'm not saying what he did was right, we both know better than that, but at the time it was legal. He broke no laws, imported what was in high demand, black humans, and was a respected member of society."

"I don't like it."

"I never said I liked it, or respected it, only that he'd broken no laws. The rich in the South wanted slaves and he had ships he inherited from his father, so, being a smart man, he delivered. You're thinking with a mind that has been conditioned to think like a modern human being and the social issues, you see, were different back then. I don't think it's fair to judge him using today's standards when they were so very different then."

Leaning against the wall, Margie said, "God has judged him."

"I'm sure he has. Listen, we're going to have to stand guard, one of us anyway, all night. So, do we do this in three hour watches or a single full six hours?"

"Let's do the full six, because I hate going to sleep knowing I'll have to get up again in a few hours."

"I'll let you have the first six then."

"Sounds good to me because they're the easiest."

"What happened back there in town?"

Margie told her tale as John scratched Dolly's ears. When she finished, he said, "You're good. Almost everyone I know would have broke out running, especially after a killing, and that would have sealed your doom. Also, you didn't go back through the market, which shows you think well under pressure."

"Do you honestly think I did the right thing?"

"You're alive and here tonight, right?"

"Why don't you get some sleep and I'll move to the front window to keep watch, because I think that's the best spot, right?"

"Yep, wake me at midnight, or when you get tired. Now, don't fall asleep on me, or you might get both of us killed. Wake me if you get a strong urge to sleep. What you did today tired you more than you realize, even if most of it was mental fatigue. Okay?"

Standing, with John's AK in her hands, she said, "I'll keep that in mind. Any idea how long we'll be here?"

He laughed and then asked, "Why, do you have a hot date or something?"

"I wish I did, just wondering."

"We'll see tomorrow. A lot depends on the Russians and how determined they are to catch us. They may think you were a common thief, and if that's the case, they'll not spend much time looking for you. But, by me using a grenade, I think they'll come."

Suddenly, realizing she'd forgotten something, Margie reached into her pocket and pulled out a poster she'd ripped from the wall of a building as she was leaving Edwards. Handing it to him she said, "These are all over town."

John read the poster and then placed it in his shirt pocket. Gazing into Margie's eyes, he said, "This will anger the resistance much more than a prison camp will. The killing of women and children is something animals would do, not human beings."

"I didn't know if I should bring one out or not. I was unsure what they'd do to me if I had one in my possession and they captured me."

John shrugged and then said, "Hard to say. I'm going to sleep, so you need to get to the window. The killing of hostages doesn't bother me personally; all of my family, except for Sandra are already dead. But, as an American, I dislike it and I'm sure the resistance will move against the Russians hard over this."

"It's wrong, but I'm a little bug and I'll do what I'm told. If you need me, I'll be at the window." she said and then made her way to the empty room.

As she pulled guard, her mind jumped in all directions, seemingly at the same time. She'd be thinking about Edwards, then memories of her late husband would jump to the forefront of her thoughts. She allowed this to happened, just to pass the time.

The wind was howling and screaming now, as rain pounded the old house. Suddenly, Dolly stood and gave a low growl of warning.

CHAPTER 12

Lieutenant Colonel Pankov walked around in the middle of the street, where John had killed the Russian troops, cursing. How could one woman, a starving one, kill this many of his men, or was she really a woman looking for her lost family? The resistance was made up of both men and women, so she may have very well been spying on the town. *She was a spy*, he thought, *or where would the grenade have come from?*

"How many dead, counting the two in the alley, Sergeant?"

Belonev said, "Ten, counting the two in the alley, sir."

"They were going to rape her, because the one shot had his penis out." Durchenko said with disgust.

"Sergeant, what we do to the Americans is not your concern, but finding those responsible for the deaths of our men is, and I want it done quickly." A light rain was falling as the new commander spoke.

"Yes, sir."

"Gather up two squads and go look for them. I should send more men with you, but we do not have the manpower to do that right now. I will send helicopter support, one aircraft, and keep the others on alert, in case you run into something big."

"That should be enough, sir." Durchenko said.

"What about me? Am I to go with the group or stay behind." Belonev asked.

"Stay, because if something happens, I do not want to lose both of you in a battle. I need one of you to remain behind."

"Yes, sir."

Durchenko said, "I will gather my men and leave now, sir, with your permission."

Waving the man away with his left hand, the Colonel said, "Go, and good hunting."

A loud crack of thunder was heard and the rain intensified as Master Sergeant Durchenko organized his men and then walked into the bushes. They left the dog handler behind, due to the rain and it showed no sign of letting up any time soon. The men were anxious, because the wind blew the long grasses and made the brush sway.

The man on point stopped and when Durchenko neared he asked, "What do you see?"

"There are no tracks, Sergeant."

"None?"

"Look for yourself. The rain has washed them all away."

Pulling out his compass and map, the Sergeant said, "Keep moving east and after a few kilometers we will move north. I suspect they will move for the swamps. The area to the north has many swamps and it would be impossible to find them, if they know the swamps well. However, the helicopter may see something from the air. Hand me the radio."

Five minutes later, they were moving again and the Sergeant had asked for a helicopter to fly over the swamps. *Maybe we will get lucky and the pilot will kill them. If he does, then I can get out of this rain and nurse a bottle for a few hours. I am too old to be doing this shit*, Durchenko thought.

Pankov said, "While we are out here, let us raid the traders and see what we can find. Hell, one or more of them may be part of the resistance. Everyone into the trucks!"

They drove to the market and as they unloaded the truck, Sally slowly made her way from her booth and walked into the wet trees behind her. The trees used to be a park, but no one had kept it up, so it was overgrown with grasses and trees. She didn't like being wet, but knew it beat a bullet in the head any day. She lay down but kept her head up to see what was happening.

Pankov yelled, "Gather all the civilians and place them next to the house across the street. I want three guards on them at all times. Then, search each booth and look for anything unusual. If you find anything, bring it to me or call for me."

The soldiers began to ransack the booths, found nothing in the first few, and then moved to Fred's booth. All went well for him, until they pulled a plastic container out from under his folding table. A private opened the container, gave a loud gasp and then stepped back. Sergeant Belonev moved to the box, looked inside and then said, "Colonel, you need to see this, sir."

Pankov walked to the booth, glanced inside the container and then asked, "Who owns this booth?" His English was fair, because he'd attended an English language course as a requirement to become an intelligence officer.

When no one replied, Pankov said, "I will not ask again. If you do not answer me, I will have all of you shot."

A woman suddenly shouted, "Fred owns it and that's him, right there." She pointed to the fat man.

Fred tried to blend in with the others, but couldn't do the job. He began to shake in fear as the Colonel commanded, "Seize that man and bring him to me."

Once he was in front of Pankov, Fred said, "S . . . sir, why do you want me?" Since Fred didn't speak Russian, he had no idea what was going on, but he had fears and suspicions.

Placing his hands on his narrow hips, Pankov asked, "Are you the owner of this booth?"

Fred started to lie, but knew it would do him little good, because he'd already been identified, so he nodded.

"Can you explain why there are human hands and feet in this container?"

"The box is not mine. I buy my meat from a man who delivers it each morning."

"Bring me the woman who identified him to me now."

When the woman neared, Pankov could see she was terrified, so he asked softly, "Is what he is telling me the truth?" Then, to get the woman's attention, he pulled his pistol.

"No, he brings his meat in from his farm. Few of us here buy any meat that is white from him, because we know what it is."

"Oh, and how did you know this?"

"By his tone. He'd say, 'I butchered another two legged hog last night,' or something like that. We didn't know for sure, so we said nothing."

Pankov said, "Take all of them, except these two to the new camp. They will be our first visitors and while it is crude, it will keep them where we need them."

"Yes, sir." Belonev replied and then yelled, "Get the civilians by the wall in the truck. Let us go, and do the job quickly."

Fred noticed everyone was watching the guards roundup the people, so he made a dash for the trees where Sally was watching. A Russian machine gunner fired and the bullets stitched down the center of Fred's back, spraying blood and bone in all directions. The butcher screamed, fell to the grasses, and his body jerked violently. After a moment or so, he stopped moving, and his blood slowly added crimson to the water puddle under him.

Pankov looked at the woman and thought, *she is not ugly and yet young enough to please my men, once clean. I must keep my troops happy or I will have problems with them eventually.*

He could see the woman was not wearing a bra, so he extended his arm and squeezed her left breast. While she didn't like his touch and gave him a sneer, he asked, "Your breasts are firm. Do you want to continue living?"

Thinking quickly, she realized if she said no, they'd likely kill her, so she said, "I can make you a happy man, sir." *I must survive,* she thought, *even if it's as a whore.*

"What do you want done with the woman, sir?" The Master Sergeant asked.

"Bring her with us, she will be useful entertaining the troops. The men use up women too quickly, but a few will enjoy this one before they grow tired of her."

While she didn't understand a word said, she was smiling when led to the Colonel's staff car, not realizing the fate awaiting her.

"What of the butcher's body?"

"Drag it to the street and then hang him from his ankles. Place a sign on his ass that says, guilty of butchering humans and peddling the meat."

"I will see to it immediately, sir."

Looking around, Pankov said, "Leave this place as it is, so some of the food and other things can go to the people of this town. I think their market has just been closed."

Durchenko and his men were cursing the rain as they moved. The rain was harder now and it angered him there were no tracks to follow in the mud. The rains had cleaned all sign of anyone passing.

The radio man walked to his side and said, "Base says the helicopter pilot is on a weather hold and we are to continue to the edge of the swamp. The commander does not want us to enter without an aircraft overhead."

"Acknowledge that I understand and we will hold on the edge of the swamp, until the aircraft is in the air."

Throughout the afternoon, the Master Sergeant wondered why they'd seen no mines or booby-traps, and was beginning to think he was on the wrong trail. He was an old partisan hunter and knew they often made attempts to scare, injure, or kill, those following, but he'd seen nothing so far.

Looks like no aircraft will be with us this day, he thought as he neared the edge of the swamp. Turning to the radio man he said, "Contact base and let them know we are at the very edge of the swamp. Ask them if we should call it a day and start fresh in the morning. And, get a weather report."

A couple of minutes later, the man carrying the radio said, "We are to spend the night here. Weather is forecasting rain all night, with dense fog at daylight. Once the fog burns off, base hopes to get the aircraft into the air."

"Give them our exact coordinates and tell them we'll contact them every hour, on the hour, and we will move in the morning when they tell us to do so." Then, looking at his wet men, Durchenko added, "Men, we will spend the night here, so move to the small clearing among the trees. I want two men on guard at all times. If I catch a guard sleeping, I will beat his ass."

The men cursed the mission and their luck to have to spend a night out in the rain. Durchenko knew a cursing soldier was common, so he ignored the chatter.

"Can we have a small fire, to cook on, before it grows dark?" A private asked.

The Master Sergeant laughed and replied, "If you can find anything dry enough to burn, sure, but it goes out at dark." *These men are such fools. It has been raining hard all day and unless they look under big trees, they will find no dry wood.*

One of the privates said, "I see a nice log over there."

He moved forward and suddenly he erupted in a sheet of fire, his body coming apart before it flew into the air. Men fell to the ground and once the noise of the explosion, as well as the dust, died down, Durchenko said, "Keep your eyes open for mines, anytime you are in the field. Is anyone else hurt?"

"We have two others down." A junior sergeant said, who Durchenko knew was their medic.

"Well, see to them, fool!"

"What if there are more mines?"

"You'll be safe enough, if you stay behind the dead man. It's not likely the ones we follow placed a mine field around here. It was designed to slow us down, so check my men."

The medic cursed under his breath and then moved to the injured men. He squatted by the first man, shook his head, and opened a bag he carried, and removed a needle. He gave the man a shot and then moved to the next man. After a few minutes he returned to Durchenko and said, "One will die, he has been hit in the gut, and the other has a slight head wound. I have dressed the head wound."

"And, Doctor Sergeant, what makes you think the belly wound will die?"

"The blast took a big chunk of his spine out and even on the base, a doctor could do nothing for him. He will be dead in a minute or two."

I think you have given the man too much morphine for his pain, so he will die for sure. I would want you to do it to me, if I was hurting and had no chance to live, Durchenko thought and then removed a ration from his pack.

Near midnight, while all were asleep, one of guards opened fire at something he thought he saw moving in the water of the swamp.

"What in the hell are you shooting at?" The Master Sergeant said as he stood, weapon in hand.

"I think I saw a man swimming toward us in the water, so I shot."

Durchenko moved to the edge of the water and saw a huge alligator dead near the bank. The body of the animal was leaking blood from a half a dozen bullet holes. He laughed and said, "Come here, fool, and see your man."

The guard, visibly shaken by the experience, walked to the edge of the swamp, looked into the water, and then said, "It looked just like a swimming man."

"Alright, everyone back to sleep." Durchenko said and then turned to the young guard, "When you are tired, it's late and dark, your eyes often play tricks on you. The next time, wake someone instead."

When morning arrived, fog draped the swamp and low areas in a veil of white that looked to go forever. The men ate and then relaxed as they waited for word from the base. The radio man neared Durchenko, who was making coffee, and said, "This fog will not be gone until around 10 hundred hours. Weather says a cold front collided with a warm one, which is causing the current conditions."

"Let them know we are ready to move when they give the word."

The rain had eased and was more like a mist now, but each man wore a poncho. The man with the belly wound had died the night before, as well as the man with the head injury. The old Master Sergeant knew head wounds were tricky and sometimes the best medics didn't understand a head didn't need to be bloody to be a serious injury. But, he hadn't known the names or anything about either of the dead, so he forgot about them. *I need to concentrate on keeping these men alive and not worry about the dead. They are beyond worrying over now*, he thought as he picked up his canteen cup.

An hour later, at 0900, the radio man neared and said, "Weather is breaking near the base, so a helicopter will be airborne shortly."

"Do they want us to enter the swamp now?"

"No. We are to wait until the pilot contacts us before we move in any direction."

Durchenko nodded and then said, "Check your gear and make sure nothing rattles. When we enter the swamp, keep a close lookout for snakes. Most of the water snakes in this part of the country are poisonous, so watch where you place your feet and hands."

No sooner had the fog dissipated than the Master Sergeant heard noise from the radio. The radio man grinned and said, "I understand."

"Well?"

"We are to wait here until the helicopter checks some areas in the swamp." The radio man said and then added, "We might not have to enter at all, not the way things are looking."

"We will enter. The aircraft is checking now to see if he can catch anyone out walking. I do not think he will be an hour checking either, so get rid of the grin."

"I can hope, Master Sergeant."

The radio squawked and when the man answered it, he spoke for a minute or two and then said, "We are to enter. He claims the area looks clean and informed you to not go more than five kilometers in to this place."

"Alright, don your packs and gear. I want a man on point with good eyes, and another man on drag."

Soon they were moving down a trail, but there were no tracks or marks indicating anyone had ever been here before. Mud was ankle deep and it slowed the men down. The chopper kept flying near and at times he'd drop low to check out suspicious looking area or to break the boredom.

The man on point covered about two kilometers when he suddenly stopped and said, "Tripwire."

Durchenko moved forward, looked at the wire, and marked it with a stick in the mud in the middle of the trail. "It is marked, so move forward, but keep your eyes open at all times."

No sooner had the Sergeant turned, than the point man took a step forward and a loud explosion filled the morning air. Durchenko was knocked to his face in the mud and there came loud screams, as debris from the mine fell from the sky. Slowly sitting up, his ears bleeding, the Master Sergeant looked around and saw over half of his men down. Unable to hear, the sergeant moved to the prone radio man and said, "Call the helicopter and ask if he can pick up the most severely injured."

When the man didn't raise his head, he turned the man over and discovered he was bleeding from his throat and as dead as it gets. Picking up the headset, the Sergeant said, "I have been wounded and cannot hear you. I am the ranking man on the ground and need you to take my wounded out without delay. I will need another aircraft, as I have many wounded. If you understand, move to my position now."

He grinned as the helicopter turned and made his way to him. Durchenko looked around, saw an uninjured private and yelled, "You, private, come and speak to the helicopter, it is time for you to earn your first medal. Come now, and be a hero."

He watched the private communicating with the aircraft and felt a dull pain starting in his lower back and his legs. He moved his hand to the spot on his back and when done, he noticed blood on his hand. The helicopter started slowly descending until the right skid was near the bank.

When the seriously wounded were gone, Durchenko said, "Get some defenses set up and cover our asses. The second aircraft will be here soon."

CHAPTER 13

Margie made her way to John, touched his right foot and said, "I have movement, but I won't swear it's not a gator."

"It's okay to wake me. I'd rather you wake me than get me killed. Let's move to your window and check out the movement."

They moved to the window together, but John saw nothing, initially. He squinted his eyes in an effort to see better, only no luck. He waited, patiently. Finally, he saw movement and it looked to be human, too. If it was a person, they were injured, because they appeared to be crawling. John expected an attacker to be bent at the waist to make a smaller target, not crawling.

"I'm goin' out there." John said a few minutes later. A long finger of lightning flashed across the dark sky, followed by a sharp *crack* of thunder, and Dolly growled.

In the flash of lightning, Margie saw blood on the fallen form outside, and said, "Go, I'll cover you. I didn't see a uniform on the person."

"Dolly, stay." He commanded, and then stepped over the fallen door and made his way to the porch. Rain was falling with more force now, and the winds blowing hard as he stepped from the protection of the porch. He made his way to the downed person and, once there, rolled them onto their back. He saw a bullet hole high in the woman's left shoulder and it'd gone all the way through, because he'd seen the exit wound before he rolled her over.

Picking her up, she might have weighed a hundred and twenty pounds; John carried her to the house over his shoulder. He used caution on the steps, because they were weak, and he didn't want to fall through. He stepped over the door and carried her into the living room. He placed her on a blanket Margie had placed on the floor.

Turning to Margie, he said, "Look her over closely and treat her injury, because I need to get back to the window."

"I've been well trained, thanks to your wife, so I'll do what I can for this woman."

John moved to the window, sat on the floor and scanned the swamp. He saw little, due to the rain, except he knew it would be a good time to attack someone. Bad weather covered movements and approaches well, and if attacked, he'd not likely know it until the last second. Dolly moved to him and placed her head in his lap. He scratched her ears.

Margie removed the woman's boonie hat, shirt, and bra. She saw the path of the bullet had hit high, into the shoulder muscle, and not the bone. Pulling some medical supplies from her first aid pouch, she cleaned the entrance and exit wounds well, removing bits of clothing and other debris. Satisfied with her work, she wiped the injuries down with some alcohol pads and then bandaged the wound. Unless the wound became infected, she'd live.

She noticed the woman was young, still in her twenties, short blond hair, attractive, but not beautiful, and was about five feet six inches tall. Her face was covered in mud and grime, so Margie washed her face and hands. *There, she looks better already*, she thought, *only she's lost a lot of blood.*

Margie then moved to John and said, "She's still out, due to shock and blood loss, I think. The bullet passed through the meaty portion of her shoulder, so she'll live. You can go back to sleep now."

John stood, yawned, and then said, "I'll do that." He handed her the AK-47.

With the coming of dawn it was still raining as hard as ever, but the wind was less forceful. John stood from in front of the window, stretched and then picked up his weapon. Making his way to the living room he asked, "How's our visitor?"

"I . . . I'm awake."

He squatted beside her and said, "I'm John, and the woman with me is Margie. You've been shot in the shoulder, but should survive. Now, who are you?"

"I'm called Sue, but it ain't my real name, only that's not important. I'm a member of the resistance, my commanders full name is Colonel Willy Williams, and you should know him."

"I know Willy and Top; are they both well?"

"They were the last time I saw them."

"What happened out there, Sue?"

"We attacked a small group of Russians in a wooded area just south of the swamps. There were ten of us and once I was hit, I crawled under some brush to hide, and after a few minutes I passed out. When I awoke, my cell was gone and a large group of Russians were unloading from choppers. I made my way into the trees and then the rains came."

"How'd ya get here?"

"Before the fall, I was an avid photographer and I wrote articles for a living. I'd been here before and had photographed the house many times."

"Which direction did you approach the house from, because I had mines on the southern trail?"

"From the west, the only way I know how to get here. I'm sure there are many trails that lead here, but that's the only way I know."

Margie asked, "Are you in pain?"

"Some, but not much we can do about that right now."

"I have some morphine I can give you for the pain, but it'll wipe you out."

"Use it, so maybe I can get some sleep, if it's safe here."

"It's as safe as it ever gets these days, which means our security is marginal at best. Take the drug, rest, and we'll leave in the morning."

No sooner had Margie administered the drug than the *wop-wop* of helicopters was heard off in the distance. John ran from the house, with Dolly behind him, and stood under a large tree, watching the two aircraft flying circles, to the south of them. After a few minutes, one of the aircraft slowly lowered until it was out of sight, but a few minutes later, he spotted it rising in the air. It continued up until it gained altitude and then flew to the south. Then, as he watched the second chopper did the same.

He walked into the house and said, "I think someone triggered one of my traps. I just watched two aircraft descend into the swamp and then leave a few minutes later. Then again, they may have been delivering supplies, so I'll go check it out."

"John," Margie said, "watch your ass out there, because if they resupplied some folks they'll be armed for bear."

"Well, I doubt it was a resupply, because if anyone is on our ass, they've only been trailing us for less than a day. Now, they may have been unloading more troops, but I don't think so. The birds I watched were in and out fast, like they do when they pick up wounded. I'll take no risks, but I'll leave Dolly with you."

John donned his poncho and left with the AK-47 in his hands.

The rain eased up and he moved through the mud to the booby-trap, except he didn't like the tracks he left in the muck. *On the way back, I'll have to cover my tracks or they might be seen from the air.*

When he neared the spot he'd placed the booby-trap, he slowed and scanned the area, but saw no one. Cautiously he moved forward, his weapon's safety off and his finger resting on the trigger. Glancing at the trail ahead, he saw a small crater where his mine had exploded. He stopped short of the crater and scanned the area. He saw part of a human hand, a foot still inside a laced up boot, and some discarded bandages. The blood had mostly washed away, leaving puddles of pink on the ground and pink stains on the bandages. However, by looking at the size of the pink bandage stains, some of the men had been hit hard. He knew from experience some men died, but it was hard to tell how many.

He pulled a stick from the water and began to move it from side-to-side in his muddy tracks as he moved back toward the house. The scratching of the mud alone would draw attention, but he hoped the falling rain would soon wash away all sign of his passing.

Margie was guarding at the front window when he returned and gave him a questioning look when he entered.

Removing his poncho, he said, "Our booby-trap exploded at some point today, but with the thunder we've had, we didn't hear the explosion. I have no way of knowing how many men were hurt, but I suspect a squad or two were taken out by choppers."

"I thought one mine couldn't do that kind of damage to a group of men."

"I had one Claymore mine using a tripwire and the second mine was an anti-personnel mine, pressure detonated. I rigged them so if the second mine exploded, the Claymore would also. I thought they'd find the tripwire easily, mark it, and then step over the wire. I planted the anti-personnel mine about a foot behind the wire."

"Nasty, huh?"

"Most of the blood had washed away, but they left some body parts behind. How's our new troop?"

"Sue is sleeping well, but she should be after I gave her the morphine. I think we can leave in the morning."

"We need a guard at this window all the time we're here. None of us should go outside either, in case they have choppers out looking for us. That means if you have to use the toilet, find an empty room to do your business. Tonight, we'll eat an early supper and then put the fire out. It's very possible they'll have infrared aircraft flying around looking for us. Gunships and helicopters both carry the technology, but we want to avoid discovery if possible, so stay inside. NVG's I'm not too worried about, because we'll be indoors."

"Comforting thought, huh?"

John gave a low chuckle and replied, "Unless they spot this place and put men on the ground to look it over, we're safe enough. From what I saw when I neared, there are plenty of tree limbs, moss and other vegetation on the roof of this house. The roof almost looks like a brush pile."

"How good is the infrared equipment the Russians have? Do you think it could pick up our body heat inside this place?"

"Honestly?" John asked and then said, "I have no idea. I know just before the fall, the United States had some awesome stuff, but I couldn't tell you about the Russians. If they're like most military units, some of their gear will be new and some old."

"What now?"

"I'll eat and get a bit more sleep."

"I've got the window, so relax and rest."

Morning arrived with Sue still in pain, but not the deep pain she'd had the day before. Overnight she'd had a fever, but it broke about an hour after dawn. She was awake now, eating a breakfast of biscuits with chocolate and hazelnut paste smeared on top. A canteen cup of hot instant coffee was sitting beside her legs. The whole meal was part of a Russian ration.

John asked, "No dizziness or faint feelings when you used the toilet this morning?"

"No, nothing. Only I hardly call peeing on the floor of an old bedroom a toilet." She gave a big smile.

Margie said, "It passes for one here. We're walking out today, so if you start to feel faint or dizzy, let one of us know."

John said, "We leave in a few minutes. The rain stopped early last evening, but we'll have some mud to deal with during the whole walk. Once out of the swamp, we'll travel overland as quickly as we can, and avoid all trails. It's still cloudy, so I expect more rain at some point today, which is good, because it will wash our tracks away."

Ten minutes later they were moving down a muddy path toward the west. John didn't want to use the same trail to leave that they'd used to enter the swamp, in case it was mined or an ambush was waiting for them. He remembered an old sergeant who once said, "Never enter and leave by the same route, because your enemies may wait and ambush you. Always leave by a different path."

Nothing was seen and little was heard, except for the occasional low splash as something entered the water from a log or from the trail. The sky remained overcast, and Margie prayed they'd not have to sleep in the swamp overnight. Just the thought of snakes and alligators filled her with anxiousness.

It was shortly after noon, when John called for a short ten minute break and they'd just left the swamp. Sue was holding up well and hadn't complained of pain, but he suspected she was hurting. Margie must have thought the same, because she removed two over the counter pain relievers and said, "Wash these down with some water. Once we get back to our base, we have something a little stronger for you."

"If you want to eat, do the job now, because we'll leave in ten minutes."

Walking to an oak tree with Sue following, Margie removed her pack and sat in the damp grass. Sue, due to pain, sat closer to the tree and leaned back against the rough gray bark.

John ate a can of pork, washing it down with a tonic drink, and then for dessert, jam on a biscuit. He then fed Dolly beef stew and a biscuit. Once she'd finished eating, he glanced at his watch, and said, "Saddle up, we need to be moving."

For hours they kept a fast walk and the miles disappeared behind them. Finally, nearing a blacktopped road, John said, "We cross one at a time, on a run. Once near the edge of the roadway, jump as far into the grass as you can. That way we'll leave no tracks in the mud beside the roadway. I'll come last, so I can cover the sign we'll leave passing through."

Margie was just about to make a mad dash across the road when Sue said, "Stop, because I hear something."

"I hear it too, now, but I didn't a second ago. Here," he handed her Dolly's leash and added, "take her, and she'll jump at the same time you do. She'll offer you a bit more protection once you're on the other side. Now wait and let's see what's causing the noise."

A lone motorcycle rode over a slight hill in the road moving south at a good speed. Then a few seconds later a convoy approached. They counted ten trucks and still they waited, to see if another motorcycle was riding drag. After almost ten minutes, John said, "Go."

Margie ran across the road and at the end, leaped high into the air, landing beyond some brush, with Dolly at her side.

Looking at Sue, John asked, "Ready?"

"Uh-huh."

"Go!"

Her run was almost an exact copy of Margie's and she landed on the other side of the brush as well.

John had just broken cover and was almost to the middle of the road when a motorcycle, moving south at a high rate of speed suddenly appeared over the hill. The encounter spooked both men, but John recovered first and fired three rounds at the bike. The motorcycle fell to its side and slid down the road with the rider's left leg trapped under it. It came to rest about twenty feet from John, who approached, shot the rider the head, and then took most of the man's gear. He then slipped an ace of spades card into the dead man's mouth.

Then he made tracks in the mud from the side of the road toward the bushes on the side he'd just left, hoping to confuse any Russians. Hopefully they'd head the wrong direction, the way they'd come. He realized it'd not fool a good tracker, not for long anyway, but might buy him a few minutes of precious time.

Going back to the dead rider, he picked up the man's pistol, a Makarov PMM, and PP-19, "Bison" sub-machine gun, with the magazine pouch, and oil can. Then, he placed the pistol in his trouser cargo pocket and the four spare magazines in his shirt pocket. It was then he noticed a dispatch pouch, so he picked it up and threw the sling around his shoulder. He placed his AK-47 strap around his neck and carried the Bison as he joined the others.

Once with the others, he handed his AK-47, along with spare magazines to Sue as he said, "You take this. Are you familiar with using it?"

"It's what I carried before, but lost it during the ambush, or else my cell took it with them. I remember having it before I blacked out."

"Follow me and we'll take the long road back home."

An hour before dark, they neared the cellar and John called out. Tom stuck his head from the doorway and replied, "Come on in! We thought you'd been captured."

"No, but it was close for a bit there." John said as he left the trees and made for the cellar. Seeing no guard he asked, "Surely you have a guard posted?"

"Kate's watching and you can be sure she had you in the crosshairs of her 30.06 for a few seconds. She has a new sniper rifle, a VSS Vintorez, with a case of 9X39 mm SP-5 cartridges, but hasn't sighted it in yet. The information we have is it will penetrate body armor. She was given five, ten round, magazines to go with the rifle and even a NSPUM-3 night vision sight. I've been carrying the night vision sight to scan the area with after dark."

"Did Santa Claus come to visit?"

"Nope; Willy blew up a convoy and they discovered a shitload of these sniper rifles, along with ammo and sights. A group passing through this area gave the rifle, ammo and gear to her. Apparently, Willy sends out groups in general directions hoping they make contact with folks like us."

Margie approached, handed her burlap bag of food to Tom and said, "Have someone put us a decent meal together, because I'm worn out."

He grinned and said, "Come on in, and John, I know a woman's who has been worried sick about you."

Later, over a meal of fresh beef stew, the first in years for many of them, John gave an update and then had Margie tell her tale of the town of Edwards. When the prison camps were explained and the poster announcing the executions shown, Tom shook his head.

"What are you thinking?" John asked, as Sandra sat by his side holding his hand.

"I think the poster is outdated and they've grown tired of killing, because it gained them nothing. Now, it doesn't mean they've turned soft, actually just the opposite. The camps, I suspect, will be well guarded and not something we'll want to attack, unless we have an advantage in some way."

"What will Willy do?" Margie asked.

"Hard to tell, because he's original in thought, but he needs this information so some of the resistance can move their families, unless it's too late."

"Is the group that gave you the sniper rifle coming back this way?"

"They said they'd be back this way tomorrow, and if we needed to contact them to be close to the spot where the dirt road intersects with the pavement. Jones, the leader, said they'd be in the area a little after sunrise."

John said, "I know Jones, and he's a good leader. In the morning, I'll take Dolly and meet him. I'll tell him what we know and have him pass it on to Willy. Hell, we don't even know where Willy is, so we can't contact him at all."

"It's on purpose, so if we're captured, we can't say where the boss is hiding, don't you see?"

"Oh, I understand easily enough, but it makes it hard to get needed intelligence to the man."

Tom nodded and then said, "Joshua, go relieve Kate. Oh, I hear ya, John."

"Sue," Sandra said, "come to me and let me take a look at your shoulder. In the conditions we live under, it doesn't take long for an infection to occur."

CHAPTER 14

Durchenko was the last man off the trail in the swamp, and he felt weak and dizzy. He'd refused to leave until his men were loaded first. Once in the chopper a medic inserted an IV and started checking his vital signs. His pain was severe and the medic gave him a shot of morphine to give him some relief. As they flew, the Master Sergeants world, gradually, grew slightly darker until he entered a deep black void.

When he awoke, he couldn't open his eyes; they felt too heavy. A feeling of serenity filled him, so he was not scared, and soon drifted back to sleep. Then he heard metal striking metal, and his eyes still wouldn't open. He attempted to stay awake, fighting the urge to sleep, only he could not.

When he next awoke, his eyes opened quickly enough, only he was confused. I am in a hospital, but how can that be and why? He thought.

An attendant saw him moving, walked to his bed and said, "Master Sergeant Durchenko, can you hear me?"

"Yes, of course, you damned fool, but why am I in a hospital?"

"You were on a patrol when someone triggered an explosive device. Your doctor will explain your injuries to you. I under-stand you were a real hero, only allowing extraction after your men were all taken off first, so I suspect you will be awarded a big medal."

"Medals are just a piece of cloth and chunk of metal. Get my damned doctor and do it now, private, or I will climb out of this bed and beat your ass."

"I will get him for you, Sergeant." The man scurried away.

Searching his mind, he remembered no mission, but it would come with time. He leaned back and closed his eyes.

A tall thin doctor, a major, entered reeking of alcohol and asked, "What is the problem, Master Sergeant Durchenko?"

"Sir, I want to know the extent of my injuries, what happened, and why I am in a hospital. I remember nothing."

The doctor said, "According to your men you are a super hero, but the first helicopter on the scene said one of your men, while on a mission, tripped a mine. Out of the nineteen men with you, nine were killed and five more wounded, some severely. You were partly shielded by men in front of you, but the shrapnel passed through them and then into you. I'm sorry, but you have lost your right leg from the knee down. We tried to save it in the operating room, but it was mangled too badly. Your other injuries will heal, so in a few days, you will be on an airplane bound for Moscow. From there you will be presented with a medal and discharged. Since you already have enough years for retirement, you will do well enough."

"The leg was all I lost?"

"That's enough, don't you think?"

"I am just glad nothing else is missing. How are my, uh,—"

"Your family jewels are just fine. I can assure you, the only part of you that will not be the same when you leave is the leg."

Durchenko started laughing.

Glancing at the orderly, the major turned and walked from the room. Durchenko sobered, looked at the private and asked, "Do you fail to see the humor?"

"I do not think this is funny, Sergeant."

"Son, men are dying here and all I lost was a leg. I get to go home, retire, and move back to the farm. Hell, I can farm with a wooden leg. I am one lucky sonofabitch, do not you think?"

Feeling uncomfortable around the senior NCO, the orderly asked, "Will that be all, Master Sergeant?"

"Yes, get out and go to work."

Now, he sounds like a normal Master Sergeant, the orderly thought as he left the room.

It was mid afternoon when Master Sergeant Belonev entered wearing a big smile. Durchenko had just woke from a nap, but smiled at his old friend, and asked, "What brings you around?"

"Why, I came to see what a real war hero looks like."

"Well, I do not feel like a hero."

"Colonel Vetrov said you were submitted for the Golden Vodka Award, with shot-glass, second cluster, and you know he has no sense of humor. If he says it, it's true."

Durchenko laughed, although it brought him pain, and said, "It is good to see you, Dmitry. It took me a couple of hours to re-member the explosion, but the man who planted it was experi-enced. He knew most men would mark the tripwire and then step over it, which is what we did."

Belonev reached into his coat pocket and pulled out a pint of vodka and handed it to his friend, "Drink if you like."

Durchenko opened the bottle and chugged about a third of it, then handed it toward Belonev, who shook his head. "It is for you, so slip it under your mattress when you're done, because the medics will take it from you if they see it."

Durchenko lowered his head and said, "I lost a lot of men, good men. I heard earlier that one of the wounded died from his injuries, so I lost over half of them." Tears began to run down his cheeks.

"Listen, I have done the same in the past, and I once lost fif-teen out of twenty. I heard you had your men removed before yourself, and that's more than most officers would do. Just that act alone makes me proud as hell to know you and call you my friend. You were thinking of your men, even when seriously hurt, and that is what makes a real leader."

"There will be eleven families back home that will be informed of the deaths of their sons, fathers, and husbands."

Putting his hands on his narrow hips, Belonev said, "Durchenko, that is enough crying and feeling sorry for yourself bullshit. You are a soldier, a brave one, so start acting like what you are. Hell, you lost a leg, so no one is calling you a coward or a poor NCO. If they do that, I'll knock them on their asses."

He nodded, wiped the tears from his eyes and took another gulp of his vodka.

"I would trade places with you in a minute. You are going home and will spend the rest of your life on your farm, while I might get killed tomorrow. Relax, rest, and sip your vodka. The men who died were all soldiers and knew the risks, so forget about them."

"I am lucky in many ways."

"Sure you are, and do not be so fast to forget it either."

They talked for a few more minutes and then Durchenko fell into a deep sleep, due to mixing alcohol with his pain medication. Belonev took the vodka bottle raised it in a toast to his old comrade and took a sip. Just before he left the room, he pushed the bottle between Durchenko's mattress and springs.

Colonel Pankov was wondering how a single American could kill half the men in Durchenko's group and yet escape. The war against the resistance was going poorly, with many more dead Russians than Americans, except for the civilian executions. The mass killings had been stopped, per a request from Pankov, but the commander had given him one year to get his prison camps into action or the executions would start again.

According to Pankov, he now had over a thousand captives and more than two hundred in the Edwards camp alone. Twenty camps were being constructed, and people locked inside as soon as the wire was strung and connected to electrical power. Electrical power was supplied at all camps by huge industrial generators. Towers were up in about half of the camps, dog teams walked the fences, and armed guards positioned at strategic locations. Vetrov thought, *I am willing to bet most of what he claims that has been started has not been done, but he has one year and then I will start my execution squads again. The only thing I have actually seen with my own eyes is the wire strung at Camp Edwards and two guard towers.*

"Sir, the forecast for today is light snow, which is being pushed south by a cold front out of Canada, but it will not amount to much. Temperatures should be down in the single numbers, Celsius. I think we will have less than an inch, but the winds will blow hard and out of the west at around fifty-six kilometers an hour, with some gusts of twice that speed. There is the possibility for property damage, downed lines, and falling limbs or trees."

"How long will this weather last?"

"Sir, the three day forecast is the same for each day, with maybe a couple degree difference on some days and the wind speeds will vary a little each day. In about four days the front will move on, bringing dryer and warmer weather."

Turning to the commander of his helicopters, Vetrov asked, "How will these winds impact your flying?"

"May put a serious damper on our daily routine, because of the gusts, only I cannot say until the winds arrive. Then, I have to decide if the mission is critical or not and cancel any that are planned during the high wind warnings. We do have wind limits, but I will inform you at the time we have to cancel or reschedule any flights."

Turning to a major from operations, he said, "Get with supply and arrange additional rations, ammo and other needs, to be sent to our bases before this storm hits. Inform all bases why we are doing this and warn them of the cold front."

The commander of supply said, "We can support what you have requested, but they will need cold weather gear and I am short of gloves, parkas, and hats."

"Damn." Vetrov said, stood and asked, "Has Moscow been informed of our cold weather needs?"

"Yes, sir, and the shipment is due shortly, within ten days."

"Ten days? Colonel, this weather hits today. When was a requisition sent to headquarters and what was the priority given?"

"Sir, I do not have that information on me now, but I'll look into it and call your office within the hour."

"You do that, Colonel, and you will also call your supply counterpart in Moscow and request an immediate expedite of this gear, by air. How in the hell do you and Moscow expect me to do my job, when I do not have the needed supplies? I want the winter clothing for my troops here and delivered no later than twenty-four hours from now, or you, sir, will be assigned to the infantry."

"Sir, I don't know if that is even poss—"

"You heard me and I am a man of my word—twenty-four hours. Now, I want all ground patrols and searches for the resistance doubled, around the clock, once we have our winter gear. The partisans will need fires to survive and that means woodsmoke during the day. Once the bad weather passes, I want flights out at night looking for the light from these flames. If an aircraft spots a fire, take the light out with rockets, because the people on the ground will be close to the fires. Tell your pilots to use some common sense and check with us to make sure it's not a fire from one of our groups. Patrol leaders need to call in with their exact map positions, as they usually do, each night."

The legal officer said, "There will be finger pointing, in the event of friendly fire losses. I suspect there will be some instances of friendly fire deaths, due to the urgency of our missions."

"Major, you and your staff determine who is at fault in any accidents. I do not expect, and will not tolerate, long drawn out court fights over guilt. Get to the bottom of it and see justice is served, if there are any cases."

"Yes, sir."

"Now, I have another appointment, so that is all. Dismissed."

A sergeant called the room to attention and Vetrov departed.

Sally was tired, hungry, and cold. While the sun was shining, the temperature was below freezing. The same day the Russians had killed Fred, she'd been caught when she returned to her stall to get the gold jewelry she kept in a cigar box. She was now, along with about two-hundred others, shivering in a barbed wire enclosure about twice the size of a football field. They had absolutely no shelter, no food and no water. The Russians simply locked them in the wire cage and walked away. This was her third day without water, food, shelter or a fire.

A truck backed to the gate and men dismounted. Huge pots, the size of trashcans, were pulled from the back of the truck, placed on the ground, and Sally could see steam coming from each container. Suspecting it was hot food, she, along with the others, ran toward the gate.

A Russian soldier yelled in thickly accented English, "Make line. You want eat, make line."

People fought to get into line and more than one was shoved or knocked to the ground as all wanted food before it ran out.

The soldier yelled again, "Enough food everyone! No fight. Fight, we take food and go."

Fighting stopped instantly.

"All get one cup. Keep cup. No get another cup." The soldier said and then removed the lid to the first steaming pot.

A soldier was handing each person a metal canteen cup as they neared the food. As she drew closer to the food, she saw each person got exactly one ladle of some kind of soup. When her turn came, she received a single ladle of watery soup, and noticed small chunks of something mixed in the broth.

A thin and ill-looking man neared the soup containers once more, he'd already had one cup of soup.

"You! Eat one time, no more. No eat two times." The soldier screamed and pulled his pistol.

"This is not enough. I need more to eat, please?" The thin man Sally only knew by Edward said as he walked toward the pot of soup.

"No, food is for all people. Eat one time."

A woman walked to Edward and said, "My husband is ill and needs more to eat than the others. Please, just one cup more?"

The pistol shot was loud and Edward gave a look of surprise as he was struck in the chest. Blood blew out his back and he collapsed to the ground screaming. His fingers clawed at the dirt as blood ran under him.

His wife screamed madly and ran straight for the guard. The pistol barked twice, each bullet hitting her, and she fell to the ground screeching and jerking.

"Now, no worry about husband. He finished. Never come close to gate. We shoot." The soldier said, and then broke out laughing. He said something in Russian and the pots were placed in the back of the truck and they left the area. Each American had received one cup of watery soup.

No one tried to help Edward or his wife, they simply walked away, except for Sally. Holding her precious soup, she squatted beside the man and knew right off he'd die. His eyes were rolled up into his head and his breathing was irregular. His fingers, no longer digging at the soil, were quivering as his central nervous system shut down.

She moved to the woman and saw one bullet had struck her in the lower stomach and the other in the shoulder. Sally knew a little about medicine, since she'd worked in a hospital before the fall as a nurses aid, and the stomach wound was fatal. The woman suddenly gave a heartbreaking scream and arched her back in pain.

As Sally moved past the man, only one finger was still twitching. She moved to the far corner of the camp and sat in the grass. Her soup didn't last long and she almost puked when she discovered a yellow chicken foot in the bottom of her cup. *I need to eat this, if I can get it down. I can eat what it takes to survive, but the first chance I get, I'm running. Please, God, help me.*

She picked up the small chicken foot with her hand and placed it in her mouth. She discovered it was mostly small bones, skin, and cartilage. Sliding the bare bones through her teeth, she ate the foot, toe by toe.

Master Sergeant Durchenko heard a visitor and when he opened his eyes, he saw Belonev standing beside his bed grinning.

"What are you grinning about?"

"I have news you will be leaving at some point this afternoon or tomorrow. According to the word I got, a helicopter is coming in with some winter gear and you are to leave with the aircraft when it returns to Jackson. From there, you will be loaded on an airliner and returned to Russia."

Durchenko grinned and asked, "Did you bring me another bottle?"

"You know I did, but you will have to drink it all before you get on the plane in Jackson. The medical staff will confiscate it, if they see it."

"That's what happened to the last bottle. I was emptying it late last night and in walked the doctor. He got mad as hell and kept talking about drugs and alcohol cannot be mixed. I told him he'd never been a real soldier."

Belonev chuckled and said, "You know that pissed him off, right? Since they wear a uniform, they like to think they are in the military."

"Most need a haircut, fresh shave, and discipline. And, besides, they are not soldiers and we both know it. Of all our troops, the medical troops need the most discipline."

Handing a pint of vodka to his friend, Belonev said, "I have shipped all of your personal belonging to your farm. I did keep your ration book to use, figuring you will have no additional use for it. If possible, in a couple of years, I will come visit you. How would you like that?"

"I would like that, my friend, but I can see something is bothering you and it is not me."

"Vetrov has ordered around the clock ground and air searches for the partisans, and my future looks bleak to me. But, there is nothing I can do but follow orders and do as I am told. It would be a shame to get killed now, with me being at retirement age. Hell, like you, I would be retired right now, if they had not extended my service to come here."

"I have known you for years and have never heard you speak as you are now. I think my injury may have changed your thinking. The Belonev I know is strong willed, determined, and a damned good soldier." Durchenko opened the bottle and took a long pull of the clear drink. He then handed it to his friend.

"I can have only one, because it is now against the rules to drink while on duty." He took a quick sip and returned the bottle.

"Just between you and I, things are not going well for the great Russian army. I think this invasion will turn into a real mess, like Afghanistan was for us years ago. It seems we never learn from our mistakes."

"We are a hardheaded country and think strength is always the answer, no matter the question. Crippled as you are, you have no need to ever worry about military service again, my friend."

Giving a loud sigh, Durchenko said, "I am not worried about me, but of my lads I leave behind. Most of these kids are just out of school and have no business in the army. The army is a hard business and you do well or die."

"Your lads, as you called them, better learn the business fast or we will be sending home a bunch of metal boxes. I feel this war is about to turn mean."

CHAPTER 15

John was at the spot where the dirt road intersects the paved road leading to town an hour before daylight. He'd brought Dolly with him, but no one else. He was squatted in some brush and she was leaning against him as he scratched her head. The weather had turned cold and he thought he'd seen a bit of snow as he walked earlier, but saw nothing now. *It's just a couple of degrees above freezing,* he thought. *The sun will be up any minute now and that should raise the temperature.*

Seeing movement in front of him, he clicked the safety off on his Bison. He watched as a man carrying an old 30.06 deer rifle neared. Dolly gave a low growl. Knowing the man was on edge, his senses keen, John said, "I'm a friend."

The rifle moved toward the sound and John slowly stood, saying, "I'm John, and looking for a man named Jones."

The gun barrel lowered and the man replied, "That's the boss. I'm Frank. So you're with Tom's bunch, are you? I was warned to watch for someone."

"Yep, I am."

First one, then two, and finally a whole group of men walked from the trees behind him. Seeing Jones, John said, "I see you're still alive and kicking."

"Well, staying that way recently has been a real task. The Russians have patrols out at night and during the day now. Choppers are all over the place, regardless of the time."

Shaking his head, John said, "Come over into the trees and let me tell you what I know is going on, and give you a dispatch pouch I took off a dead motorcycle rider. There are some interesting things in the pouch."

Twenty minutes later, John was done speaking and Jones sat quietly. The orders in the pouch instructed all units to increase the frequency of their patrols, take captives and to fully interrogate those captured. It ended mass executions, but allowed immediate killing of those caught bearing arms. Tanks and other vehicles were to be placed at the intersections of remote roads and check points established. It also explained in detail how to establish a prisoner camp, when to feed and water prisoners, how much food and water each was to receive, and what to do with anything of value recovered from a prisoner. As far as John was concerned, the pouch held the whole Russian game plan for the near future.

John asked, "I wonder what Willy will say once he reads these Russian orders?"

"He'll be pissed and while we've already learned of the camps, the food they intend to give our people will starve most of them to death. I doubt the diet in these orders is even 800 to 900 calories, and a person needs more than that to stay alive."

"So, what do we do?"

"Willy wanted confirmation of the camps starting before we do anything, but I know what he'll want now, or at least think I do. We need to hit and destroy these camps before they're fully manned and operational. Once they have lights, electric fences, machine-guns, guard towers, and are full of troops, we'd never overrun one without a serious loss of life. It'll be too late to do much then."

"We can harass the workers with sniper fire, at least until Willy decides what kind of action we need to take."

"Do it, and if I get word one way or the other about an attack, I'll send a runner to you. Out of all our cells, I've only located about a fourth of them. Oh, before I forget, Davie, bring me your spare toy."

Davie walked to the men, squatted and opened his pack. He then removed an ugly looking gun of some sort that had an over-sized revolving cylinder. Seeing the confusion in John's eyes, he grinned and said, "This is a RG-6 and it shoots six 40mm grenades. It's semi-automatic and able to launch two grenades a second, or something like that. Ugly, it surely is, but I've not used one yet to see how deadly it is. I was to leave it with your group earlier, but to be honest, I wanted the extra protection as we traveled toward Vicksburg. Now that we're heading home, I want you to have it."

"Do you have any grenades for it?"

"More than just a few, but our supply is limited. Once you use what I give you, you'll be on your own for ammo after that, so use it sparingly." He then pulled a vest out that had many pockets, and each held a grenade.

Calling another man forward, Davie took a crate from the man and handed it to John. "This box isn't full; only a little more than half of the grenades remain. I've kept the rest for us. These are the first RG-6's I've seen, but I suspect the way things are heating up, the ammo will soon become common."

Jones looked at his watch, stood, and then said, "We need to be moving. So, it's time to put your sniper to work and I want to wish you good luck."

"I suspect with our sniper and this RG-6, we'll keep them busy at Edwards." John extended his hand and shook with Jones.

Once back with his group, a meeting was held and John explained what was to happen. Kate smiled and said, "Give me a few shots and I'll have my new sniper rifle, with night vision scope ready to use."

"Try to shoot an officer, if you see one, and only wound him."

She gave a deadly smile and replied, "I know how the game is played."

John handed the RG-6 to Tom and said, "Since you carried an M-79 before, this will be a step up for you. As far as I'm concerned, a 'blooper' is a 'blooper', but figure you'll enjoy using it. I have a vest and a few more rounds in the crate I packed in earlier."

Tom grinned like a kid in a candy store with a pocket full of money.

John and the rest waited in the darkness, behind a hill, as Margie and Tom checked the prison camp to see if workers were still on the job. It would do little good to kill a few men, unless they created a great deal of confusion in the process. Joshua, much better than an average shot, was using Kate's old 30.06 and once she started the show, he was to join in, but be selective in his targets. The first priority was to kill or injure officers, then sergeants, or workers that looked to have specialized skills. Finally, worker bees would be taken out.

It was snowing hard and the temperature was well below freezing. Tom had argued to wait for better weather, but John knew any dedicated commander, especially one with headquarters on his ass, would have his troops out working, no matter the weather conditions. Besides, the weather conditions in Russia were harsher than this, so it should be just another workday for the troops.

Tom and Margie returned a few minutes after midnight and grinned. "Got a shitload of 'em working tonight. The place is well lit up too, just as clear as daylight." Margie said.

"Joshua, you and Kate move to positions you think will give you the best shots. Tom, did you see any tanks or other armor, in or out of the wire?"

"Nothing that I saw and I looked for it, too. I did see their fuel dump and hopefully I'll take it out in a few minutes."

"Keep in mind, with Kate using her suppressor, they may not know what is going on at first. All they'll see is men dropping. With that said, if you get a good shot into a group, Joshua, after Kate opens the dance, take it."

"I'll take out the fuel and ammo dumps." Tom said with a big lopsided grin.

"Now, let's move people, and get to your positions. Remember, no shooting until Kate drops a man, so keep your eyes on the compound."

Ten minutes later, as John watched the compound an officer fell to the dirt, unmoving. A man moved to his side and then suddenly fell over the first man. Confusion resulted and men began to run in all directions. Joshua fired and a man fell, and then Tom fired and a huge explosion filled the cold air and flames rolled into the sky. A machine-gun opened fire, from the back of a truck, but the gunner soon fell over and John suspected one of his snipers had taken him out.

He heard a *bloop* and then a massive explosion sounded and flames burst to the sky. The ground shook as the ammunition went up, but John knew Tom had been lucky, because the ammo wasn't all stored in one spot. It was likely his round struck an open door to a storage building or an ammo truck parked near the dump. Three more explosions rocked the ground, one after another, and John was confused. Surely the Russians had ammo bunkers for explosive storage.

Tom, seeing the trucks by the ammo bunkers, fired, hitting one, but had no way of knowing the other three vehicles carried ammunition and explosives, too. The night sky was suddenly daylight, as the trucks exploded. Seeing a large electric fence around a group, he sent a 40 mm grenade into the wire, blowing a huge hole. He then blew the wire wide open in two other locations. Civilians screamed as they ran out of the prison compound, but many were killed or wounded in the process, because the Russians were firing at anything that moved.

Colonel Vetrov ran to the camp, wearing no shirt and began to shout orders. Officers and enlisted men scattered to do as he commanded. He held a pistol in his left hand and when Sergeant Belonev arrived, he said, "Take a company of men and search the area around this place. Use night vision goggles and bring me the heads of those responsible for this!"

"Yes, sir." Belonev replied and then thought, *Stand out there like a fool in the light, because if you stand there too long, we will get a new commander.*

From on a hill, well over two hundred yards away, Kate brought the cross-hairs up on Vetrov's chest, took a deep breath, and as she released it, she gently squeezed the trigger. The sound of her shot was low, more like a thump than the sharp crack of a rifle shot. Moving the scope back to her target, she saw he was down. Another man ran for Vetrov, so her rifle coughed once more and the man fell screaming to the ground. Through the scope, she saw the top of his head was missing.

Belonev ducked behind some sandbags the second the first shot struck Vetrov, and watched as a private he didn't know ran toward the colonel. The runner collapsed with most of his head, from the ears up, missing. "Sniper!" The Master Sergeant yelled.

Two others attempting to get at the Colonel were down, and then the Sergeant realized the sniper was playing an old game. Down an important person and then shoot everyone who tries to save him, only to kill your first victim eventually. "I think I know where that shot came from," he said, and running to a machine-gun, he pushed the dead gunner out of his way and sent a short stream of bullets toward the spot. He fired five more times, before he was knocked to the side and realized he'd been shot. His face was in the grass and he smiled as he looked at the snow covering most of the ground around him. Then his world turned gray before he entered complete darkness.

Glancing at his watch, John saw it was time to withdraw, so he pulled a whistle from his neck to his lips and blew three long blasts. The others would either hear the whistle blasts or realize no one else was firing and leave. He heard the low thump of the RG-6 and when he glanced toward the base, something exploded, sending more fire into the sky, and most likely killing more Russians.

John left the area and once away from the light of the base, started a slow trot that would allow him to cover some distance. The winds were high now, with the cold cutting through his coat and chilling him. Snow was falling harder, and he knew they had to return to the cellar before the snows stopped or even a child would be able to follow them.

Seeing a shape nearing, John yelled, "Civil!"

"War!" The voice replied with the proper countersign.

"Is that you, Tom?"

"Yep, with the rest right behind me. I'm on point. Let's move straight to the cellar or we'll not be able to return until this snow melts."

"Any wounded?"

"No, no wounded but we had one fatality, Kate. I'll explain more at the cellar."

The distance to the cellar was short, but with the gear they were packing, all were tired when the remains of the old house were seen. They slowed to a walk and then stopped at the edge of the trees. "Joshua, I want you and Sandra to check the cellar out. If it's clear, we'll do the house next, so move."

Once at the cellar, Joshua entered with Sandra riding his ass, but they came back out in just a minute or so. They then ran to the house and entered. Minutes passed, with John growing apprehensive, and then both exited to wave all clear.

"Everyone but a guard, Margie, will go into the cellar. Margie, I'll send a replacement out for you in a couple of hours. Stay in the trees where you can see the cellar clearly." John said.

After all were seated in the cellar, John asked, "Okay, what happened to Kate, Tom?"

"First, I am sure she was killed, because her body was torn apart by a machine-gun, large caliber, and I checked her closely. The rifle was ruined, but I did manage to grab the night scope and her gear."

"I saw the machine-gun and fired a few rounds toward the man. I'm sure I didn't kill him, but did take the man out. Joshua, did you see the gun?"

"Uh-huh, and I hit him, too, but not sure how much damage I did. I saw him fall and he was unmoving when I left. I was aiming for the center of his chest, so he might be dead."

"What in the hell did you hit with that grenade launcher on your last shot?"

Tom laughed and said, "Hell, I don't have any idea. I fired at a truck and something inside went up."

"Okay, I want all of us to eat a little something and then get some rest." John said, and then moved to Sandra's side where he asked, "You okay?"

"I'm fine. I'm not sure what Tom hit tonight, but he blew half the damned base up from what I could see. I know at least three men burned to death because I saw them burning as they ran from the flames."

"The Russians will turn mean, shortly."

"Gas?"

"Not sure what they'll do, but poison gas is certainly a possibility."

"I'm tired of fighting. I want to go home, cuddle up in front of a good movie, and sip some wine with you."

"Well, baby, that won't happen anytime soon. We don't have a home, there are no televisions that work, and no wine." He leaned over and kissed her forehead.

"Hold me tonight as we sleep; I need to feel you near me."

John put his arm around her and pulled her close. In just a few minutes, both were asleep.

"John, wake up." He heard his name called. Opening his eyes, he saw Tom squatted beside him. Looking at Sandra, he saw she was still sleeping, so he lowered her head to the blanket as he asked, "Trouble?"

"I don't think so, but we have a visitor."

"Visitor?"

"Let's go outside so we can talk. I don't want to wake these folks. I have to warn you, it's colder than a witches left ankle out there right now. I'd guess the temperature is close to zero, or below."

Donning a jacket, John walked out and asked, "Now, what's this about a visitor?"

"She's in the trees with Margie. She was given a coat, so she's okay."

"She?"

"A woman named Sally, and she claims she had a food booth in Edwards, which Margie verified and knows the woman. According to her, she was a prisoner at the camp we hit tonight."

John saw the snow was still falling and nearly an inch was on the ground. He thought for a moment and then said, "Go and tell Margie to bring her to the cellar and you take the next shift. It's too damned cold to talk to her out here. If anyone followed her, you've the best eyes to spot them."

"Not a problem, so go back inside the cellar. Hell, ain't no reason for all of us to be cold."

John had just removed his jacket when Margie entered with a woman. The woman looked scared, and she kept glancing around the cellar. *She's had it pretty rough and recently too*, John thought.

"So, how many others escaped tonight?" John asked.

"All of us made a run for safety, but a lot were killed by the Russians. I'd guess maybe twenty-five out of two hundred made it out. Once out, we scattered in all directions."

"How'd you find us?"

"I saw a man with a gun move past me and I tried to follow him. Finally, remembering this place, I figured y'all were heading here. At times, in the low light, I'd see a footprint, but it wasn't often because the snow is covering them."

"How'd ya know of this place?"

"I used to know a black man by the first name of Joshua who lived here off and on. This farm was once very successful, but most left it alone, since black folks owned it. Joshua and I went to school together. Then, after the fall, I lost touch with everyone."

"Well," John said with a slight smile, "Joshua lives here again. He's one of us and we're a resistance group."

"Lawdy, that's good news. After the way the Russians treated us, I have a lot of revenge on my mind right now. Can I join you?"

"Do you have any military experience?"

"No, never been in the military, but I'm a hunter from way back, and was a police officer for about five years, back in my younger days. I can hit a man-size target at hundred yards with open sights."

"I see no problem, but our life is filled with death, injury and hardship, so let me know for sure in the morning. Right now, eat a little, but not too much or it will make you ill."

Margie said, "I've a biscuit and some jam she can have, as well as tonic water."

John had just dozed off when Tom woke him once again and said, "Russian aircraft flying low overhead, spraying something.

Due to wind drift I didn't smell or feel anything. I did see a slight discoloration of a vapor against the night sky and especially around the moon. The snow has stopped and it's partly cloudy overhead, but still cold."

"Gas, it's likely poison gas." John said, and then stood, "Gas, find your masks now! Margie, give Kate's mask and gear to Sally."

"What about Dolly?" Sandra asked.

"She'll have to make do without. Maybe we can leave the area before the droplets hit the ground."

Tom yelled, "Don your chemical warfare suits and masks. We need to get out of this cellar, because the gas will settle in low areas. Move, folks!"

CHAPTER 16

Vetrov awoke in a hospital, and it took him many long minutes to remember the attack, due to the pain killing drugs in his system. He looked to be in post recovery, so he raised his head and looked his body over. Other than a bandage on his chest, he saw no other signs of injury. A doctor, seeing him awake, moved to his side and said, "Colonel, you have sustained a serious chest wound, but your prognosis is excellent. We expect a full recovery in a few months."

"Months? That will not happen, doctor, and I shall return to my unit tomorrow."

"I suspect you will be flown home to Moscow for recovery, so you will not be going back to your unit any time soon."

"Oh, I disagree, Captain, and as the anti-terrorism commander, I am in charge, not you. You work for me, so remember that fact. I will continue to work out of Edwards until I fully recover."

"Sir, I must protest and as the—"

"As a man who works for me, you will do exactly as ordered, understand? Now, I want you to collect the members of my staff and we will have a meeting in my private room. If you have need of help gathering the men, see my executive officer."

"He is dead, sir."

"Then have Master Sergeant Belonev assist you."

"He was seriously injured and will not be doing any talking for days. He took a round in the chest as well, and his lungs were slightly injured. He should live, only he will face some severe pain first. He needs to leave on the first plane to Moscow for better treatment."

"Gather up those you can find and get them to me as soon as possible. Oh, and Master Sergeant Belonev will recover here with me, not in Moscow."

"Yes, sir." The doctor replied and then left the room.

An hour later, Vetrov was conducting his first staff meeting since the attack. He felt weak, but if he returned to Moscow after suffering so much damage during the attack, someone would have him imprisoned or killed. He'd stay on the job or die trying. Currently he had a difficult time organizing his thoughts and his mind was dulled by drugs.

"A total of twenty-two personnel were killed near the prison camp, five others working in the fuel storage area are missing, and we are not sure yet of the exact count of those working in munitions. We have confirmed five more dead and six missing from the ammo explosions. Most of those missing were truck drivers and it is not likely they will ever be found." A major from supply replied.

"How many dead partisans were found?"

"One, a woman."

"Do you mean to stand there and suggest all this damage was done by a single woman?"

"Oh, not at all, sir. We found brass from at least six other positions around the camp. We currently have a dozen teams out looking for them, only blowing snow has covered their tracks."

"Recall the teams. I want every aircraft available that can fly out delivering poison gas. Plot a circle, say twenty miles around us, and stay within that area. Deliver nerve gas and do it in alternating sections or grids. Then tomorrow fly over the grids missed today. I hope they will run to the grids we miss today, thinking they're safe. But use some common sense and do not spray upwind of us."

"Sir," the Major said, "The operations executive officer has taken command, since the commander of the squadron was one of our dead. He attempted to rescue you, after you were hit, except he took a bullet to the head. I will pass the word on to him, and order it started immediately."

"See the dead man is submitted for an award, since he died trying to save his commander, and get him a *posthumous promotion, if possible*. Now, what other damage was done?"

Once again the supply officer said, "We lost most of our aviation fuel, maybe forty percent of our munitions, and other buildings have suffered damage, including this hospital building. Additionally, about a hundred and seventy-five of the prisoners were killed."

"How many of the twenty-five got away clean?"

"We have recaptured fifteen, so our total prisoner loss is a hundred and ninety."

"Fifteen are nothing and we'll find the others at our leisure, later. Kill the remaining prisoners in revenge for the attack, but do it in a gruesome manner, so it attracts attention. We must show the partisans what we are willing do in retaliation when other camps are attacked."

"Yes, sir, but any idea of how to kill them? I am a supply officer and not an infantry man."

"Burn them alive or decapitate them in public, hell, use your imagination, Major. Only do the job today. Once they are dead, hang the bodies near the main road with signs around them, stating they are in retaliation for the attack on the base. What is your name?"

The Major, a pencil pusher, felt squeamish at the thought of killing innocent people, gave a loud gulp, snapped to attention and replied, "I am Major Anosov and I will see to it this morning, sir."

"Tell the operations officer if he does a good job with the delivery of the gas, he will be the new commander."

Belonev was awake and had been for some time. He was sharing a room with another senior sergeant and so far he had no idea who the man was. The man had been brought in after surgery and placed in a bed on the other side of the room. Drugged and sleepy, the Sergeant heard two orderlies discussing the attack. When he heard part of the hospital was hit, he asked, "Can one of you see if a Master Sergeant Durchenko has left or is safe? He was in the wing of the hospital that was hit, I think."

"Sure, let me go see." A private said and then quickly disappeared.

"What is the extent of injuries to the man by the wall?" The Sergeant asked.

"Massive burns, so it does not look good for him. I think I heard seventy-five percent of his body was burned, which most do not survive."

"Any idea where he got burns like that?" Belonev was getting sleepy.

"Truck driver on a fuel truck. I heard he ran out of a fireball in flames, but they managed to get the fire out. Personally, shoot me any day before burning me. If he lives, he'll suffer some horrible pain in recovery. Burns bring horrible pain even to the survivors."

The private who'd left returned, lowered his head and said, "The ward Master Sergeant Durchenko was in sustained total destruction, and he is currently listed as missing in action. Seems a fuel truck was passing the hospital when it exploded during the attack. He may be someplace, but they have not found him yet."

"There is always confusion following a big attack." The Sergeant said, and then drifted off to sleep, thinking of his old friend.

The next time he awoke, the orderlies were removing the injured man. Belonev did not ask any questions, because the blanket over the man's face answered all questions; he was dead. The orderly, seeing the Master Sergeant awake said, "Master Sergeant Durchenko's body was found under a wall. The doctor said he died instantly, if that helps any. I am sorry you lost your friend, Sergeant."

Durchenko dead, it seems impossible, because he was so full of life, Belonev thought, and then said, "Get the hell out of my room, boy, and leave my ass alone."

"Yes, Master Sergeant." The orderly scurried out.

Major Anosov sat in his supply office dreading the executions of the civilian captives, but could find no way to avoid the nasty task. Finally, he decided to give the responsibility to his lieutenant.

"Lieutenant Bortnik, come here please."

The young officer walked into the office, assumed the position of attention and asked, "Sir?"

"I want you to take two trucks. Load our fifteen prisoners in one and a machine-gun in the other. Take them to the road where it enters town and shoot all of them. Then place signs written in English on each body. Warn others we will kill those involved with the resistance. Hang their remains on light poles or telephone poles. My orders come from Colonel Vetrov and must be obeyed."

"Uh, when am I to do this, sir?"

"Immediately."

Saluting, Bortnik said, "I will leave now, sir."

The Major waved a casual salute and warned, "Do the job properly, or the next time our army shoots prisoners, you and I will be standing beside them."

"Yes, sir." Bortnik said and paled at the thought of murder.

"Now, go."

The lieutenant quickly gathered up two trucks, a squad of men, and a machine-gun crew. Then, they moved to a temporary tent that was being used to house the prisoners. He walked into the tent and ordered in fair English, "Everyone get into the truck on the left. We are taking you to a new place to stay until we can re-build the camp. Once at the new tent, you will be fed and given a bed."

The prisoners smiled at the thought of a good meal and warm bed to sleep on. They'd been getting a cup of soup a day to eat and sleeping on the grass. Most climbed into the back of the truck willingly, but a pregnant woman and a small child had to be assisted.

Bortnik had attended college in the states a few years back, as an exchange student, and once in Russia, he'd forgotten most of his English. As the driver beside him shifted gears, he thought, *may God forgive me for what I am about to do, but I cannot kill these people in cold blood. I know I can kill another soldier in a battle, except these are old men, women, and children.*

Once at the spot, which he'd previously pointed out to the drivers on a map, the lieutenant climbed from the truck and said, "Everyone out, now."

As soon as all were out of the truck, including the pregnant woman, Bortnik said, "My commander wants all of you killed, but I cannot do this." Since he was speaking in English, none of the Russians understood a word, nor did they know why they were selected to transport the people.

"Why are we here, and where is the food and shelter?" An old man asked.

He is old and must not understand the danger, Bortnik thought and then said, "Behind you are the woods; run, because you are now free. In the future, avoid the Russian army."

A woman beside the old man grabbed his hand, turned, and started to run for the forest. The rest followed. Yelling in Russian to be heard by all of his men, Bortnik said, "Let them go. They are to be freed."

A sergeant shrugged his shoulders and said, "They are your responsibility, sir, not mine. I simply follow orders."

After ten minutes had passed, Bortnik said, "I want three long bursts sent into the woods."

As soon as the machine-gun grew quiet, the Lieutenant ordered the trucks returned to the camp, never realizing the people he'd just released were running toward an area sprayed with deadly nerve gas, just an hour before. Within twenty-four hours, not a single released civilian would be alive.

As soon as he returned to camp, Bortnik reported to the Major.

"I heard the machine-gun fire. Are all the civilians dead?"

"No sir, I did not kill them." He was standing at attention, his eyes straight ahead.

"Did you return them here?"

"No, sir, I released them."

Slamming his hand down hard on the top of his desk, Major Anosov screamed, "You damned fool! Now your actions have caused the deaths of both of us. Colonel Vetrov warned me if the job was not done properly, he'd personally shoot me."

"S . . . sir, I'm a soldier, not a murderer. I could not do what was asked of me."

"Let me ask you a personal question, if I may, Lieutenant?" Major Anosov began to walk slow circles around the younger officer.

"Yes, sir."

"Do you believe in God, Lieutenant?"

Once behind Bortnik, Anosov pulled his pistol and held it flat against his leg, but continued walking.

"Yes, sir, I practice my faith, which is why I could not kill those—"

At the word, those, when he was behind the lieutenant, Anosov raised his pistol and fired into the back of the man's head. The man fell to the floor, quivering as his body shut down. The Major glanced at the blood and brains spattered on his desk and shook his head at the stupidity.

He walked to his desk, opened the top drawer and removed a bottle of vodka. He gulped a quick drink, picked up a framed photograph of his beautiful wife, and placed the barrel of the pistol in his mouth. Tears rolled down his cheeks as he pulled the trigger. His blood, bone and gore joined the lieutenant's to run down the wall. The frame fell to the floor, spattered with blood, and the glass shattered.

A sergeant, who'd been outside stringing barbed-wire, ran into the building, his pistol in hand, and discovered the two dead men. He picked up the phone and dialed a number and said, "Send an officer to Major Anosov's office. There has been a serious accident."

"The attack on this base has cost me the lives of forty men, thirty-eight directly and two suicides for failure to carry out their duties. I no longer hold a single prisoner and all that were released, by the damned fool Lieutenant Bortnik, are dead by now. Moscow will want to know what I have to show for the expense, so what will I tell them, gentlemen?"

All were standing around his bed, heads lowered as if in prayer, but not a one spoke.

"I want answers, damn it!" He shouted.

"Sir, may I suggest we strike another town and round up the civilians. Since you are the overall commander for the fight against the resistance, you have the authority to collect anyone you wish."

"Lieutenant Colonel Zheglov, I want you to take a company of men and hit whatever town that you wish. I want at least a thousand people collected and I want it done quickly. If you fail me, I will add your name to the growing suicide list I have."

"I will not fail you, sir."

"Have the alternate sectors been sprayed with the nerve agent?"

"Yes, sir, and while we have counted some dead deer, horses and cows, the only bodies discovered were civilians, most likely the ones released from here."

"I want intelligence to determine, by checking with supply, if we have lost a great number of chemical biological suits, masks and filters over the last year. I want a count down to the last mask filter. It may be gas is not going to do the job."

"Is that all, sir?" Zheglov asked.

"One more thing; I want armor and troops on the major roads. I want helicopters in the air as our troops travel, too, so they can respond to the first hint of trouble. Jackson has a few fixed wing aircraft, so call on them to provide support. Get me a team of jets and place them on standby. Zheglov, you are free to go now, but the rest of you stay."

Zheglov left the room and moved toward his office. In his office, he picked up the phone, called an old friend and said, "Give me Colonel Izhutin, sergeant."

A minute later a voice said, "Lieutenant Colonel Izhutin, how may I help you?"

"Anton, Kolya here. How are you?"

"I am on the promotion list, how about you?"

"Good, I am glad to hear the news; so what day does your promotion arrive? I will not put mine on for another six months."

"I have three months, and then I will be a full colonel."

"I am happy for you my friend. Listen, I need a favor."

"Name it and if it is legal, I will do it. If it is illegal, I will consider it."

"Colonel Vetrov needs prisoners, so I need you to round up a thousand for me. Do you think you can get than many?"

"Kolya, for you I can get twice that many."

"Seriously? Can you get that many?"

"Sure, but not quickly. I can have a thousand by the time you get here by truck and the others within 24 hours. Why all the prisoners?"

"Let me just say ours are gone. We were attacked and they escaped. We need others to replace them."

"Sure, Kolya, I will have my troops start busting doors down. When can I expect to see you in Jackson?"

"I will leave in a few minutes."

"I will have a vodka bottle ready. Spend the night, Kolya, and tomorrow we can round up the rest of these trouble makers. How does that sound?"

Laughing, Zheglov said, "Get a big bottle and I will be there in a couple of hours. I am bringing armor with me, so we will take a while getting there."

"Stay safe and take no chances. The resistance is growing bold."

"Goodbye, and I shall see you in a little while." Zheglov hung up the phone and called for his Master Sergeant.

When the man arrived, the Colonel said, "I want every available truck ready to move within the hour. I also want a tank ready to leave as well. Tell the crews we are going to Jackson and we will be spending the night."

"And the purpose of our mission, sir?"

"To pick up prisoners, Sergeant, prisoners. I want to leave soon, so stress the one hour time limit. It is now, 10 hundred hours."

At 11 hundred hours, on the dot, the convoy was leaving Edwards and moving toward the highway. Once on the main road it was a straight shot right into the capital city and there would be no other traffic. The trucks, if traveling alone, could do the trip in a little more than an hour, but the tank would slow them down. However, the firepower of the tank made it a nice addition to the group.

CHAPTER 17

John and the rest left the relative safety of the cellar, wearing chemical suits and masks. They moved under a heavy growth of oak trees. The wind was slight, but with heavy gusts at times. Finally, Tom said, "Move toward Edwards, but remain in the trees as much as possible. I think we'll be safer near the camp."

"I want Margie on point and Sally bringing up the rear."

Ten minutes later, as they moved through the trees, John glanced behind him and saw no trace of Sally. *Where in the hell has she gone?* he thought, and then stopped.

Tom ran forward to get Margie.

"She was right behind us," Sandra said, "but she claimed she was having some problems with her mask. I think her hair kept it from sealing well."

"Why didn't anyone say anything?" John then began to run the toward the last place he'd seen her.

He found Sally in the dirt, her mask beside her, twitching and gasping for air. Squatting and pulling an atropine injector from his chemical warfare suit, he pushed the needle end against her thigh, felt it inject her, and heard her gasp.

Dolly lay beside her and was trying to breathe as well. So John removed the atropine injector from Margie's suit and placed on the dog's thigh. When the needle entered, she gave a cry of alarm, but John was able to sooth her with his voice. She seemed to know he was trying to help. *I don't know if atropine works on a dog, but will know in a few minutes*, he thought, as he petted Dolly on the head.

The others arrived and Tom asked, "How far along is she? Any slobbering, shaking or breathing problems?"

"Yep and if she lives, it all depends on if I got the atropine into her quickly enough. I suspect we'll know in less than ten minutes. I want two long limbs to make a stretcher, because we'll take her with us, even if she dies. I don't want any bodies this close to the cellar." He then moved into the trees, looking for the right limbs.

"What about Dolly?"

John stopped, shook his head and said, "We'll have to pick her up on the way back, if she's still alive."

Sandra knelt beside Sally and then said, "She'll be incapacitated for either a short or long time, even if she lives. Atropine doesn't work the same way on all people. Some it helps right off, while others it might take much longer. Has she peed, pooped, or vomited yet?"

"Huh?" Tom asked.

"Those are indicators of the nerve agent working, and eventually her lungs will stop working."

Rolling the woman on her back, Margie said, "The front of her pants are still dry, but wouldn't she be foaming at the mouth, too? I don't see anything to indicate she's shit her pants either."

"Involuntary salivating is one of the symptoms, yes."

"I don't think she's been exposed long. Should I put her mask back on her head?"

"Uh-huh, but listen to her breathing and make sure she doesn't start puking or she will choke to death with a mask on her face."

"Move straight north, near the main highway. I think it might be the closest clear zone. They'd try to avoid spraying the road." John said as he returned with two long straight limbs.

He then pulled two long sleeve shirts out of his pack, ran a different pole in each arm, so the bottoms of the shirts were touching. He then buttoned the buttons on the front of each shirt. "Help me place her on the stretcher." He said, looking at Tom.

"Joshua and Tom carry her for an hour, then we'll change to me and Sandra. After that, Margie and Tom. Hopefully, after that, she'll be up and moving." John said and then quickly added "let's move, with Margie on point and Sandra on drag."

Two hours later, as they neared the main highway, Tom said, "Traffic coming."

"Try to see if any are wearing chemical gear. I don't want to remove our masks, until we're damned sure the air is safe."

"A damned tank is leading, but it's not running well. Do you hear the engine?"

"Uh-huh, and he'll never get far, not running like it is."

The tank pulled from the road and stopped almost in front of the small group of partisans. The top hatch opened, a man's head came up, and then he moved up and out of the tank turret. He jumped to the ground and stood talking to someone in a staff car. A few minutes later, a wrecker moved to the tank and mainte-nance men dismounted from the back. The convoy, with the staff car, continued to move east toward Jackson.

"None are in chemical/biological gear, so this area must be safe. We can remove our masks." John said in a whisper as he re-moved his. The air smelled sweet and tasted fresh to him.

When Sandra removed her mask, sweat ran from the rubber around her chin. She gave aloud sigh at the relief it brought her. John gave her a nasty look, and she understood she'd made exces-sive noise.

"Keep the noise down as we wait for more of the tank crew to climb out. Once a couple more dismount the tank, we'll attack. This tank must be destroyed and crew killed." John said whisper-ing.

Five minutes later, two other members of the tank climbed out, opened a bottle of vodka and began to pass it around. They were laughing and playing grab-ass as soldiers the world over are prone to do when the sergeants and officers were gone.

"In a few minutes, we'll toss two grenades. Tom, you throw one at the wrecker, while I do the same with the tank. Immedi-ately following the explosions, move to the men and take them out. Any questions?"

Silence followed.

Both men removed grenades and pulled the tape holding the spoons in place. Looking around and seeing all were ready, John tossed his grenade, noticed it hit the turret with a loud *clang*, and then bounced to the ground, near the men. The Russians were standing in confusion as if not understanding what was going on, when both grenades exploded. Screams were heard and dust filled the air near the two vehicles.

Bursting through the brush, the small group began shooting into the fallen forms. Once the Russians were dead, John ordered the group back into the woods. He then stuck the ace of spades card in a dead Russian's mouth. He tossed a grenade into the cab of the wrecker and then ran for the brush.

Tom had moved to the top of the tank, dropped two grenades down the hatch, heard a loud *clang-clang*, and jumped to the ground where he started running. He was still running, almost beside John, when the grenades exploded and a flash of blinding reddish-white light shot straight up, out of the open hatch.

Moving to the group, Tom screamed, "Deeper, into the woods now, before the fuel and ammo blow on the tank!"

They moved about fifty feet when they heard a loud explosion, quickly followed by a series of secondary explosions. A second loud blast sounded, and looking over his shoulder, John saw the turret spinning high into the air. Then, it grew quiet, except for the crackling flames of the fires.

"Let's move, and take the long way back to the cellar!" John ordered.

Dolly and Sally were both alive and laying on blankets under a large oak. The sun was bright, the winds gentle, and the temperature was close to seventy. Neither of the injured were back to normal yet, nonetheless, they'd grown no worst either. Both were breathing better and Sally's mind was much clearer.

Sandra sat on an old stump and said, "They'll get stronger over time, but right now they're lucky to be above ground, both of them."

"When do you think they'll be able to move?" Tom asked.

"Why?" John asked and then added, "Are you thinking what I've been thinking?"

Tom nodded and replied, "Probably; we need to move. We've staged two attacks from here and I'd feel better if we moved on."

Sandra said, "They're able to move today, as long as we keep the pace slow. Keep a close watch on both of them, in case they try to meander from the path. While their bodies are in fair to good shape, their minds are still unable to concentrate for long periods."

"Okay, we'll move further south and find a place to hole up for while. We'll take what supplies we can on the first trip, but come back for the rest later." John replied and started stacking things against the wall nearest the entrance. "Dolly will be on a leash, so she'll stay with me."

"Any priority on what supplies and gear goes first?" Margie asked.

"Guns, ammunition, chemical/biological gear, explosives, and first aid items first. Then food and comfort items." John said, and then picked up an ammunition can.

"Let's move, and I want Sandra on point and Joshua on drag."

Tom moved to his side and said, "Once we get in place and settled, I need Sandra to look at a tooth that's bothering me."

"Is the gum inflamed?"

"Nope, but it hurts like a sonofabitch and I think it needs to come out."

"She'll take a look at it in an hour or so. Can you wait that long?"

Tom gave a low chuckle and replied, "Sure, it's been bothering me for a month, off and on, so another hour is nothing."

"Let's kill the chatter until we find a new place."

Joshua neared and said, "Tom, take my place on drag for a couple of minutes. I need to talk with John."

Tom moved back and then Joshua said, "I used to hunt, oh maybe five miles south of here and we had a rough log cabin we used. Now, it ain't much, but the last time I was there the roof didn't leak, unless it rained. Want to check it out? Has four beds made into the walls, a wood stove, and an outhouse."

"Take the point and get us there. Have Sandra drop back with the rest of us."

He nodded and moved forward.

A little over an hour later, the group watched the cabin as Joshua and Tom moved forward to check the place out. John was sure if Joshua hadn't pointed at the place, they would have walked right by. Brush was thick all around and long grasses grew on the cabin roof. Three windows were seen, but shutters were closed on all three.

Tom waved them in and Joshua opened the plywood door to the building. He then moved inside, where he opened all the shutters to allow fresh air to circulate. Dust covered an old wooden picnic table and cobwebs were in the corners of each wall. An old newspaper and some beer cans, remains of a better time, littered the floor. As Joshua turned to walk out, a mouse ran by him and in a zip was out the door. He grinned.

It only took Tom and Joshua a couple of hours to return to the cellar and remove the remainder of their gear and supplies. They'd all pitched in while the two were gone and cleaned the cabin. John noticed a layer of dirt on the roof and decided to ask Joshua about it when they returned. Finally, as they placed the last box on a bunk bed, he asked, "Joshua, why the dirt on the roof?"

"My brother read in some western fiction book that in the old days settlers covered their cedar shingles with dirt, to keep the risk of fire down from chimney sparks, so we did the same. I had no idea it'd end up growing grass."

"Well, it makes sense, because dirt would also protect them if Indians tried to burn them out, too." Tom said, and then continued, "Sandra, can you look at a tooth of mine?"

"Sure, but step outside in the sunlight."

They left and few minutes later, she returned for her medical bag and said, "I have to do an extraction, so I need one of you guys to help me."

Joshua smiled and said, "Not so fast. My daddy and I used to keep a quart of whiskey right about here." He said and then lifted a wooden slate on the floor. He smiled, pulled out a bottle and said, "Brand new, too; ain't never been opened. Give Tom a snort of this before you start to work on him and he'll be easier to deal with." He handed the bottle to Sandra.

John laughed and asked, "You don't have a couple more of those around here, do you?"

"One more," he said, "but it's hidden in the rafters of the outhouse, or was. Let me go check."

When Joshua walked outside, Tom was sitting on a stump sipping a canteen cup of whiskey. He grinned at him and said, "Good Kentucky bourbon, it was the best in the world."

"Was is the key word." Joshua said.

"Drink that up. As soon as that cup is gone, I'll pull the tooth."

As he neared the outhouse, a copperhead snake slithered off the trail, where he'd been sunning himself, and moved into the bushes. Opening the door to the small building, Joshua expected to see another snake, but was not prepared for what he did see. He blinked rapidly a few times and then looked again. Sitting on the seat, but fully dressed, was a woman holding a pistol in her right hand, while in her left she held a baby about three years old.

"Good, yer an American. Iffen you'd been wearin' a Russian uniform I'd have sent ya to hell, mister." She spoke with narrow eyes and Joshua believed every word.

"Listen, I won't hurt you any." Right then, Tom screamed and he knew it wouldn't help matters.

"Y'all torturin' Russians in there?"

Joshua gave a dry laugh, which he didn't feel at all, and replied, "No, one of our men is having a bad tooth pulled."

"I counted six of y'all, so is that all of ya?"

"Yep, six. Do you have a name?"

"Mollie, and the baby is Ruben. Do ya have any food, mister?"

"I'm Joshua and if you're hungry, come with me into the cabin and we'll feed you. We're a mixed group of men and women."

"I saw that."

"Come, and you can eat." He said and then added, "Let me get something, before we go." Joshua reached to the rafters and removed the bottle of whiskey. He then walked for the cabin.

Glancing over his shoulder, he saw the woman following him with the baby riding on her hip, and thought, *this woman has seen some rough times and I have no doubt, if I'd been a Russian, she would have killed me.*

They passed Tom, who ignored them, and Sandra who smiled at Mollie. Entering first, he said, "I found Mollie and her baby, Ruben, hiding in the outhouse."

"Lawdy," said Sally, "that's a stinky place to hide."

"She thought we were Russians."

"Mollie," John asked, "have the Russians been around here?"

"I got here yesterday and I ain't seen nobody, but y'all. A week or so back, they attacked our group, killed us all, except fer me and Ruben. I've been scared to death and prayin' hard some Americans would find me."

"You're safe now; well, as safe as it gets anymore." John replied.

Margie handed Mollie a Russian ration and said, "I know you're hungry, so dig in."

Opening the container, she began feeding the baby first. She glanced at Margie and said, "Thank ya fer the food. Little Ruben was beside himself with hunger."

"You must be hungry, too." John said.

"I always feed my boy first. There is plenty of food here, so I'll eat after Ruben."

"Mollie," John asked, "where is your husband?"

"Franklin was caught when we hit a convoy, oh, mayhap six months back. The damned Russians put him and twenty hostages in an old church, soaked it with gasoline and burned them to death. It's not a pretty nor good way to die, sir."

"No 'sir', because I'm just John, okay?"

"That's fine, iffen that's the way ya want it, because it doesn't matter much to me anymore. My only goal is to keep me and Ruben alive until this war stops."

Sandra and Tom entered and sat on different bunk beds. Blood was seen on Tom's chin, but he said nothing. Sandra said, "Pulled a molar, so he'll start feeling better in a few hours. The whiskey helped him, and he's feeling little pain right now."

"Joshua, I want you on guard outside. It wouldn't pay for all of us to be caught in here."

Joshua stood, picked up his weapon, and moved to the door.

"If you see or hear anything, let us know. The Russians are looking for us, so they'll come, eventually."

The man nodded and walked out.

Once outside, he leaned back against an old pine and scanned the area as he let his mind drift from one thought to another. His father had been forced to kill his mother, when the fall came, because she could no longer get her medications. Mother had always been sickly and as far back as he could remember, she'd been in and out of the hospital. Toward the end, she had stage four cancer and was in some serious pain. In less then three weeks her prescription medications were gone and his father had turned to giving her whiskey from his liquor supply. A month later, the alcohol now gone, he had nothing for her pain. He'd walked into her bedroom one night and shot her in the head with a 12 gauge shotgun.

His father quit eating and he wasn't in the best of health to start with, so within a month he'd died. His last words to Joshua where, "I didn't kill your mother out of hate, son, but love. I should have died with her that day. I would have too, but I don't think suicides enter the kingdom of Heaven. God has forgiven me for killing her."

Then his mind shifted to his wife and kids. He'd gone off to work one day, right after the fall, and when he returned, they were gone. He'd found no bodies, no blood, and no signs of a fight.

Even now, he had no idea what had happened. He suspected his wife was taken for sport, but his missing kids, well, they had him stumped. A feeling of grief struck him hard, but he put his family out of his mind and remembered other things.

Tom exited the cabin, walked to Joshua and said, "We need to place a few mines and tripwires rigged to claymores around this place."

CHAPTER 18

Colonel Izhutin sat in his office sipping vodka with Colonel Zheglov, as they discussed the prisoners that were rounded up within the last two hours. It was late in the day, after 15 hundred, but darkness would not come for about two more hours.

Izhutin asked, "We rounded up three thousand for you. Is that enough or do you spend the night and collect more tomorrow?"

"These are enough, and my trucks will be full on the return trip. If possible, Anton, collect another two thousand during the coming week."

"Do you have enough food and shelter for so many people?"

Laughing, Zheglov replied, "No, of course not, but we do have a large fenced in area we can place them. We feed them little, surely not enough to live on, and provide them with nothing else. But our workers have started building barracks for them and we will have a limited supply system in place for their support within a month. I think by the end of the month, they will be taking in about a thousand calories a day."

"Are they to work?"

"Some will, once we sort through all of them and determine their skills, if any. However, that is a long time down the road—perhaps a year or more. Have the tracks for the train been repaired between here and Vicksburg? If so, perhaps you can send me additional prisoners using trains."

"Yes, the tracks are serviceable and trains have been using it, but not frequently. Each train has a company of infantry to act as security. At times the rails have been loosened or completely removed, so we have to move slowly. However, I think if we shackle a few prisoners to the front of the engine on the trains, maybe the partisans will leave the tracks alone." Colonel Izhutin replied and then asked, "More drink, my friend?"

"No, no I've had enough already." Standing, Zheglov added, "Thank you for the help. I am sure Colonel Vetrov will wonder where I have been able to round up so many people. As for shackling prisoners on a train, hell, give it a try."

Grinning over the top of his vodka glass, Colonel Izhutin asked, "Oh, and what will you tell him?" He then downed the remainder of his drink.

"I will simply ask if it matters. They will make him happy and right now he's the most important man in this region, bar none."

Extending his hand, Izhutin said, "Have a safe trip and call me if you need anything else. It is always an honor to help an old friend. Now, I have assigned extra trucks to help you transport your prisoners, but they must return tomorrow to pick up those we cannot transport today. You and I together do not have enough trucks to move all of them at once."

Shaking hands, Zheglov thought, *bullshit, you will remember this and when you need something from me, you will bring this up. Because that is how life works, my friend.* Finally he said, "We will take all we can now and pick up the others later."

Zheglov walked from the office, called out to the senior sergeant and said, "Get the prisoners loaded, because we need to get moving. I do not want to be caught on the main highway after darkness."

They were a little less than half way back to the base at Edwards when the sun went down. Zheglov noticed the sergeant riding in the front of his staff car flipped the safety off his weapon. The man then donned NVG's so he could see in the darkness.

"Sergeant, radio all drivers to be alert and for their guards to prepare for an ambush. While I do not think we will be attacked, there is always a chance."

"Prepare for ambush, sir? How do you want that done?"

"Just as you have, safeties off and NVG's on their heads. I want everyone awake and alert for danger. I have discovered it pays to always expect the worst."

An hour later, the motorcyclist riding point never felt the wire stretched across the road that struck him in the neck and decapitated him. As his severed head rolled into a ditch, his motorcycle fell to its side and began to send sparks high into the air as metal struck concrete. A second or two later the bike flipped high into the air and landed in the median of the highway.

Machine-gun bullets walked the length of the convoy and then back again. Grenade launchers gave their familiar *thump*, as 40 mm grenades were sent into targets. Trucks exploded, sending pieces of metal, tires, and prisoners high into the air, along with the drivers and guards.

"Faster, move faster, we must ride out of the ambush zone! Sergeant, radio my message now." Zheglov yelled, and then pulled his pistol.

Suddenly the driver of the staff car took a bullet to his head, spraying blood and brains on Zheglov, and the car went out of control. The sergeant attempted to control the car's direction with the steering wheel, but the dead man's foot had the accelerator to the floor. The car slipped around trucks and entered the passing lane. The sight of a staff car moving alone, brought more partisan fire on the vehicle, and the sergeant screamed and then slumped.

The car ran off the road, struck a ditch in the median and then flipped three times. It was during the second flip, when Zheglov was ejected and landed in the grass, unconscious. The car then lay still as dust filled the air. A minute later, fire was seen near the engine and flames grew quickly. The injured sergeant, his leg caught in the wreckage screamed for help.

The trucks from the convoy, those still moving, rolled past the staff car without a second thought. All drivers were concerned about survival, not risking their necks for some colonel that rode their asses all the time. Grenades still exploded, screams were heard, and bullets continued to strike the big vehicles. One was seen to leave the road at a high rate of speed, knock down a fence, and then collide with a huge oak tree. It suddenly burst into flames, either from a ruptured gas tank or a 40 mm round. Shrieks of fear and pain were heard, but not for long, because it exploded. The resulting fire set the woods aflame as well.

The trucks continued to move away from the ambush site and within a few minutes the survivors were moving, as fast as the governors on their engines would allow, for Edwards. The scene of ambush grew quiet, with the exception of crackling flames, small secondary detonations, and the moans and screams of the injured. Out of the blue, Zheglov's staff car exploded, sending a huge rolling ball of reddish-black flames high into the air. With the explosion, the injured sergeants screams stopped.

Many long minutes passed before Colonel Willy Williams walked from the trees and yelled, "Check out all the trucks and re-move anything we can use. Shoot all the injured and no captives." He then moved to the closest truck, discovered the driver dead, his bloody head slumped over the steering wheel and the guard laying half out of an open door. His feet were were entangled in the dash of the vehicle. Willy sent a round into the man's head, just to be safe, because he saw no blood.

He and some of his men moved to the rear of the truck and looked inside. A young partisan, barely over 15, turned his head to the right and puked. The back of the vehicle was covered in blood with body parts littering the floor. The dead civilians, most thrown to the rear of the cab when the truck struck a guardrail, were laying in unnatural positions.

"We had no idea what they were carrying, so don't let this get to you son." Willy said to the young man who was wiping his mouth clean of vomit.

A man neared and said, "We've found a bunch of civilians in these trucks, but no supplies. What do you want us to do with the people?"

"Check all the trucks and remove any civilians that are able to move on their own. If they can't walk, put 'em down. Take every pair of NVG's and spare batteries you can find."

"Y . . . you mean, kill them?" The man asked.

"That's exactly what I've ordered, Lieutenant, or do you have a problem with my orders?"

A pistol shot was heard and then the Lieutenant said, "That's murder, sir."

"Phil, how long do you think someone seriously injured will live in a prison camp? These folks were going to Edwards and they don't even have housing for them. They will be given no medical treatment and simply dumped on the grass inside the wire. It might take some of these folks days to die and they'll do so in great pain. Now, do as I asked, because I'm doing this to be merciful, not because I'm a killer."

Phil muttered under his breath as he walked off and started giving orders to his men.

"Let's hurry folks, because choppers will be overhead shortly. I want to be miles from here before they arrive."

A woman neared Willy and reported, "The officer from the staff car is alive, but with a broken neck."

"Take me to him, Lieutenant."

A few minutes later, in the median, Zheglov met the eyes of Colonel Willy Williams.

"I speak your language." Willy said as he squatted beside the injured man.

"Will you now kill me?"

"I have not decided, but you deserve to die."

"I am soldier obeying orders."

Willy laughed and then said, "Is that why you were carrying people instead of supplies or soldiers? Do not insult my intelligence, Colonel. You were carrying innocent people gathered up to fill your prison camp."

"I hurt. Can you not give me anything for the pain?"

Pulling his pistol, Willy said, "No, we will give you nothing for your pain. My medics think your neck is broken, so to make sure you are removed from all future battles, I must do this."

"Plea—"

The two shots were loud as both bullets struck Zheglov's knee caps, shattering them. The Russian screamed, but more out of fear than pain, because he actually felt nothing from the neck down.

"Colonel Williams, we have choppers in the air!" Someone shouted.

"Disperse, and do the job now! Break into small two man teams and meet back at our base when you can." He placed his pistol back in the holster and said to Zheglov, "You may live, Colonel, but you will never use your legs again and I pray your neck is truly broken. Tell your boss we will resist the Russians until no single American lives. We will have our country back!" He placed an ace of spades card in Zheglov's shirt pocket.

Hearing the sound of the chopper, Willy broke for the trees at a hard run. Once under cover, he squatted beside three of his men as the chopper landed on the highway, close to the staff car. He watched as men exited the chopper and ran to each truck, and two made their way to the staff car, stretchers in hand. A gunner was scanning the countryside, his nerves obviously on edge. Another chopper circled overhead.

Suddenly Willy had a change of mind. He motioned to a man beside him that he wanted his weapon. Taking the RG-6 in his hands, he waited.

Minutes later, two men walked toward the helicopter, packing Zheglov on a stretcher. The other men were boarding on the other side. As the stretcher was placed inside the aircraft, Willy quickly fired two grenades from the RG-6. One struck in the cockpit area and the second struck the tail boom. The resulting explosions were loud, and then the fuel went up with a loud swoosh. Engulfed by flames, two human torches moved from the flames walking aimlessly as they screamed. An explosion vibrated in the trees and a giant ball of fire suddenly appeared where the aircraft had been resting on it's skids. The two burning men, were knocked to the ground by the detonation and remained unmoving.

Turning to his men, Willy said, "Move, but take the long way back to camp."

The chopper flying overhead saw the explosion from the aircraft on the ground and quickly radioed the main base to report the aircraft down. Then, the aircraft commander zoomed down to tree top level as they searched for partisans. Spotting a small group of three men, the door gunner reported, "Three men at your three o'clock position, sir."

"Fire, fool, and if you kill them all, a bottle of vodka will be given to you."

The *rat-tat-tat* of the machine-gun was heard and the gunner walked the bullets into the men. Dirt, grasses, stones, blood and bones flew high into the air as the bullets passed through two of the men, but the last seemed unharmed.

"Go around, go around now!" The gunner screamed into his intercom system.

When they returned, two men were seen on the ground, but the third was gone.

"Start circling slowly, sir." The gunner said as he kept his eyes on the ground and his finger on the trigger, ready to spit lead death at the last man.

Slowly the aircraft circled and was about to turn away, when Willy stood from some brush with a smile on his face and the RG-6 in his hands. The Russian gunner saw Willy a second too late and before his mind could register what his eyes were seeing, the *thump* of a launcher was heard on the ground.

The big 40 mm round struck the chopper in the engine area and then exploded. Smoke began to stream from the engine and flames were shooting from access panels. The aircraft fought to gain height, and was running rough and shaking violently as the pilot made an attempt to get to the highway to land. The pilot was about ten feet from the ground when the engine seized and it dropped hard to the concrete.

On impact both the pilot and co-pilot suffered severe back injuries, but the pilot quickly reached up with his right hand and hit the fire agent discharge button, which shot a thick fire preventing foam into the engine compartment smothering the flames. He then turned all power switches off. If the aircraft was leaking fuel, the sparks of any electrical device could cause an explosion.

The gunner crawled from the chopper and took his machine-gun with him, guarding against any ground attacks. The man had a cut over his left eye, where the edge of his helmet had struck him when they slammed hard to the ground. He removed his helmet and pulled his first aid kit open. Removing a bandage, he soon had his injury wrapped.

Five minutes later, a helicopter arrived with Colonel Pankov as the senior officer on board the aircraft. A team of medics jumped from the aircraft and moved to the downed bird.

Then more and more choppers landed and infantry troops began to secure the area. As soon as the troops were off the aircraft, each chopper returned to the sky, flying in lazy circles. A Lieutenant Colonel walked to Pankov and said, "We have secured the area, sir."

"Thank you, Yakubov, now have some of your men remove our dead. Be sure to get me a body count of our troops."

"What of the dead civilians, sir?"

"Leave them where they lay. Pour gas on each truck that is beyond repair and when we leave, burn it all."

A medic neared and said, "The co-pilot has a broken back, we are not sure about the pilot's back and both gunners sustained injuries, with one having a concussion."

Pankov walked to what remained of Zheglov's helicopter and realized they'd never find enough of the man to bury. Three fourths of the aircraft was gone and the only bodies seen were two men laying on the pavement, burnt to a crisp. Both were so badly disfigured by the fire, their own mothers wouldn't recognize them.

Smoke from the fire still reached for the sky, but thinner now than just minutes ago.

Two hours later, dozers from the base cleared the highway and the troops returned to base. Pankov was pissed about the attack, but not overly so, and returned to his room. Once showered to remove the smell of death from him, he had supper in the officers mess and returned to his quarters for a few drinks. He picked up a book and begain reading when there came a knock at his door.

A young lieutenant was standing in the hallway when he asked, "Yes?"

The young officer saluted and said, "Colonel Vetrov has asked to see you immediately, sir."

"Return to the Colonel and inform him I will be there as soon as I get my boots on."

"Yes, sir."

Pankov closed the door and thought, *What does the damned fool want from me now? I suspect he wants an update on the partisan attack*, but why at this hour? He placed his feet into the boots and then moved for the door, thinking, *Well, he cannot blame this last attack on me, it was all Zheglov's idea.*

He entered the hospital ward to find Vetrov looking sour and pissed, staring at his hands. The Colonel looked up and asked "And, where in the hell have you been? I expected a report from you right after you landed."

"I showered, had a bite to eat and had no idea you wanted to speak with me, sir. You sent no word to me, nor did you say anything at the staff meeting this morning." *Like I can read your small brain.*

CHAPTER 19

Three days later, as John and Joshua scouted in cold weather, they spotted men moving toward them. They crouched in the bushes and waited for the men to get closer. Seeing they were Americans, John said, "That's close enough. Who are you and what do you want?"

The man on point stopped, swung his weapon in John's general direction, but said nothing.

Long seconds passed before the man called out, "Bill, come to me."

A minute later a tall man with black hair, said, "I'm Bill and was sent by Willy Williams. We need to talk, if your name is John or Tom."

"My name is John. What does Willy want?"

"He wants a strike on Russian railroad traffic started immediately. If possible, derail the engine and other cars when you do the job." Bill removed his pack and sat it on the ground beside him.

John smiled and said, "We can do that."

"In the mean time, all other rail lines will be hit, too."

"We'll start tonight. Was that all he wanted?"

"Nope, I have a few pounds of C4 explosive for you to use on the job." He pulled a paper-wrapped bundle from his pack, handing it to John.

"Do you have time to eat?"

Shaking his head, Bill said, "No, I have to get back. I'll inform Willy you'll start this evening."

Donning his pack, Bill and the rest disappeared into the trees.

Glancing at the low clouds overhead, John said, "Let's get back. It looks like rain or snow coming, and we've a mission to prepare."

Once back at the cabin, they discussed the mission and how to do the most damage with the least effort. Ideas were kicked around and around, until John said, "I like Tom's idea and think it will cause the most damage with the least danger to us. We move at dark, only Dolly will stay here to give you a little more protection."

At dark, three of them were moving north toward the railroad and it was quiet. A light drizzle fell, so each wore a poncho, and the weather was cold. It was perfect hypothermia weather with temperatures in the mid thirties. According to Sally, a train pulled into Edwards each night near midnight to offload supplies for the military. Civilians were not allowed on the trains and the only traffic was military. The only dangerous part of the mission, so far, was crossing the main highway, which they did one at a time. They'd encountered no problems and a little before 2300 hours arrived at the tracks.

They quickly placed two Claymore mines facing each other on the opposite sides of the tracks and ran the wires from the mine on the far side, under the steel beams and covered them with small rocks. Then fifty yards down the track, east, they placed some C4 which Tom rigged up to blow on command.

They then ran the wires from their explosives to a ditch that ran parallel to the tracks. They'd be in the ditch when the C-4 and Claymores blew. Joshua moved a distance behind to cover their rear as they did the dirty work. Once the explosives were detonated, he was to join the other two in shooting up the train.

At 2345 hours they heard the train approaching and a bright light was shining from the engine. The speed was low, approximately twenty-five miles an hour, and when it neared, John spotted people on a platform in front of the engine. *They're using captives to make sure the train isn't attacked; well, it won't work today*, he thought as he picked up the clackers for the Claymore mines.

"We let the captives go by and when I yell now, we blow the mines. Hopefully no civilians will be killed. Okay?"

"I'll squeeze when you give the word."

As John waited, he decided to set the explosives off a second before the engineer's door reached the mines. John thought his forward speed would have him in the kill zone and most of the hostages out, but no matter where the civilians were, this train would be destroyed.

The engine ran over the C4 and kept moving and just before the engineer was between the two mines, John yelled, "Now!"

Both mines exploded, riddling and knocking the engine off the tracks, where it quickly fell on its side, smoking. Tom exploded the C4 and two flatbed cars loaded with troops flew high into the air. He then picked up his RG-6 and sent 40 mm grenades into the five remaining cars.

Joshua opened up and heard his bullets hitting cargo cars and pinging off into space. Then one car exploded, a large fireball lighting up the darkness as clear as day. Screams were heard from the engine, so John ran to the train. The engineer was dead, his bloody head almost ripped from his neck. He quickly untied the prisoners and told them to go. They scattered into the winds in ones and twos and some had minor injuries, but he couldn't help them.

Russian bodies were spread all over the place and all were dead. John pulled an ace of spades from his pocket and placed it in the open mouth of a dead Master Sergeant. He then used his right foot to close the dead man's mouth.

"We need to move and do the job now. I'm sure they'll have choppers up looking for us shortly." Tom said.

The drizzle had changed to rain so they began a distance eating trot to put some distance between them and the tracks. At the main highway, they crossed as a group, to lessen time needed to cross, and were soon back in the trees.

An hour later, choppers were heard overhead, but they simply stopped and hugged a tree. Minutes later the aircraft moved away.

Lightning flashed across the sky, lighting the area, and a few seconds later a loud *boom* or *crack* was heard. They never slowed and soon saw the safety of the cabin in front of them. It was pouring rain now and each was tired, wet and hungry. John wanted to dry off, eat a little and then get some much needed sleep.

Walking up to the door, John knocked twice, waited a second and then knocked twice more. Sandra opened the door and asked, "Well?"

"The Russians are short a train and a large number of men. I'll tell all of you about it after we dry off, get something to eat."

"There is some stew on the stove. We opened a few rations and placed the canteen cups on the edge of the stove to keep warm."

As soon as they'd changed into dry clothes, they each took a canteen cup from the stove and started eating. John told his story as he ate.

When he'd finished, Sandra said, "Sounds like it went smoothly."

He laughed and replied, "It did and that scared me, too. Most missions have something go wrong, but not this time."

"We're lucky, that's all." Tom said. "I think because they've never been attacked before we got away with it, this time. We need to space the attacks out and hit them on different days and not show any routine. If they get the rhythm of our attacks, we're dead meat."

"Yep, I know, so tonight we'll hit them again."

"Tonight? Have you lost your mind?"

"Nope, I honestly don't think they'll change much in 24 hours. It takes time to make changes, and then we'll hold off for a week or ten days."

"Are you taking the same people?" Sandra asked.

"Nope, I'll take Joshua and Sally. Sally needs the experience and Joshua is a proven hand in the field. Now, Tom, make out a guard detail for those that remain behind. The three of us need to get some sleep."

"You should take the RG-6, because it makes a big difference on the train cars."

"We'll take it," John said and stood as he continued, "because it adds firepower to the group. The key is to avoid any injury to those held captive on the platform riding in front."

"Hell, let the engine go." Joshua said.

"Can't do that, because it's a valuable piece of equipment. The engine must be blown and any fuels, petroleum or liquids destroyed. Plus, any troops we can kill are an added bonus, because it keeps them out of the field looking for us."

"When do we leave?" Sally asked.

"At dark, so get some sleep."

At 2000 hours they were ready, with the mines placed, and all three wide awake. They'd walked nearly two miles closer to Edwards to avoid using the same ambush spot. Just past the mines, they'd pulled the tracks out about four inches, which would cause the train to derail. They had no idea of the train schedule, none were printed, or even if one would run this night, but John thought they would, to make up for what had been lost the night before. All faces were wearing camouflage paint and they'd be hard to see if explosions resulted from their attack. Dolly lay near John's feet.

It was two hours later before Joshua lifted his ear from the steel track and said, "Something coming, but I can't tell if it's moving east or west."

John looked both directions and saw a pin-point of light to the east. "Looks like they're trying to resupply Edwards again tonight. Look to my right. Do you see the light?" *Vicksburg gets most of their supplies shipped up river, on the Mississippi*, he thought.

"Uh-huh." Joshua said and then grinned.

"Move back into the brush. As soon as the Claymore fires, come up shooting."

"Train coming?" Sally asked.

"Yep, from the east moving toward Vicksburg. I want you down low, behind that log, and do your shooting from there. They may be ready for us this time, so we need to be more careful." John said as he squatted and picked up the clackers.

The train was moving fast down the tracks and Joshua knew they were afraid of an ambush, so he relaxed a bit. *If they were well prepared for an ambush, they'd not be traveling so fast*, he thought.

Again, there was a platform of some sort welded to the front of the train and a dozen captives were seen chained in place. John waited until the platform was well past the Claymore mines and then squeezed them. The mines thundered in the air and the smaller mine gave a dull *boom*. The train continued moving, until it hit where the track was pulled apart, and then it derailed. The locomotive engine exploded, sending flames, dust and smoke high into the air. Screams were heard all along the train—but most came from the front, on the platform.

Joshua stood and sent out 40 mm rounds at the rate of about one a second, and then ducked to reload. Explosions shook the ground, fires erupted and men screamed as they burned to death inside the derailed cars.

Sally opened up with her AK-47 and began to walk her bullets down the short train. When her weapon was empty, she inserted a fresh magazine and did the same thing again.

From between two cars on their sides, a machine-gun opened up, with deadly results. Sally screamed and rolled to her side where she began to jerk and twitch, the top of her head gone.

Joshua fired one 40 mm round and the machine-gun grew quiet.

"Sixth car seems to be fuel, take it out!" John yelled.

Bloop, went the PG-6 and a gigantic fireball rolled to the sky. Burning fuel began to move into the other cars, forcing soldiers out into the open. Taking his time, John killed as many as he could. It was then he heard a jet fly over.

"Break contact and haul ass to the south and do it now!" John screamed.

"What about Sally?"

"She's dead; move!" John glanced at the brain of the woman and knew she was gone.

Joshua took two steps when something slammed into his back and fell to the ground. John, stopped, looked back, but heard his friend yell, "Move, don't worry about me! Go!"

John suddenly had a change of plans and moved west, toward Edwards. He had just cleared a fence when he saw the jet diving to where he'd been a few minutes ago and something fell from both wings. A few seconds later, the area straight south of the tracks was engulfed in flames.

"Napalm," John said aloud and then thought, *damn me. It's a good thing I wasn't still moving in that direction. I don't like leaving Joshua like this. If he's captured, he'll tell them where we're at. Move, we'll have to relocate again.*

The jet made another pass, guns firing and bullets zinging in all directions. John kept running, until he'd covered about two miles and then turned south. Part of him wanted Joshua to survive and yet he really hoped the man had been killed. He knew the Russians would be hard on any prisoner they took involved with the resistance. It was more likely a slow death awaited him.

The highway was bare, not a thing seen, and John was wearing NVG's, so there could be no surprises. The deaths or loss of both his friends ate at him hard, but he ignored his emotions and kept moving. He crossed the road as quickly as he could, jumping at the last second to cover where he entered the woods. He then scattered a few leaves around where he'd landed. Slowly he moved toward the cabin.

Once at the cabin, he knocked once, then three times before he entered. Tom was guarding in the trees and seeing John return, he entered the structure.

"Margie, go pull guard. I have to talk with John about the mission." Tom said as he touched her left foot.

She yawned, sat up and wiped the sleep from her eyes. Five minutes later, she was gone.

"Where are the rest?" Tom asked.

"Dead if they're lucky, captured if they're not."

"Tell me what happened."

John told his story and left nothing out. He paused at the end and said, "I don't know how badly Joshua was hit. He yelled for me to run, so I did. I suspected, obviously he did too, that the plane was going to drop napalm or use rockets. The only reason I'm still alive is I ran west instead of south and it took the pilot a bit to determine where we were. The whole south side of the tracks was in flames when I looked the last time. I know Sally was dead, because chunks of her skull and brain were missing."

"What now?"

"We move and we do the job within an hour. If Joshua talks, this place will be swarming with Russians, and we don't want to be here. He'll talk, so the only question is, when? We're making one trip out of here, so what we can't pack, we leave. Once everyone is out of the cabin, you and I will make some booby-traps."

In a loud voice, Tom said, "Everyone up and get ready to leave! We've got to move now."

"Leave?" Sandra asked.

"The Russians may be here soon." John replied.

All were soon putting on their boots, grabbing gear and ammunition. John said, "Don't overload yourselves, because we have to move fast. Load up on food, ammunition and medical supplies. Take your chemical biological suits, masks and filters. The rest we leave."

Mollie asked, "Can we go with ya?"

"Uh-huh, as long as you can keep up with us. Do you think you can carry Ruben five to ten miles?"

"Tom, I ain't got any idea, but we'll damned sure see, now won't we?"

John said, "Tom, go relieve Margie and have her gather up the gear she needs. I want to be gone within twenty minutes."

Placing a hand grenade with the pin pulled, John wedged it between two boxes of ammunition, tied some two pound fishing line they used for trip mines to a shotgun with a broken stock and ran the line to another grenade. He pulled the pin and slid the grenade inside an empty bean can he'd found. The can was taped to a support leg on the bed. The idea behind the trap was, someone would pick the shotgun up, the line would pull the grenade from the can, and it would explode.

Then going outside, he planted a few anti-personnel contact mines on the trail leading to the door, and finally walked about fifty feet down the trail and placed a Claymore with a trip wire, and inserted anti-personnel mine on the other side, just like he did in the swamp. Then, moving down the trail another fifty feet, he lined the side of the trail with three contact mines, hoping when the claymore or one of the other mines exploded, the Russians would jump to the sides of the trail for safety.

Finishing, John called out, "Let's move, people, and head south. I want Margie on point and Tom on drag. Come, Dolly." Packs were quickly donned and the group began to move south in the darkness.

Over the course of the night and morning, they took turns packing little Ruben, since Mollie was packing her fair share of the supplies as well. John was beginning to respect her, because she wasn't a complainer and he'd never liked a whiner.

Near noon they stopped for a quick bite to eat and were deep in the woods, but a small clearing was near. The clearing was maybe a hundred feet long and half that in width. After everyone had eaten, Ruben was walking around throwing rocks.

Suddenly, Dolly gave a low warning growl. John looked around, but saw nothing out of place. He scratched her ears, but she stood, watching the child.

Ruben moved to the clearing and bent over, picked up a small stone, and tossed it about six feet. He was moving forward, as Tom watched, when suddenly there was a detonation, a scream, and Ruben was thrown to his back. Dust filled the air around him and his loud shrieks were heard.

Mollie stood and screamed, "Ruben!" She started toward her son, but Tom grabbed her.

John yelled, "Stop! He's in some kind of minefield or something. Let me check it out." Then, turning to his dog, he said, "Stay."

John moved toward the clearing and off to the left he saw a green PFM-1 Butterfly mine. Glancing around he saw many of the mines scattered over the field, so they were likely dropped by a chopper as it flew over. Using caution he made his way to boy, who'd stopped crying and was either unconscious or dead. Looking closer, he determined the youngster was still breathing. Ruben's right leg was missing from the knee down and he was bleeding heavily. Pulling a cotton cord from his shirt pocket, John placed the line around the boys leg, just above his knee to slow bleeding. He tightened the cord with an unopened pocketknife, by placing it under the line and then twisting it, finally tucking the loose end of the knife under the tourniquet. He picked the boy up and stepping carefully, made his way back to the others.

"It was a PFM-1 Russian butterfly mine, and the field is full of them."

"Oh, my baby! Is he dead? Is my baby dead?" Mollie asked as she moved toward the child as John handed him to Sandra.

"Keep her ass away long enough for me to see what we have on our hands here. I can't work if she's going to be in my face." Sandra said as she pulled her medical bag to her side.

Margie placed a blanket on the ground beside Sandra and said, "Put him here, John."

As Mollie neared, John said, "Come sit with me, because the boy will be fine. He's lost a leg, but give Sandra some room to work on him. I don't think he's in any serious danger of dying, because those mines are designed to maim and not kill."

Mollie's eyes were darting all around as she attempted to see the extent of her son's injuries, but finally, after a few seconds, she did follow John and sat on a stump. She placed her head in her hands and began to cry softly.

Sandra glanced at John and slowly shook her head. Her hands were covered in blood and a spurting artery had sent a long line of blood from her hairline, across her cheeks and nose, to her chin. She bent back over the boy and started working on his mangled leg. A few minutes later, she stood and said, "He's gone, Mollie, I couldn't stop the bleeding. I'm so sorry."

A loud animal-like wail came from Mollie and she moved to her son. She raised the little boy's head, smoothed his hair, and said, "Come back, Reuben, momma needs ya with me. Do ya hear me, son?"

Tom looked at John and said, "Come with me, we have a shallow grave to dig."

CHAPTER 20

The Russians doctored Joshua to stop the bleeding and then threw him in the back of a large truck. His feet and hands were tied, but he was unconscious and unaware he'd been captured. Sally's body was thrown in the same truck with Joshua, but most of her brain had fallen out as the troops dragged her body to the vehicles.

The commander of the small relief force, Major Gagarin said, "Keep checking, because the pilot claimed he saw many American's burning in the napalm."

"If so, the bodies may not exist now, sir. What was the count he gave to the base?" Senior Sergeant Delov asked.

"Over fifty."

"I would never call an officer in the Air Force a liar, sir, but I have been here since we first arrived and never encountered over ten Americans in any attacking partisan group. Perhaps he is mistaken with his estimate."

"It matters little, because I will report fifty dead, we have one for proof and one captured." Gagarin replied, knowing he'd reap the benefits of his report. "How many dead and injured do we have? Additionally, determine how much we lost in supplies, gear, and material."

"The petrol tank is completely gone, we have thirty-five dead and forty wounded. Most of the wounded are suffering from burns that came from the exploding fuel car. Of the contents of the cars, I would estimate we've lost forty to forty-five percent, mostly due to fire. However, we recovered an RG-6 and an old AK-47 from the two we have in custody."

"Good work, Delov, and when we return come by my quarters, it seems I have a bottle of vodka I no longer want."

"I will be there for sure, sir. We should be done searching within thirty minutes or so."

Two hours later, Joshua awoke startled and then realized his hands and feet were secured to something. His chest hurt and he was sitting in a large metal chair, with a single bulb burning overhead. Glancing around the dimly lighted room, he saw an IV bag and the line ran into his arm, and little else, except a wooden box near the door. He was completely naked, chilled, and saw a bloodstained bandage on his chest. The bullet had struck him about an inch below his collarbone, so he knew his injury wasn't fatal.

Two Russians entered and in perfect English the smallest man said, "I am Lieutenant Dyomin, your interrogator. This big monster beside me is Private Vasnev, and he is the muscle behind our little talks. Let us begin by you telling me your name, shall we?"

Joshua looked at the big man and quivered because he was closer to seven feet than six, and he must have weighed three hundred pounds, all of it muscle. The big private was wearing a dull smile, like someone who has, at best, borderline functioning. *Lawdy, I hate to piss this big bastard off, but here goes*, he thought and then replied, "I'm not telling you shit, asshole."

The lieutenant said, "Now, think about what I have asked, which is not much. I only want your name. If you refuse me once more, the private will eventually convince you to answer. Why not avoid unnecessary pain?"

Joshua spat a glob of bloody mucus toward the Russian, but missed. The Private raised his huge fist and didn't miss as he struck Joshua hard on his injury.

Screaming and hoping he'd pass out, he saw the world turn gray and then black.

How long he was out, he had no idea, but when he open his eyes, Dyomin asked, "Your name, please."

"Bubba, Bubba Lee Claremore." He manage to get out. He then glanced down and his injury was bleeding again. *These jokers will kill me anyway, so I'll lie to them*, he thought.

"Why are you, a black man, fighting for white men? Do you not see they are using you so they can return you to bondage?"

"You're wrong, peckerwood," he replied, "because the only white men that are my enemies speak Russian. May God bless the United States."

Vasnev moved to the wooden box and removed a steel pipe. He slapped his hand a few times with it, testing his grip. He moved to Joshua's side and waited.

"Now, Bubba, we can do this the easy way, or the hard way, and it does not matter much to me how we do it, because you will talk when I'm done with you." Dyomin said with a false grin.

"Go to hell, you vodka slurping piece of—"

Dyomin nodded and the Private struck Joshua hard on the left leg and the bone snapped. With his fists clinched tightly, Joshua screamed and twisted in the chair. Reaching down, Vasnev began to slowly rotate the foot, which brought excruciating pain. Screaming louder, as tears formed in his eyes, he wasn't sure he could take much more. Then he began to pray aloud. First, he prayed for God to save him and then he prayed for Him to end his life. Once again, he blacked out.

When he next awoke he was wet and looking down he saw wires leading to his balls. He met Dyomin's eyes and asked, "W . . . what are the wires?"

"Well, my friend, the wires are connected to a hand cranked generator and while the pain, from what I understand, can be se-vere, it will not kill you. Shall we start this conversation once more?"

"Y . . . yes." Joshua saw the wires were connected to a box with a rotating handle, so he knew Private Bad-ass would love to turn the crank.

"Who is your leader?"

"Willy is the name we know him by and nothing else. I was told in case we got captured we couldn't tell what we didn't know."

Pulling a small pad and pen from his shirt pocket, the Lieu-tenant asked, "His rank?"

"Full colonel."

"Where can this Willy be found?"

"I honestly don't know."

The lieutenant nodded to Vasnev and he turned the crank hard and fast.

Due to the water on him, the electrical current didn't just go to his balls, it shot through his whole body and he lost complete control of his whole nervous system, as he jerked and twisted violently in the chair.

The interrogator held an open palm toward Vasnev and he stopped. Giving Joshua a minute or two, Dyomin asked, "Where can he be found?"

"I . . . I'm just a . . . private, how much . . . do you . . . think I know?"

"Much more than what you are telling me. Private Vasnev, remove the first three finger nails on his left hand."

Pulling a pair of pliers from the box, the big man moved to Joshua and pried his fingers from the balled fist. The pain from the removal of the nail, added to his electrical shock and his bullet injury was too much and once again he passed out.

How long he was out, he had no idea, but when he awoke, he was in a field with others. Unlike them, he was chained to a support pole and the prisoners were all on the other side of the compound, because no one wanted to be associated with him. His hands were also chained together, with about three feet of chain between his wrists. *They did a half-assed job, because they've broken my leg and don't see me as a threat now. They know I can't escape.*

The bone from his shin was clearly seen and no effort had been made to set the break or even wrap it. *Death is my only option now, because I'll not get far with a broken leg.* Pain filled his whole body and he had a hard time focusing his eyes.

I have to resist, for no other reason than to show these bastards what Americans are made of, so they'll learn to respect and fear us. He looked around and it was night, which surprised him, because he'd been captured during the early morning. He saw some of the guards watching and then a man pointed at him and said something to another man. The man walked away at a fast pace.

Going to tell the Lieutenant I'm awake for another round, I bet. His right hand throbbed and when he looked, all five nails were missing and the whole hand was covered in dried blood. *I can't take another interrogation, because it'll kill me. I need to end this shit the first chance I get, so I can die much faster than the way they're doing the job now. I don't fear death nearly as much as I do the pain of torture. I just can't take it.*

A few minutes later, Private Vasnev showed and yelled something in Russian. The gate was instantly unlocked and opened. The huge man walked to Joshua smiling and used a twisting motion of both of his hands to show he intended to twist the broken leg.

When the Private reached for Joshua's feet, to drag him to interrogation, the wounded man threw the loose chain between his hands over Vasnev's neck, and then crossed his arms as hard as he could. Something broke in the Russian's throat and he began chocking as blood ran freely from his mouth and nose. Two guards near the gate yelled and then moved toward Joshua with their bayonets reflecting in the light.

The thrust of the first soldier entered the quivering body of Vasnev, but the sharp point on the second bayonet struck Joshua in the left side of his chest and he howled with pain. Then, with the two Russians standing on each side of him they began to stab him repeatedly, until Lieutenant Dyomin yelled, "Stop, you damned fools, do not kill him! Stop! He has important information I need."

Both guards stopped and snapped to attention. The bayonets on their rifles were covered with blood.

"Sir, he killed Private Vasnev!" The taller of the two said.

"Vasnev, like the two of you, is expendable." He moved to Joshua's side and then squatted. The black man's eyes were open, but unseeing, so the Lieutenant closed them with his fingers. Vasnev was dead, his mouth filled with blood, and the bayonet had entered the very center of his chest. The Lieutenant stood and said, "Get a truck and remove both bodies. The dead partisan you can dump on any street in town, but take Vasnev's body to the mortuary. Damn me, the first prisoner I have had in almost a year and you fools killed him."

"I am sorry, sir, but I was attempting to save a comrade."

"Yes, yes, yes, but what am I to tell Colonel Vetrov? He will be filled with anger."

Knowing he was in trouble, the guard said, "I will get a truck."

Half an hour later, Lieutenant Dyomin was standing in front of his commander, along with Major Gagarin, and Vetrov was so mad his face was scarlet. He was still in bed, but the IV was gone, and he was healing. He leaned forward and asked, "Do you expect me to believe an average size black American killed Private Vasnev? Hell, that man was the biggest man in the whole Russian army! Then, two idiotic guards killed the prisoner before you could get any information of value from him? You got his name, Bubba something or the other, and that is all?"

"Sir, he crushed the throat of Vasnev, using the chains on his hands. However, at one point, when he was near insane with pain, he mentioned a cellar five miles south of here. He said it was his father's old place and the remains of a house still stood. He said the locals call it "The Plantation," in a joking way. Also, he mentioned a Colonel Willy Williams, but his last name did not come out openly. Just before he passed out the last time, I asked for Willy's name and he gave it, unknowingly."

"So, there must be a million American's named Williams."

"He called the man, Bro Williams, which means the man Willy is black as well."

"Maybe, but Christians call each other brothers and that is the same, right?"

"When I attended college in the states, I learned black people use bro or sister to associate with each other. Often the women address each other as 'sistah.' Christians use the more formal 'brother' when addressing each other."

"It is a terrible language anyway, English is, and full of nonsense."

"Yes, sir, but I ran a computer check on a Willy Williams, Negro, and I found three of them in our data base, which you know was stolen from the American Department of Defense."

"And?"

"The first Willy Williams died almost five years ago in a car accident. The second was injured on active duty and retired a major for medical reasons. He was injured when his parachute failed to open properly. The last man was in the U.S. Army Special Operations and a member of the elite Green Berets."

"Surely you joke? I have heard of their special operations, of course, and the Green Berets, but I know little about them."

"It is my opinion," the Lieutenant said as he met Gagarin's eyes, "that the special forces group he belonged to was equal to our *Spetsnaz.*"

"Would you agree with that, Major?"

"Yes, sir, I would. Before the formation of Special Operations as a specific organization, the Green Berets were called Special Forces. They earned a hard reputation in Vietnam as being good at any assignment given to them, but America didn't use them as they should have. I consider any prior members of their special operations units to be dangerous men, sir."

Handing a thick folder to Vetrov, the Lieutenant said, "I printed all the information I could find on the man and he is well trained."

Gazing into Dyomin's eyes, the Colonel asked, "Do you have any idea where this Williams is now?"

Shaking his head, the Major replied, "No, sir, we do not, but we know exactly where the cellar is and want your permission to go there. Lieutenant Dyomin and I found it on a map."

"Then stop talking with me, gather up a company of men and go visit the cellar. I would suggest you have some helicopters or jets flying cover for you. If you run into Williams, there will be a fight. Try, if possible to bring some prisoners back so we can learn more about the partisans." For the first time in weeks, Colonel Vetrov almost felt like his old self and even smiled.

The trucks had problems the minute they pulled up in front of the old house beside the cellar. The truck in front suddenly exploded as the bumper pulled a tripwire, which triggered a Claymore mine, killing most of the men in the cargo area. Those that were not killed, were injured. The second truck's front right tire contacted an anti-personnel mine, which exploded and severely damaged the front quarter panel of the truck.

"I want a mine detecting team to sweep this area and do the job now!" Major Gagarin yelled, pissed that men had died and they'd not even left the trucks yet.

As the team worked, Lieutenant Dyomin said, "As the teams sweep your area, dismount the trucks, but stay near. If you step away, you might discover a mine."

One man, a private, moved about four feet, beside an oak tree, to pee into the grasses. He'd just unbuttoned his trousers, when he felt his left foot tangled in something, so he moved his leg slightly. He spotted a sudden movement in the limbs of the tree and a split second later, saw a limb moving toward him, and on the branch was four spear-like stakes. Three of the four stakes entered his body, with lowest about an inch above his penis, the second in his belly and last in his chest. He gave warbling scream and danced madly on the stakes.

"Medic!" Someone screamed.

"Help . . . me." The injured man managed to get out between his clenched teeth.

"The medic is coming, so you will soon be fine."

"I—h..hurt."

The medic neared, scanned the ground around the man, and saw the almost invisible two pound fishing line on the man's left boot. Placing his medical bag on the ground, he saw immediately the man would die. The barbs sticking out his back were soaked with blood and debris, and already the injured man was leaking blood from his ears, nose and mouth. The medic reached into his bag, pulled out a needle and filled the syringe with morphine. *I'll give him too much of the drug and it will kill him without pain*, he thought as he moved to the front of the man where he could insert the needle in a vein in his arm.

The medic took two steps, when the ground gave way and his right foot fell into a hole. Inside the hole were sharpened oak stakes, smeared with dried human dung, so his foot was immediately impaled on one. He screamed, tried to jerk his foot up and out, but he was unable to do the job. Two men moved to his side and using pure force, they jerked his foot free. He screamed and then passed out, as the injury bled profusely. One of the men, knowing the medic was in pain, picked up the syringe and injected the morphine into his right arm.

The man standing with the stakes through his body had stopped screaming, only now he was whimpering like an injured animal. The whimpers were low and could barely be heard. One of the men moved to the man's side, nearest the tree, and unknowingly stepped on a mine. There was a loud detonation, the air filled with smoke and detritus, and men screamed. The one who'd activated the mine was now short a leg, the man working on the injured medic had taken the blast in his face, and the man standing beside him was killed instantly.

Dyomin yelled, "Everyone stay where you are until the area is cleared of mines and traps. Damn fools! " He then moved close to the tree and said, "You men, remove your comrades and place them in the truck. Once in the truck, I want a medic to work on them."

When the men hesitated to move, Dyomin pointed with his right index finger as he said, "You, you, you, and you, get those men and do it now."

A few minutes later, the four were in the back of the truck and a medic climbed inside. He worked on the man with the missing leg, then the man with the injury to his face. He checked the man that had the injuries from the barbs in his chest, but he was dead. Finally, moving to the medic, he found no serious injury, but the man was dead, too. He stuck his head from the canvas cover and said, "We have two dead, one has lost his leg, and the other has most likely lost his eyes. Actually, his face is so mangled he must have some brain injuries. We need a helicopter to remove our wounded, sir. We have ten others injured from the second truck alone."

"Radio man, contact the helicopter and have him land on the road approaching the house. There are no trees in the way and the area is clean."

"Yes, sir."

Dyomin turned and walked to the Major where he said, "We are not dealing with a group of ignorant partisans that are angry, sir. We are dealing with professionals who are as calculating as they are deadly. We have over twenty dead and ten wounded, and we have not even stepped from the driveway yet."

CHAPTER 21

Ruben was wrapped up in his blanket and placed in the grave John and Tom had prepared. Mollie stood crying beside the hole and quivered, devastated by the death of her only child. Removing his boonie hat, Tom asked, "Do you want to speak a few words, Mollie?"

"I— I can't."

"John, you say something then, from the Bible." Tom said.

John cleared his throat, held his hat in both hands, and said, "We are troubled on every side, yet not distressed; we are perplexed, but not in despair; persecuted, but not forsaken; cast down, but not destroyed; always bearing about in the body the dying of the Lord Jesus, that the life also of Jesus might be made manifest in our body. Knowing that he which raised up the Lord Jesus shall raise up us also by Jesus, and shall present us with you. For which cause we faint not; but though our outward man perish, yet the inward man is renewed day by day. For our light affliction, which is but for a moment, worketh for us a far more exceeding and eternal weight of glory; while we look not at the things which are seen, but at the things which are not seen, for the things which are seen are temporal; but the things which are not seen are eternal. This I say in the name of Jesus, our Lord and Savior, amen. This is from 2 Corinthians 4."

"T . . . thank . . . you." Mollie fell to her knees beside the grave as Tom and John filled it with dirt.

When they were finished, John whispered, "Let's leave her alone and let her have some time with her son."

Tom nodded and they walked away.

An hour later, they were moving again and Dolly was walking beside Mollie, as if she felt the pain the woman held inside. The weather had turned cold just before the funeral and now it was starting to spit snow.

"Any idea where we're heading?" Tom asked as he slipped back to walk beside John.

"I know of an old junkyard, oh, maybe another mile, that may be okay to use for a few days. It's off the beaten path and I don't think the old owner ever made much money from the place. It looked rough on it's best day."

"How do you know of this place? I mean, it's a bit out of the way and you drove some nice cars from what I remember."

"I had an old car I was restoring. It' was a 1957 Chevy, but I quit after a while because the parts were too expensive. Most of the parts had to be ordered from California. I originally got the car from Mister Myles, who owned the junk yard."

"Well, let's hope we can rest there a bit, because for some reason, I'm beat today."

John gave a slight grin and then said, "I've not slept a deep sleep since the fall. Now, let's be quiet until we get to where we'll spend the night."

About a mile later, Margie, who'd been on point, returned and said, "Spotted what looks like an old junkyard. The house has burnt down and the barn is on it's last legs. But on the top of a hill, maybe a hundred yards away is a garage, or so it looks to me."

"Uh-huh," John said, "that's the garage. Let's move there, because we can see the whole area from there."

As they walked, Tom warned, "Stay off the road and in the grass."

The road was dirt and Tom was checking the surface as they walked, looking for tire prints or foot prints, but saw nothing. Stopping half way to the place, he said, "John, take Sandra and check it out."

John smiled at Sandra and then motioned toward the garage with his head. Handing Dolly's leash to Tom as he walked by the man, he said, "I suspect it's empty, but this is the best way to find out."

They neared the building slowly, with John checking the dusty road for any sign as Tom had, but saw nothing. At the door, he pointed to himself and then indicated for her to wait outside. Sandra nodded.

The door squeaked on rusty hinges as it opened, so he waited a few minutes before entering. When he did enter, he was scanning the inside from side-to-side looking for movement, except he found it clean. He then check out back and in two sheds at the rear.

He walked back to Sandra and said, "It's clean and looks like nobody has been here in years." He then waved to Tom and the others.

They walked inside and looked things over closely. There was an office, with a sofa, two chairs and an old wooden desk. The top of the desk was marred and discolored by cigarette burns. Cobwebs were in the corners and spiderwebs were seen near a broken window behind the desk.

The others soon joined them and Tom asked, "Find anything we can use?"

"Most of the tools are gone, but I did find some welding gear, scrap metal and a cutting torch. Overall, I have to say no, nothing we can use, unless you want to put a car together." John replied.

"I'll stand guard while the rest of you eat something. Once you're finished, someone come and relieve me so I can eat." Tom said.

"Will do." John said, and then lowered his pack to the floor. His back ached, but it usually did after carrying a pack all day. He dusted off a water bucket and then turned it up-side-down. He sat on it and grinned when Dolly placed her big head on his thigh. He scratched her ears and rubbed her head.

Sandra moved to his side, sat in the floor and then pulled out a Russian ration. The rations were good, so she shared hers as they talked. Unlike before the fall, they chewed the food well, enjoying the taste as long as they could. Every minute or so, John would feed Dolly a bite, and he enjoyed having her near. The dog was the only thing, besides Sandra, he had of the old days and as a result, they were both precious to him now.

Tom ran into the building and said, "Have a tank with maybe twenty men heading our way."

"How far off?"

"Quarter mile, maybe."

"Which way are they approaching?"

"Straight down the road like they own the place."

"Everyone get out the back door, while I rig some surprises for our visitors. Sandra, take Dolly with you." John said and pulled out a hand grenade. "Go straight after you leave this place and wait for me, oh, maybe a hundred yards out."

As soon as they left, he spotted some gas cans and walking to them, he was surprised to find a little gas in them. He poured the gas on the floor and then rigged his grenade to explode when someone tripped his thin fishing line. He hoped the added gas fumes would increase the damage by the grenade.

He could now hear the noisy motor of the tank and peeking from the door, he spotted the head of the tank commander sticking from an open hatch. He lined up the sights of his bison and fired, smiling as the bullets gave loud *pings* and *zings* as they struck around the man. Finally his head was struck and his body instantly fell from view, as blood and brains spattered on the turret behind him.

A machine-gun opened fire and started to riddle the wooden building. John ran with all his strength, suspecting a cannon shot, but it didn't happen. He flew out the back door and ran into the woods. Once with the others he noticed the machine-gun had stopped firing, so as they moved he listened for a cannon shot, but heard nothing. A few minutes later, he heard the grenade explode and knew he'd killed at least one more Russian.

John ordered, "Move at a slow jog and keep it up for a couple of hours. You'll run into a creek in a couple of miles; move downstream once there and stay in the water."

After about a mile, John said, "Take everyone and keep moving with the stream. I'm going to double back and see if we're being followed. If so, I can get a look at how many are on our asses, see how they're armed and if they have a dog. I'll take Dolly with me."

Dolly and John broke from the main group, went up the side of the creek and entered the woods. Then, at a slow jog, he moved toward the trail, but closer to the garage. He quickly identified the spot they'd entered the woods, so he moved back into the brush to watch. His wait was short and just a few minutes later, three Russians and a single dog moved down their trail. Since he was downwind, the dog never knew they were there.

The dog handler carried a pistol, but no long gun and the other two were armed with AKM assault rifles. John knew the rifles carried 30 round magazines, and his Bison gave him more firepower than them. He carried 60 rounds in his magazine and being a submachine-gun, his 700 rounds a minute beat their 600, so he had them outgunned—only slightly. *But I need to take all three of them out with the first burst or I'll lose my ass. I'm glad the dog handler has his animal on a leash and it looked like it was looped around his wrist. If I miss one or two, the shit will hit the stump*, John thought as he stood and started moving at a jog to the spot where they'd entered the creek.

Twenty minutes or so after he'd been at the creek, he heard and then saw, movement toward him on the trail. The dog had his nose to the grass and was moving at a steady pace. Once they were in close, about twenty feet, John raised his Bison and fired. A storm of bullets struck the three men, but the dog got loose and moved right for John; Dolly lunged and met the dog head on.

Around and around the dogs went, flying into the air at times, as each made serious attempts to kill the other. John dropped his Bison, which hung from a sling around his neck, and pulled his pistol. He could see blood on Dolly's right shoulder and the other animal had blood on it's neck. Finally, the dogs broke free and Dolly stood giving a deep growl, her hackles up, and her blood-stained teeth showing. Blood tainted saliva dripped from her chin.

Raising his pistol, John fired two fast shots and the Russian dog collapsed to the grass, unmoving. John called Dolly to his side. Petting her, he checked her for injuries. *It looks like a deep claw mark on her shoulder and a couple of bites that are bleeding on her legs, so she was lucky*, he thought. He then moved to the three men, where he discovered they were dead. Returning to his dog and pack, he pulled out his medical kit and dressed her wounds. Of the three, the shoulder was the deepest injury, but the punctures from the bites would have to be cleaned and dressed better once he met the group.

He then returned to the dead Russians, took their gear and weapons, and booby-trapped all three.

"Come, girl." He said and took off at a slow trot.

Sandra looked at John and said, "She'll be fine. I gave her a local, sewed part of her shoulder together, and the bites I covered with triple antibiotic ointment."

Tom asked, "Was that all you saw, just the three men on the tracking team?"

"Uh-huh, and they were alone."

"What now?" Margie asked.

"We keep moving. We need some miles between us and the garage. We'll keep moving until close to midnight, then sleep for four hours, and start moving again. I want all ears in the air as we move. Since they know the general direction we were moving, they'll have birds in the air looking for us. Right now, we'll head due west, so let's get out of this creek and start in that direction." John said, and then gave a weak smile.

"Why the smile?" Sandra asked.

"I was thinking of how much I loved this part of the state before the fall of our nation. It was so special to come out and hunt during deer season, you know?"

Tom said, "You're still hunting, only men now and not deer. Let's move. The longer we stay here talking the longer we'll have to walk tonight."

Hours passed and it was well after dark when the group stopped to rest and eat. They all gathered under a huge oak to eat. The night was cool and the low clouds John had seen earlier could bring snow or rain. He knew if it snowed it would never amount to much, because Mississippi never got over two inches in all the years he'd lived in the state.

"John, do you know of anyway to protect ourselves from infrared or thermal detection?"

"Only stories and none that really work, why?"

"I've heard the only thing that really works well is rain. For some reason rain makes the screens look cluttered and hard to see the heat on the ground. From what I've read, the infrared systems in choppers are a handful for just two men to operate, and usually the chopper is used to find folks. They then radio troops on the ground to engage the enemy. Of course, if we run into a gunship, the party is over, because they're designed to kill."

"I've heard wool blankets mask human heat, but it seems to me the wool would absorb the heat and make you a bigger target. I've also heard space blankets or casualty blankets work, but only for a minute or two, because after that the edges of the blanket will start to glow from escaping heat. I saw a movie once, while on active duty, and a guy tried to get away from an aircraft by swimming, but on the screen he was clearly seen, and his movements in the water glowed behind him, leaving a trail."

"Let's just pray we never run into that problem. The next time we hook up with Willy, we need to find something for choppers." John said.

"We're wearing mostly new BDU's from the batch Willy gave us and I heard, but can't confirm, that BDU's were treated with something that cut down on thermal image readings. I think it reduces the amount of body heat given off. I even remember reading something about it on a label sewed on a BDU shirt one time."

"Well, even if it does, 80 to 90 percent of a person's body heat exits from the top of their head, so I hope our boonie hats were treated with the same shit."

Tom laughed and said, "Then the feet will give a good clear reading and so will the hands."

"The problem," Sandra said, "is the human body is almost a hundred degrees and the surrounding areas are cooler, so your body heat would stand out clearly. The only place in the world where it might be easier to hide, might be on a hot road at night or in desert sand. They'd both be pretty hot, but you'd have to be one lucky sonofabitch to find a road at the right temperature."

"I think a space blanket would be the best or just not moving. The risk with not moving is they might smoke your ass anyway, because they know something is alive."

"I heard they don't get a reading in a house or under canvas, but I hope to never have to find out."

As they talked, they ate a quick meal and were soon on the trail once again, moving west. As they walked, a light sprinkling of rain started to fall, so everyone donned a poncho. There were many bright flashes of lightning but no loud thunder, so they continued to move. After a couple of hours, the trail became slippery and more than one fell and regained their feet cursing.

It was shortly after midnight, when Sandra, who'd been on point said, "I have a house in front of me, and I see a light inside."

"Did you spot anyone moving around?"

"Not outside, but I saw two different men walk by the window."

"Well, it ain't Russians, or a guard would have been posted."

Tom said, "It could be a different cell, so do we knock on the door or what?"

"You can knock on the door if you want; I don't think I'd try it, because they'll likely shoot your ass." John replied.

"Why don't we stay behind shelter and call out to them? If we can explain who we are, they might let us stay the night." Margie said, and then wiped the rain from her face.

"Okay, we'll do as Margie suggests, because I can't think of a safer way to do this. I'll go forward with Margie. John, you stay here with Mollie, Sandra and Dolly. Once we're inside, we'll come back for all of you. If you hear shooting, don't join us, because we'll try to withdraw."

"When do you want to do this?" Margie asked.

"Why not right now? The longer we stand here the wetter we'll get, if that's possible." John said and then added, "Come on."

He let her lead and near the edge of the trees was an old farmhouse that was way overdue a paint job, and some of the windows were broken. The light was clearly seen in what may have been the living room.

John called out, "Hello the house. We're needing shelter from the rain."

Minutes passed before a voice said, "Keep walkin', we're full for the night."

"Do you know Willy Williams? If not, how about Top?"

Again, it was a couple of minutes before the same voice said, "One of you move toward the door. If we see more than one, we'll start shooting. I want no weapons on you, which means no pistols or rifles, understand?"

Handing his rifle to Margie, he stuck the pistol in the small of his back and stood. Even in the darkness, he felt vulnerable as hell. "I'm coming in, but keep your fingers off the triggers."

"Come."

He walked across the clearing, half expecting to be killed any second, and when he stepped on the porch and it gave a loud groan, he cringed at the noise. The door opened and short man with a shotgun said, "Get in here."

John entered but remained by the door.

"Hell, James, that's John and I know him well." Top said with a big grin.

"Can I bring my people in, Top? It's pretty wet out there."

"Sure, John. You did it properly, James, but John's a good man and one of our cell leaders."

John pulled the pistol from his back and placed it back in his holster. Top broke out laughing and said, "Still don't trust worth a shit, do ya, John?"

"Nope, never have and never will, I guess. How have you been doing?"

"Not so good. Here about, oh, a week back a chopper caught us on a hill in the middle of the night. I suspect they were using thermal imagery, because they shot us to hell and back. Out of twenty, five of us survived the attack. But, that was miles from here."

"Tom and I were talking about the same subject earlier. Do we have anything to protect us at all?"

"Not really, not as far as I know. I'm to meet up with Willy in a couple of days, so why don't y'all hang around and go with us?"

"I think I'll do just that."

CHAPTER 22

Lieutenant Dyomin stood looking at the garage where his men had set off the grenade planted by John, and the young officer was seething. He'd warned the first troops in the door to do the job slowly and to check for danger as they moved, but they'd kicked the door in and entered in a rush. A few seconds later came the explosion and he had three dead men to place on the truck beside the dead tank commander.

Damn fools. Do they think the Americans are idiots? I have stressed we are fighting well trained soldiers, but they cannot accept that in their small brains, Dyomin thought as he watched a squad of men returning from the woods. He'd sent them after the team tracking the Americans and from what he could see, they'd been killed or seriously wounded. Just the fact that bodies were being packed out and the dog was nowhere to be seen, added to his apprehension.

Senior Sergeant Delov, leading the group, walked to the Lieutenant and said, "Three more dead men and we lost our dog, too. I found where a single man waited to ambush them. The tracks indicate he had a dog with him. Our dog had blood on his teeth and head, but a pistol killed him. To me, it means we have at least injured their dog."

"Vetrov will shit! We have seven dead men and all we did was injure a dog? We must have better results or the Colonel will start taking heads. I want these men to break into small groups and search for the partisans."

"Which group do you want me to join, sir?"

"You stay with me. Make sure each group has a radio, plenty of ammunition, and rations for a few days. Stress to them we must find the Americans and the group that finds them will be greatly rewarded. I want your experience behind the communications, so we have some control on each group."

"What kind of reward, sir, because they will surely ask?"

"Promise them women, vodka and a few days off. I have yet to see an infantryman who did not enjoy that sort of thing. Also, tell them Colonel Vetrov will mention them by name in communications with Moscow and a medal can be provided, as well as a promotion. We have got to start doing better or we will all end up in a prison someplace."

Delov came to attention and asked, "Will that be all, sir?"

"No, contact the flying squadron and have them keep a helicopter in the air at all times, night and day. If possible, try to get a bird or two with thermal imaging capability, so we can go on the offense. We must be aggressive without being stupid, and thorough without being slow. The aircraft are not to attack the partisans, but radio the locations to us. I want us to get the credit for killing the Americans, not the helicopter crews."

"Yes, sir, I fully understand. I will take care of your request immediately." The Senior Sergeant replied. *Typical officer, wants the credit for the kills when the aircraft could just fire one missile or use his cannons to kill a houseful of partisans. It is all politics for officers, and I am glad to be enlisted.*

Waving his hand, to indicate to Delov to handle the situation, Dyomin thought, *In the time they have been gone from here, even if they walked fast with no breaks, they must be within twenty miles. I will have the crews start twenty miles out and work inward. We will either check each building or send a missile into it. If I handle this properly, I am sure to make at least one promotion out of this war, or an early death.*

The radioman and Delov walked to the Lieutenant, where the radio operator handed the headset to him and said, "The operations officer for the squadron wants to speak with you, sir. He needs some additional information about where to start this search."

Dyomin quickly explained his idea to the Major on the other end of the radio and then waited for a reply. He knew the operations officer had to get the commander's approval before the search would start.

Finally, the Major said, "We will start looking today. We currently have three aircraft with thermal capabilities, but two are down for maintenance. I expect to have all three in the air before the end of the week."

"Good. I appreciate your assistance, sir, and I think by working together we can achieve a great deal of success against the partisans."

"We shall see, Lieutenant, but you have our support."

Dyomin replied, "Thank you, sir." He handed the headset to the radioman and then said, "Get the teams moving and do it now."

As the teams walked in the general direction of John and his small group, Delov wondered, *How many of these men will return alive? Most of my soldiers are boys and this game is about to become deadly.*

The radio operator yelled out, "Lieutenant Dyomin, we are to return to base right away by order of Colonel Vetrov."

"Load up the remaining men and let us move!"

Colonel Vetrov was in his office, his right arm in a sling and in pain, but the war was not going well for him. Over the last few weeks he'd lost well over a hundred men and had killed less than a dozen Americans, including the prisoner they'd had. His aircraft kept breaking down, his motor pool was having vehicle problems, and supply had yet to provide winter gear for his troops. He had a list of problems on a sheet of paper in front of him and beside it, on the same paper, a list of things going well. He had two things going well that he'd identified; his troops were all healthy and the attacks on the trains had ceased. He was unsure if the attacks had stopped because he now placed a tank on a flatcar to protect the trains, or if the partisans had moved on to other ripe targets.

Lieutenant Dyomin stood at attention in front of Vetrov and nervously licked his lips. The Colonel had exploded when told of the deaths of seven more men, but then grew quiet. It was the silence that scared the young officer.

"So, you have how many teams out searching for the American's, Lieutenant?"

"Twelve, sir, and I think by using the helicopters and my men, we can at least find the partisans. Then, working together we can kill them and maybe even get a prisoner or two."

Vetrov looked at his papers, shook his head and then said, "Dyomin, I hope you realize both of our careers are riding on your teams right now. I am damned sure if we do not have some good word for Moscow soon, heads will roll, and they'll start with ours."

"Y—yes, sir."

"I want a helicopter to take you to a team, so you can keep an eye on how things are done. I also want Delov dropped off with another team. Now, listen to your Senior Sergeant, because he has been in the army longer than you have been alive. That means use the radio before you fight, and I want you to stress to your men that the partisans are experts with mines and booby-traps. Do you fully understand what your orders are?"

"Yes, sir, and I will discuss all plans of attack with my sergeant before I take any action."

"Good. When you are in the field, keep in mind I will fully support you and if you have need of something, let me know. We must take the offensive and start improving our partisan body count, or our careers are over. I've warned you of our careers twice in this meeting, because the situation right now is most grave."

"I will do my best, sir." Dyomin replied and knowing the conversation was over, he saluted and left the room.

He found Delov talking to a guard at the prison camp gate and informed him of the Colonel's orders, leaving out he was to discuss any attack plans with the sergeant. He then said, "Arrange a helicopter, just one, to take us both into the field as soon as possible. We'll be delivered to two different groups. Once on the ground, contact me, and let me know you're in place and ready. Then, hopefully, we can find our targets."

Thirty minutes later, both men were in flight. Delov was dropped off first, to a group of men near a creek, and Dyomin was released on the edge of a large field. The temperature was cool, but not really cold, and a light rain fell. After he'd been on the ground for half an hour, Delov contacted him and informed him they were moving.

Slowly the rains increased in intensity and all teams were forced to seek shelter for the night. Most of Dyomin's men felt uncomfortable with the young officer along and they complained about it among themselves as they made shelters from their shelter-halves. A guard was placed and the rest turned in for the night, some too tired to even eat.

It was near four in the morning when Dyomin was awakened by the radio operator. "Sir, one of the helicopters reports movement about 3 miles from us."

The Lieutenant took the headset and spoke for a few minutes with the crew. Finally he smiled, handed the headset back and said, "Get the men up and ready to move. One of the aircraft with thermal imaging discovered a man coming and going from a rundown house near us. It seems he was looking for, or collecting, wood for a fire."

A junior sergeant, who'd been the leader the day before, asked, "How many men are at this house, sir?"

"They have no idea how many are in the house; the images would be blocked by the building, but if they saw one clearly, there will be more inside. The aircraft cannot see inside buildings or other structures well and my guess would be less than ten men. Most of the cells we have run into have between six and ten men, right?"

"Hell, I have no idea, sir. I have yet to see a partisan, but I know they are good with mines and booby-traps."

"You will see some this morning, Sergeant, and that's a promise. Get the men up and moving. I want them to eat and be ready to leave in less than an hour."

"Yes, sir." The Sergeant replied and began waking his men.

A little more than an hour later, the Lieutenant called the helicopter crew and asked them to stand by as they carried out the assault on the house. He was informed by the pilot that he had enough fuel to remain overhead, and another aircraft was to join him at sunrise. Dyomin grinned, because two choppers almost guaranteed success.

"Move the men toward the house, Sergeant, and make sure you place a man with good eyes on point. I want him to watch for mines or booby-traps. If he sees anything unusual, he is to stop and wait for me to evaluate the situation."

"Understood, sir. Private Antipin, you have point and Private Zverev, I want you to bring up our rear. I want both of you to remember to keep your distance as we move, and Antipin, stay alert or we will be shipping your body home to momma. Let us move, people, but watch your spacing as we travel."

Grunts and groans were heard as the men donned their heavy packs and moved in behind Private Antipin. Since they were not on a trail, the point man encountered no mines or traps, but he moved slowly through the woods. He held a compass in his left hand and tried his best to maintain the heading given to him by the Junior Sergeant. Just as dawn was breaking, he spotted the house and came to a stop.

He observed the building and other than smoke coming from the place, he saw nothing. He looked for guards, saw none and then reported to the Lieutenant.

Antipin and Dyomin moved forward, both held their guns at the ready, because the situation looked too easy. Both men scanned the countryside, saw nothing out of place, and then they returned to the group.

Dyomin contacted the chopper and was informed there were now two aircraft on station. He informed the pilot that he intended to attack the house within a few minutes and once the attack was in progress, he was to assist if needed.

"I want Private Zverev to move before the rest of us. He will move to the window and toss a grenade inside. As soon as the grenade explodes I want all of us to enter and do the job quickly. However, I want the Sergeant and Antipin to move to the rear of the building to make sure none slip out the back. It's a two level home, so we will have to clear both floors."

"When do we move, sir?" The Sergeant asked.

"Now, but I will give you ten minutes to get into position." Dyomin looked at his watch and said, "On the hour the attack will start. Any questions?"

"Are we to remain at the rear at all times during the attack?" The Sergeant asked.

"Yes, do not move from your position until we have cleared the house and one of us waves you in."

The Sergeant nodded and then said, "Come with me, Antipin."

While they waited, Dyomin said, "Once the grenade explodes, Zverev, you kick the door in and we will enter."

He has me doing many things in this attack, and I wonder if it is because he trusts me or if I am expendable? the Private thought as he pulled a RGO grenade from his pack. *He should have Krayev walk to the window and fire two or three 43 MM grenades from the GM-94, if all he wants is dead Americans. Hell, the grenade launcher can fire three rounds fast too,* he thought and then cursed his luck for having so little rank.

"Let us move, it is time." Dyomin said and started forward. Zverev hurried to the front of the men and he'd just moved to the window when something struck him hard in the middle of his chest. He dropped the grenade and fell to his knees, as the sound of a single shot was heard. After a split-second, he fell forward, landing with his face in the mud. *If this is death*, he thought, *it is not so bad.* His world slowly turned to different shades of gray, until he was surrounded by darkness.

Dyomin glanced at Zverev and picking up the grenade the man dropped, he pulled the pin and tossed it through the window. Two more loud rifle shots were heard and a man dropped each time. The grenade exploded, sending smoke and dust from the broken window. Screams were heard inside the house and then the Sergeant and Antipin were heard firing at the rear. Someone kicked the door open and they began to enter.

Rifles started barking the minute they entered and seeing movement to his left, Dyomin twisted and saw an American with a pistol. Out of reflex, the Russian fired and saw the man knocked back against the wall, his body quivering as he fell to the floor.

The men began to yell as they cleared the house room-by-room.

Once the lower floor was cleared, the Lieutenant yelled, "Next floor, let us go!"

The first man on the stairs, unknowingly, pulled a thin line forward a few inches with his right foot, and the staircase exploded into flames. Dyomin's world instantly turned black.

Dyomin lay on the floor dazed and it was a few minutes before he was able to move. He sat up, looked around and saw most of his men were uninjured. With the Lieutenant down, most of the men were unsure what to do next. Blood ran down his arm, but he slowly stood and said, "Pull all bodies out of the house now!"

"Ours and the Americans?" Someone asked.

"All, and do it now."

A few short minutes later, ten dead Americans and two Russians lay beside Zverev. One of the dead was Private Krayev, the GM-94 man.

Pointing at a private near him, Dyomin said, "Go through the house and move to the Sergeant. Let him know the second floor has not been cleared, but I will have the helicopter destroy this building."

"What now, sir?"

"Take the bodies and move them into the woods. Then we will have the aircraft destroy this house."

A lone figure stood near the upper rear window of the house and watched as a lone Russian moved into the woods. A couple of minutes later, two other Russians joined the man and they all moved toward the front of the farm house. As soon as all three men were gone, the woman opened the window and threw out a rope. She then lowered herself to the ground and made her way toward the woods. Once in the woods, she'd try to link up with their guard, who was a sniper in a huge oak about a hundred and fifty yards away.

Colonel Vetrov listened closely as Lieutenant Dyomin explained his attack and the results. They'd found five more American bodies once the house was brought under fire by the helicopters, so the attack looked like a great success for the Russians. There were fifteen dead partisans and only three Russian dead.

"You have done well, Lieutenant, and I think your career will go far, but we have only started to clean house, or so to speak. Much more must be done before we can say we control this area, but you have done well. I want many small teams, just like yours, out in the field, with overhead support from either jets or helicopters. I think by working together, we can soon train others to use your tactics in the whole state."

"Thank you, sir."

"Now, get a shower, some hot food and a little rest. At 0400 in the morning I want you to lead your group back into the field. Well done, Lieutenant, and you will find a fresh bottle of vodka in your quarters."

"Sir?"

"Yes, Lieutenant?"

"How many teams will be out at once, I mean in the morning, when I leave?"

"A dozen will be inserted at different compass points before dawn."

"How many aircraft will be overhead? My concern is having sufficient air cover for all the teams."

"That is a problem for the operations officer and his executive. However, keep in mind, our biggest problem now is not aircraft but fuel. The last few tanker cars were destroyed by the Americans. I do know we will have enough aircraft in the sky to support two fights on the ground at once, if that makes you feel any better."

"It does, sir. My concern is protecting my men in the event we start a fight with a much larger group."

"I understand, but the past shows the Americans in small groups. They usually hit and then run, so your biggest problem may be finding anyone to fight with, not running into a larger force. Any other questions?"

"No, sir."

"Dismissed and the best of luck tomorrow, Lieutenant."

CHAPTER 23

John and Top sat at a table in the kitchen and listened to Cheryl and Esom explain the attack on their house. Esom, not much of a talker, allowed the woman to explain most of the story and nodded at times. She then held up the GM-94 and said, "I found this on the ground floor once the Russians left and just before I was sent out. Harold told me to get out and find you, which I did, but soon after the house came under attack by a chopper using cannons. I could hear screams from inside the house and I wasn't even close."

"Cannons are devastating to anything they fire on, and will make short work on a building." Top said and then took a sip of his coffee.

"It damned sure didn't take it long to tear that farmhouse to hell and back." Esom said.

"No, I guess it didn't. Listen, you two get some food in you and sleep. I'm sorry about what happened to Harold and the rest, but we're at war and these things happen."

As soon as the two left the room, John said, "Looks like the Russians have finally got organized." He pulled Dolly's head to his lap.

"One attack doesn't mean much, but I suspect they'll soon be out in force, knocking on doors. So, let's beef up our security around this place, plant a few surprises and have Barbara get a warning out to the other cells. Now, we both know we can't contact everyone, but we'll do our best, and hope it's good enough. Willy will just love the fact the Russians are now on the offensive, because this way they'll bring the fight to him."

Willy Williams had lost even more weight than the last time John had seen him and his thin face broke into a smile after Top told all he knew about the Russians. He thought for a few minutes and then said, "Ring each house with mines, booby-traps, and I want a good shot in a tree keeping watch during the day. Now, I'll remain here, but we're going to stir up a hornets nest, because we're going after the Russians."

"While they'll think they're on the attack, we'll turn the table, huh?" Tom asked.

"I want toe-poppers, punji spikes, and booby-trap wires across streams, but under water. I want empty houses fixed so if someone opens the door, a trap with three stakes on it will swing down and injure those entering. The traps are simple to make, and I'll draw out some diagrams of the surprises this morning. However, to protect our folks, mark each house the same way and then pass the marking on to me. If we see the marking, we'll enter by another door."

"Another good door trap is to mount an anti-personnel mine at the same level as the doorknob, so when the door swings full open, it contacts the mine mounted on the wall, and the resulting explosion takes a few folks out of the picture." John added.

"Yep, I'd forgotten about that one, and I've seen it done a time or two. Also, don't forget to use a side-closing punji trap, where the trap is mounted on a hinge. When someone steps on it, the hinge causes the iron or wooden stakes to swing up contacting the person's leg. It's like a teeter-totter except it produces pain. Be sure to smear all barbs and stakes with human waste, because severe infections will result to those injured." Willy said, and then asked, "Any other ideas?"

"We have some unexploded bombs and the like, do you want those rigged as well?"

"Use everything we have and even rig boulders, logs, flip snares or anything that can be used to slow them down. I want the Russians scared shitless to enter the woods."

John stood and looking at Tom said, "Looks like we've some traps to place."

Four days later, Willy said at the morning meeting, "We lost two more houses before we could get traps in place. The roughest part is the loss of twenty good men and women, who can't be replaced. These were our friends and in some cases, members of our family, and according to the survivors the same routine was used each time."

"A grenade through the front window, door kicked in following the explosion, then a fight for the house. Once the Russians withdraw, an airstrike is called on the cleared building." John said.

Tom shrugged and said, "There really isn't much we can do against that, other than traps and guards."

"I think," Willy said, "over the last few months we've grown complacent, since the Russians have left us pretty much alone. Now that they've come visiting, we're caught with our heads stuck up our rears."

"Most all we know of have been warned." Barbara said, and quickly added, "I know, because I warned them personally."

Willy took a sip of his coffee and then asked, "How are the traps on the roads and trails going?"

"We've barely dented the roads, because there are just too many of them. All the houses have been ringed with traps and mines, but we're still working on streams, trails and logging roads." Tom replied.

"Oh, I know it takes time and I'm not mad about it, just wondering is all. Tell all to keep up the effort and we'll soon own the countryside." Willy said and then asked, "John, are you still interested in something to fight Russian choppers with?"

"I sure am."

"Earlier this week, we were able to get our hands on a few LAWS rockets that should work, except I have no idea how well. I've never heard of anyone using it for anything except tanks. Keep in mind, you'll have to catch a chopper loading or unloading troops to use it, because it's limited to around 3,300 feet, which isn't very high."

"It beats nothing; how fast can we get them into the hands of our cells?"

"We can deliver them quickly, and we can send a short note along that it's to be used only for choppers at low level. How does that sound?" Willy asked.

"Good to me, let's get them out as soon as possible, Barbara." John said as he grinned at the woman.

"Why me?" She asked.

"You're the only one who knows where all the cells are located."

"Good point," Willy said. He thought for a couple of minutes and then spoke again. "John, I want you to go with her, because we need more than one person who knows where all the groups are. If Barbara gets seriously injured or killed, we'll be lost."

"Some of the troops that go with her know, right?" Tom asked.

"No," Barbara said, "I take out different groups when I go in different compass directions. The main idea is if a man is captured, he only knows so much and can't tell what he doesn't know."

"Makes sense to my old head." Tom said and then smiled.

Two days later, John was in an old shack of a house, handing out a LAW, when a guard ran in and said, "I just saw a chopper fly over us and then it sounded like it's pitch changed once over the trees."

"Have you noticed any other choppers around?" John asked; since it was just barely after dawn, he was surprised.

"A guard reported hearing one last night, when he went for water, but no, not really. It's usually quiet around here."

"I'd suggest you prepare for an attack. If the chopper landed, it's up to no good and you can take that to the bank. It's likely your guard was seen using infrared and this house was marked to check out."

"We're ready, but first they have to get through our mines and booby-traps. Once they come for the house, we've a tunnel dug that leads us to the river. We'll be long gone before they enter this place."

"I pray for your sake, you're right. We can stay and help, if you want, Allison."

"No, we're in good shape. I don't intend to fight them anyway, so we'll kill and wound as many as we can and then run."

"It's your choice, but you can't win against aircraft, anyway you look at it."

"They've always used ground troops first, for some strange reason, so I know what to expect. Go on, you two get out now and we'll prepare for our visitors. Frank, see these two through our gap, seal it, and then return."

"What do you mean, seal it?" John asked.

"Once you're clear, he'll place a few quick mines to keep the Russians honest. So once outside, don't try to come back in or you'll ruin your day."

"Let's go," Frank said, "because we don't have much time. I want to get back before the Russians arrive." He picked up his rifle and began to move for the back door. John and Barbara, along with five other men, followed.

Once outside the wire, John thought for a few minutes as they were checking the map and then said, "We're going to hang around long enough to see how this fight goes." Then, pulling a LAW from a pack, he added, "I may get a chance to use one of these."

"Well," Barbara said, "let me know where you'll be, because I damned sure don't want to be behind you when it fires. Have you ever seen the back blast from one of those things?"

"It'd hurt you, and that's for sure. Now, every one needs to get camouflaged well from the choppers and no matter what happens, wait until I start to move before you move. Most of you can get back in the trees, but I'll need someone up close to me to protect me as I try to launch this thing."

"I'll stay with you." Barbara said, and then smiled.

"You think I'm crazy, don't you?"

"What I think isn't important right now. I'm curious to see if you can down a helicopter with a LAW."

"I don't see why it won't work, if I lead the bird enough."

There was a loud explosion, followed by a scream from the front of the house, but it was impossible to determine exactly where it had occurred. Gun shots were heard from inside the house, and then the chopper appeared and made a run for the structure. He'd made his run from the other side, so John never had a clear shot, but bullets were heard striking the old structure.

"Get out now!" John said under his breath.

The helicopter turned in the blue sky and lined up for another run for the building. Once again, John never got a clear shot. He decided then to wait for the Russians to be picked up or for the chopper to hover overhead near the building. He needed the aircraft almost stationary before he could fire, because he felt uneasy about how much to lead. He also realized if he missed, his group would then become the hunted.

It bothered him that firing from the house stopped after the one pass by the chopper and he saw no movement at all. Then, out of the blue, a small group of Russians moved toward the front door and were lost from his view. Two other men moved to a position behind the house and waited, with their weapons ready.

Lawdy, I hope they're all using the tunnel or Willy will soon be short some troops, if he's not already, he thought.

The biggest Russian in the group waited until Dyomin tossed in a grenade and it exploded before he kicked the front door hard with his right shoulder. The door swung full open, the doorknob contacted a mine secured to the wall, and an explosion filled the morning air.

Five men were down, two bleeding profusely from their mouths, and another was dead. Lieutenant Dyomin had just turned to order his men into the building when the mine exploded, knocking him on his ass on the porch, and his ears filled with a loud ringing from the blast. He looked around and saw two more men staggering and leaking crimson.

"Medic!" Someone yelled.

A medic appeared, moved to the seriously wounded and started to work. Other than his ears ringing, Dyomin, felt fine and could find no injuries. He moved out of the way and started walking toward the radio operator.

Other men passed him at a run, moving for the now open door.

The ringing in his ears had Dyomin in a confused state and he didn't realize there were no shots fired by either side, and there should have been.

Finally, Junior Sergeant Norin reported, "They went out using a tunnel, sir."

"A tunnel? Where does the tunnel lead? Has anyone gone into it?"

"We don't have anyone who's willing to enter the tunnel to see, and I suspect it's booby-trapped anyway."

"Sir, I have an important message from the helicopter. He said he spotted two groups moving from the air. One is further away than the other, and the closest one is near the stream."

"Tell him to kill the men near the river, because it is the closest, and I think the tunnel leads to that area. They would want to keep the tunnel short, to escape faster."

"I have instructed him, sir."

"Tell him to make two passes at the group and then come here to pick up my badly wounded. I am sure if he uses a rocket attack on them or machine-guns, they will fall quickly."

The radio operator spoke into his headset, grinned and said, "He is starting to line up his attack now."

The men near the river, thinking they'd made a clean getaway, waded the shallow stream and started into the trees.

Frank suddenly yelled, "A chopper has lined up on us!" The man pointed in the direction of the aircraft and all could see it was turning to start its approach.

"Spread out now and do it fast! Run!" Allison screamed and then ran wildly through the woods, jumping over logs, brush and accidentally through a blackberry briar patch. His hands and legs were ripped by the sharp thorns in the patch, but he knew distance was all they had between them and death. Just as the chopper passed over him, in a steep dive angle, he saw one puff of smoke followed by a second. The two rockets exploded near the high bank on the river, so he slowed his running a little, in an attempt to catch his breath. *The bird is firing blind now, because he's lost us in these trees*, he thought and then yelled, "Form on me, men!"

One or two men near, formed on him quickly, since they were closer and one of them warned, "Here comes the chopper again!" They all fell to the ground and heard the cannons begin to fire. Behind him, Allison heard the rounds hitting and turning his head, he saw dust and clumps of soil thrown six feet into the air. Fortunately, his men were in advance of the bullets.

Ten minutes later, with Frank on point, they moved toward another house Allison knew of, and it would shelter them until he decided what to do. They'd been forced to leave most of their supplies, but he'd worry about that once they were safely away from the area.

John lay absolutely still until the second pass was completed and then he knelt beside a huge oak to watch the chopper. The bird slowly moved to the house, the gunners alert and scanning the woods, and hovered near the Russian men as they lined up the injured to load on the bird.

When one man moved to the front of the chopper and held his rifle over his head, John knew from experience the man would slowly lower his weapon as the chopper started down to pick up the wounded. Once the skids touched the ground, John would attempt to make a killing shot. But suddenly, he decided to allow the Russians time to load some injured men, so he could kill more than just the crew, if he hit the damned thing at all.

When the skids touched the ground, the LAW was already extended and since he'd sent Barbara and the others out, he knew no one was behind him. He lined the sights up and waited patiently as two stretchers neared the aircraft. Once the first stretcher was inside, with the second being loaded, he fired and watched his rocket take the chopper right in the engines. It rewarded him with a huge explosion and men in flames were seen running inside the fireball, just before the fuel went, too. The chopper came apart and pieces in various sizes were thrown in all directions. The ammo was going off when John placed the now empty LAW into his backpack to carry out. Smaller detonations were heard as he stood and started running for his group.

He'd remembered where empty LAW containers left behind were booby-trapped, so he'd always carry out all he carried in, but it was lighter now with the rocket fired.

Lieutenant Dyomin was mad as hell as he watched his men help extinguish the burning men and knew he'd not only lost more men, but a helicopter as well. He had a number of dead before the chopper was hit, and now he had a good six or seven more to add to the total. He'd caught sight of the rocket just a split second before it struck, and was surprised, not thinking the Americans had any defense against aircraft. It'd been a costly learning experience, so from now on, he'd send in choppers first, and then his men would do a body count after the attack. He also knew he needed some mine detector teams along to clear the way through the protective rings around the houses. *So, you've grown smarter, have you? It will do you little good against the might of Mother Russia. How many men or helicopters I lose matters little to me, because the end is what matters*, he thought, not realizing he was starting to think like a real Russian commander.

The radio man neared and said, "The second helicopter said we have to return to the point we inserted before he'll do an extraction now. He seems to think this place is ringed with more rockets."

"Tell him we will withdraw to the pickup point and for him to remain ready to assist us on the way back. Sergeant Norkin!"

"He is dead sir, along with Senior Sergeant Delov. Both were burned so badly they could not survive, so the medic put them to sleep."

"Private Antipin, take point and lead us back to where we started this whole mess."

"Yes, sir." And, as he turned and started walking, the men lined up behind him for the trip out. All went well, until they were about fifty yards from the spot they were inserted, and being a little off the trail was intentional by the man walking point. The last thing he wanted was to step on a mine on his way back to the base. He had no way of knowing even the sides of the trails had been mined and booby-trapped, and for this very reason.

He'd just taken a step, when his foot struck a treadle board and before he could react, the opposite end of the trap swung up and four sharpened stakes entered his chest. He screamed and struggled against the fire-hardened stakes, but they were barbed and three of them had passed through his chest. Sticking from his back, the bloody points were a reminder to all near him that they were not safe yet. The medic neared and inserted a fatal amount of morphine into Antipin, knowing there was nothing he could do to help the man. *He will die anyway, so I will end his pain.*

"You," Dyomin said, pointing a private standing near, "take the point, and watch where you put your feet or you will be the next one to go home in a metal box."

CHAPTER 24

John sat at the table as Willy had a small staff meeting at the kitchen table. The shooting down of a chopper was great news, and Willy kept shaking his head at the thought.

Finally, John said, "My dad was career army and I got the idea from him. Seems during the Vietnam War, the Viet Cong shot at our helicopters with damned near anything they could find, including rocket propelled grenades. I figure if a grenade would do the trick, a rocket for damned sure should work."

"Oh, I'd heard stories like that, mostly at a table in the club as the old sergeants told war stories. I guess you taught us something new today, huh?"

"What has me concerned is this; I may have caused the Russians to change tactics now, and I don't think we'll find any choppers coming near houses, unless it's to fire on them."

Willy asked, "Sergeant Thomas, please tell John what you know about Thermal Imagery."

A new man to the small group said, "I'm a sniper and at times I have to hide from the choppers that I suspect can see in the dark. In Afghanistan, the bad guys learned to hide from infrared and thermal equipped aircraft by covering themselves with wool blankets. It's not real good in the long run, because eventually heat will start to become visible as it leaks from the edges of the blanket. However, if they only make a pass or two, well, it works. If they stay looking for you, then they'll likely be looking for human forms and not just heat. Now, I know that sounds iffy, but it's the best idea we've come up with yet. The real key is how well trained the man on the other end is, how determined they are to get your ass, and how much fuel and time they want to spend in one area looking."

"Thanks, Thomas, we'll give it a try."

"Oh, and don't wear the blanket, or it'll be 'hot' from your body heat. I carry mine tied loosely on the top of my pack. When I need it, I pull it from my pack and throw it over me."

Willy grinned and said, "I've sent word to all cells that we will no longer defend houses against attacks, because like John, I suspect the Russians will use aircraft against structures now. I want everyone to bug out when an attack is imminent. We will, however, always leave one man behind with a LAW, to attempt to down a bird. If we can start taking out choppers, it'll worry the hell out the Russians."

"Sounds good to me," John said and then added, "but the man left behind better have some big balls, because it scared the living hell out of me."

"Oh, the commander at Jackson is about to go on a tour of other bases, to meet the commanders, so it's a grip and grin tour, and to check their readiness to combat us. Our intelligence section now has a few men and women working on the inside, doing manual labor or jobs the Russians don't want to do, like burning shit, cleaning hospital patients, or filling sandbags. One such man saw a folded paper drop from the Colonel's jacket, as he got into a car, and brought it to us straight away. It was his complete schedule for the trip, as well as the names of those going with him. It seems he flew to Edwards a long while back for an extended visit, and now intends to travel back by car. I think John's use of the LAW has him concerned."

"It'll be too big a convoy for us to tackle." John said.

Willy laughed and replied, "He'll be traveling with a motorcycle in front and one in the rear. He'll be riding in a liberated car, with three other men. There is a Major Galkin, which we think is his air operations officer, and Lieutenant Dyomin, who seems to just be an infantryman. The driver will be a Private Aptekar and riding security, or shotgun, is a Master Sergeant Belonev. They'll leave in three days."

"What do we know about any of those men?" Sergeant Thomas asked.

"One of our contacts, who cleans up patients in the hospital that mess their pants or pee the bed, said both Vetrov and Belonev were hospitalized recently, due to the night attack John and his group did on the prison camp. Both had gunshot wounds and are almost fully recovered now. The Major is a big drinker of Vodka and consumes about a pint a day, so we know his reflexes will be slow, as well as his mind. The Lieutenant is just your normal ground pounder, and he will be the most dangerous one in the group. The driver, Aptekar, I'd imagine, is some poor bastard they ordered to drive, but he does work for the Lieutenant."

"What are the chances the schedule might change, I mean when the Colonel realizes he's lost his itinerary?" Tom asked.

"He might change it, hell anything is possible, but a visit like this takes a lot of coordination. Commanders have to be available, motorcycle escorts and vehicles lined up, billeting and feeding of the visitors has to be established by each base, so I think he'll change nothing. If he's not left the base recently, then I suspect he'll know it fell from his pocket and think it was lost on the base. He likely feels he's got a good handle on base security, so he'll not suspect we know anything about it. But, if he changes the schedule, we'll show by the road each night until he does leave. Any questions?"

John said, "Do we know the time he'll leave?"

"At dusk, 1700 hours, but we want our attack to occur under the full cover of darkness, so we'll hit him about halfway to Jackson, his first stop. I suspect, since the man is based in Jackson, he'll want to pick up a few more men to take along, and that will mean more vehicles. More vehicles mean more security. As a result, we have to take him out before he reaches the city."

"My folks can find a good ambush site, if you want us to do it." John said.

"Good, you do that, John. Now I want all the supplies we'll need for this attack rounded up and ready to go in two days. We want to take Vetrov alive, if possible, but if not, he has to die. He is the brains behind the movement against us and a serious threat.

If we kill him, it'll buy us some time to get better organized, before the Russians bring in a new man. Any questions?" Willy said and then took a long drink of his now cold coffee.

Willy then moved to the coffee pot, pulled it from the fireplace and filled his cup. Looking at the group, he said, "Since there are no questions, dismissed. John, scout the area today."

"Yes, sir."

John left Sandra behind and was a bit surprised when Sergeant Thomas joined them. "I've been assigned to your cell, since your sniper was killed."

Shaking hands with the man, John said, "Everyone, this is Thomas; he's to be our sniper."

After the new man was welcomed, John said, "I want Thomas, Tom, and Margie to go with me to scout out an area. The rest of you get some hot food in you and some rest. Three days from now we'll be going on an important mission."

Ten minutes later they were moving north, toward the main highway that ran from Vicksburg to Jackson. The weather was cool, skies clear, and little wind. Each wore camouflage makeup on their faces, hands, and necks. Tom now carried the GM-94 grenade launcher, with an M-16 slung over his shoulder. Thomas had his sniper rifle in a protective pouch, over his shoulder, and packed a sawed off 12 gauge shotgun, which had the stock removed and a roughly made pistol grip in its place. John had his Bison and Margie an AK-74, which John had taken from one of the men he killed a while back with the dog.

They moved silently through the trees and stopped often, to listen and scan the countryside. Thomas was on point with Margie bringing up the rear. They soon entered a part of the woods that had a wide path, perhaps before the fall it had been a logging road, and they moved parallel to it, out about twenty feet. They'd gone about a hundred yards when Thomas signaled for them to hide.

John moved into the brush and squatted, so he could part some bushes and clearly see the trail. A few minutes later, a lone Russian walked by, obviously the point man, and a few minutes later a group of ten soldiers were counted. John waited until the man walking drag passed and then stood a few minutes later.

He waved everyone to him, and once they were there, he said, "Tom, mine the trail. We'll return by a different route."

Twenty minutes later, they were once more moving north.

The remainder of the trip to the road was uneventful and once there, Thomas said, "We can string some barbed-wire across the highway the night of the attack and maybe take the lead cycle out of action."

Tom, pointed to the other side of the road and added, "The short slope, on the other side, would be a good place for a few men, so they can shoot anyone that exits the car from that side. Up there, they'll be out of our line of fire."

"I was thinking our main force could be in that group of trees in the median, but we'll need some people covering the traffic coming from the other direction too." John said.

"They could do that job from here, don't you think?" Margie asked.

"Yep, now let's get back to Willy."

They'd just turned and moved into positions, when a chopper flew low overhead. John had looked up, out of instinct and met the eyes of the door gunner, who immediately pulled his gun around, but was unable to squeeze off a round. However, the aircraft instantly banked the other direction and all knew the pilot was lining up to attack.

"Break and scatter, we'll meet down the way about a mile."

"Run!" Thomas yelled as he began moving through the brush at a run.

They flew in all directions, and just a few seconds later the loud explosion of a missile was heard, followed quickly by a second. Shrapnel flew by John, striking tree trunks and cutting bushes, but none touched him. He added more speed to his run and moved for the densest part of the trees.

He heard a woman scream and knew Margie was hit, but they could do nothing for her until the chopper left the area.

On the next run, the big cannons on the chopper came alive, throwing lead into the brush and trees at an unbelievable rate. Tree bark, dirt, rocks and other debris filled the air and dust blocked John's vision. After the run with the guns, the aircraft circled once and then left.

John yelled, "Stay where you are, until we're sure the chopper has left the area!"

Ten minutes later, John stood and looked around. The trees were torn to hell back off his left side and to his right, but there was little damage in front of him. "Let's check on Margie."

They found her laying on her back, her eyes open and she was blinking. Squatting beside her, John asked, "Where are you hit?"

"Upper. . .back." She replied and then groaned.

"I've got to roll you over onto your belly to treat the wound, okay? It'll hurt, so prepare yourself."

Tom walked to them and then Thomas arrived a few seconds later.

Thomas said, "I'll guard near the road, just in case they send any troopers here to look for bodies."

"Go." Tom said.

"Sliver of metal in her back, and I'm going to pull it out. Now, Tom, prepare me a dressing to use as soon as I get it out. It's missed her spine and hit in the area of the shoulder bone, so it has to hurt."

"Need some morphine?"

"No, because she needs to try to walk back, if she can do the job."

"I'll . . . walk."

John grunted and worked the metal in her back, which brought a loud scream. Finally, it pulled loose and blood began to flow. He applied a bandage, wrapped her up and said, "You're lucky it didn't go all the way through, because I think it might have killed you."

"Well, by God, I don't . . . feel lucky." She replied.

"You'll live." Tom said and then added, "We need to get moving."

Helping her to her feet, John said, "If you start to feel faint, let me know, but place your arm around my neck and let me hold onto you. We're in no hurry, so take it slow and easy."

Tom pulled Thomas from guard and placed the man on point, as he brought up the rear. Once again they were moving, only, John prayed the Russians wouldn't send troops. He knew if they were followed, Margie would be left behind. The unwritten rule was, the unit must be saved and no one person was worth the lives of the others.

The next hour passed slowly for Margie and she was experiencing the worst pain of her life. She could feel blood running down her back, but knew they had to keep moving. John held her arm around his neck, and his other arm around here waist, so he knew she was bleeding. *We've got to place some distance between us and the attack site*, he thought and kept moving.

Thomas waited for them and when they were beside the man, he said, "Check her injury. If she's bleeding badly, we'll leave a trail a kid could follow."

Not removing the old bandage, John placed a new one on top and wrapped her once again. The blood was a trickle and very little was seen on her shirt. "If they bring in dogs, we're screwed." He said.

"I've not seen many dog teams out. Most of those I have seen were guard dogs, so maybe the one you killed by the stream was a fluke." Tom said.

"Get her up and let's move. I don't like being out here after that attack. I've got a bad feeling and I always listen to my feelings." Thomas said and then scanned the area.

"I hear ya, brother." John said and then lifted Margie to her feet.

"How much more?" she asked.

"We're about half way, or do you need some rest?"

"I'll keep moving as long as possible, because I agree with Thomas."

"Let's go. Thomas, you bring up the rear while John takes point. I'll help Margie for the rest of the trip."

All went well until they could see the house, and then Margie collapsed to the grass.

"John, I need your help." Tom said.

John neared, looked down at Margie and said, "Help get her onto my shoulder and I'll pack her as far as I can. I'm not as strong as I once was, but the house is less than a hundred yards. Here, take my Bison."

They walked to the house and once on the steps, two men came out and took Margie from John. He noticed she was now dripping blood, but still breathing as they took her to what passed for a hospital.

All three entered and Willy asked, "What happened?"

After explaining the attack and what they discovered, Willy said, "We'll use the spot for our ambush. Now, we've counted four choppers around this place today and that's a lot. I imagine the Colonel has ordered more sorties flown, looking for us. It's very likely the chopper that hit you will return to base with an inflated number of known partisans killed, when they actually injured only one. They may have thought you were in the woods after crossing the road."

"Why would we cross the road?" Tom asked.

"They may figure you were checking out the Edwards Base or the prison camp."

"We were moving, that's for sure. I *never* want to be near a target when a cannon is fired again. It's pure hell, and I feared I'd lose my mind." John said.

Sandra neared and said, "Dolly is doing fine. She's been sewed up, given an IV and is now sleeping."

"Too early to know about Margie?"

"She'll live, but have some serious pain over the next few weeks."

Moving to a side room, that before would have been a bedroom, John lowered his pack to the floor and said, "I need some rest. I'm tired, hungry and sleepy." He then sat on the floor and leaned his head back against the wall.

"There are some beans and biscuits on the stove. You rest a bit, while I get you something to eat. It'll have to be cold, because no fires during the day. Willy said if the Russians want us, they'll have to work to find us."

"It'll do. I love you, Sandra, and wish things were different."

She squatted beside him, ran her hand over his face and then kissed the top of his head before she said, "Better days are coming, but I do pray each night that we'll both live long enough to see them."

"I do as well, but I don't know if God hears us."

Standing she replied, "Let me get your food and remember, God hears us, except he doesn't always give us what we want." She walked from the room.

When she returned, just minutes later, John was asleep. She placed his bowl on the floor, covered it with a small plate and curled up beside him. Sandra missed the times they used to share at home, the wonderful foods, the conversations and the loving. She fell asleep thinking of the prime rib and soft music they'd shared the year before the fall.

The night of the ambush, all were a bit nervous, because most knew it wouldn't go as planned. They had learned, through combat experience, you can plan your ass off, rehearse all year long, and yet you couldn't add the human element of your enemy. Often the best plans were useless once a fight started, because how your enemy reacted to your attack made all the difference in the world. John had seen some strange behavior from his enemy, like the time he'd shot one man a least a half dozen times and the man kept coming for him, or the time a man was ablaze with flames and tried to get in close to him. It proved to him that you can never tell what a human will do when the shit hit the stump, and there is no way to plan for it either.

You simply adjusted during the fight. Like the night Kate was killed or when Joshua died. I really thought things would go to hell once Colonel Parker died, but Willy has done a great job. It goes to show that we have to train our subordinates to take over in the event of our deaths, just like we did on active duty, he thought as he looked his gear over one more time.

"Saddle up, let's get this show on the road. John, you're on point, and Thomas, I want you bringing up our rear. Esom!"

"Yo!"

"You're our sniper and I want you with three others on the other side of the road, like I discussed this morning. Try not to kill the Colonel, but take him out if the job needs done."

"Let's move, folks."

CHAPTER 25

Vetrov finished his meal in his quarters, showered and changed into his best uniform for his trip. He wore all his medals, wings and other badges he'd either earned or been awarded for some achievement or the other. He stood looking at himself in a mirror; he was a vain man, and thought, *Looking good for an older gentleman. When I return to Moscow the women will surely love my looks and the fact I am a successful war hero.*

Private Aptekar entered the room and said, "Sir, we are to depart in fifteen minutes. I have two bottles of vodka for you and Major Galkin, along with ice, in the rear seat. Additionally, the officers mess has provided some special foods for your trip. Will you be returning here when the inspection is completed, or staying in Jackson? I ask only because Master Sergeant Belonev needs to know so he can arrange better quarters for you and assign an aide."

"I will stay in Jackson, once we've completed the inspection, but keep this room open for me in the event I decide to visit again. Oh, and before I forget, Lieutenant Dyomin will not be joining us on this trip."

"I will inform the Sergeant, sir."

Fifteen minutes later, they were loaded in the car, with the two officers in the rear seat and the two enlisted in front. Master Sergeant Belonev carried a Bison for protection and Aptekar had a AKM, with a 30 round magazine. Extra ammunition for both weapons were stored in ammo boxes between the two men. Additionally, each enlisted man carried four RGO hand grenades.

"Private, I want my flag on the front bumper."

"Sir, we thought it safer not to post your flag." Belonev said.

"I did not ask what you thought, Master Sergeant, I gave an order. Post my flag now."

Aptekar got out and posted the Colonel's rank on the car, knowing it would be a bullet magnet in the event of an ambush. *His vanity will get us all killed if we run into any partisans*, the private thought as he returned to his seat in the staff car.

Master Sergeant Belonev picked up a hand-held radio and ordered, "Motorcycles, move into position now. Let me know when you are ready to move."

The Sergeant heard the vodka bottle open in the back seat and the tinkle of ice in glasses. *They had better not get drunk on this trip, because I think we are in for some trouble. This is a piss-poor escort for the man that runs the anti-partisan program for the whole state. Hell, if the Americans have word on this move, they will hit us with everything they have to kill or capture Vetrov, because I damned sure would*, he thought as he slipped the safety off his weapon.

"We are in position now, Sergeant." The radio squawked.

"First motorcycle, stay a hundred yards in front of us and the other rider should stay the same distance behind. Any sign of trouble, radio the base and inform them instantly. As soon as base acknowledges your radio report, close in on us. Do you both understand your orders?"

"Yes, Sergeant."

"I understand my orders, Sergeant."

Belonev looked at Aptekar and nodded. The Private started the car, slipped it into gear, and began moving.

As they moved for the entrance gate, Master Sergeant Belonev silently prayed, "Lord, I ask for your protection on this trip. I have a gut feeling things will turn rough. I've spent many years in the army and would like to live long enough to retire. I know I have not practiced my religion in years and I am not a good Christian, but keep me alive, please. I will try to be a better man and Christian in the future, amen."

The two guards at the gate snapped to attention and saluted Colonel Vetrov's staff car as it left the base.

The first few miles were hard on the Sergeant, and his attention was on the darkness that surrounded them. *When*, he thought, *will the partisans strike? I just want to go home to my Alena. I want a simple life and to live as a farmer. I am not asking for much.*

"What was that, Sergeant?" Aptekar asked.

"I asked if you are keeping your eyes on the rider in front of us."

"Oh, I am, and you can believe me, too." He wanted to say more, but couldn't, not with the officers in the backseat.

"Sergeant?" Colonel Vetrov asked.

"Yes, sir?"

"Would you enjoy a drink?"

He must be getting drunk, because when sober he'd never ask an enlisted man to drink with him, he thought and then said, "Just one, sir, because of my duties." *I can hardly turn down an offered drink by my commander.*

A few minutes later, Vetrov's hand appeared over the seat, with a tall glass. Belonev noticed the glass was almost full and had very little ice.

Taking the glass, the Master Sergeant said, "Thank you, sir."

When the two officers went back to talking, the Sergeant took a big gulp of his drink, mainly to settle his nerves, and then placed the drink between his thighs. He then placed NVG's over his head and began to scan the countryside. He saw little, except a doe deer and her yearling standing beside the roadway eating the lush green grasses.

There suddenly came a bright flash of lightning, followed by a sharp crack of thunder. The Master Sergeant, took another long gulp of his vodka and continued watching the sides of the road through the greenish tint of the goggles. A gentle rain began to fall, and picking up the radio, Belonev said, "Reduce speed by 15 kilometers an hour."

Both motorcycles immediately reduced speed.

Wanting to get rid of the glass between his thighs, Belonev downed the rest of his drink and placed the empty glass on the floor. The *whack-whack* of the wiper blades running almost put the senior NCO to sleep, but just the thought of an ambush quickly filled his body with adrenaline. *Come on, hit us if you are going to do the job, because I would rather get it over with*, he thought as he watched the cyclist in front of him.

The motorcyclist in front, Private Babanin, was a young man of eighteen on his first military assignment. He'd become engaged right out of secondary school, but really didn't want to marry, so he'd joined the army. He knew eventually he'd have to serve anyway, so he'd decided it was a good way to avoid marriage and to get his military service behind him. He'd played his girlfriend for a fool, using her to satisfy his sexual urges, and then deserted her. He'd told her the army had contacted him demanding he appear for active duty right away and he had to serve. He chuckled as he remembered the hot night they had shared just before he left for service.

He was enjoying the ride, even if the rain did sting his face as it struck, and his speed was low, 64.4 kilometers an hour. He'd hoped the pace would be much higher, because he had a deep love for speed. He was wearing NVG's to see the sides of the roadway clearer, and his headlight was almost blacked out with wide tape, which allowed a flat narrow beam to hit the road surface. But with the goggles on, he could usually see the road clearly beyond the reach of his light. Tonight, the clouds covered most of the moonlight and at times his vision with the high tech gear was limited at best. The goggles, from what little he knew, absorbed light from all natural sources, and somehow used it to present a clear view in the darkness. His mind was that of a farm boy, which was all he'd ever been until a year ago.

Private Babanin never saw the thin wire stretched across the highway, which cut his head from his body as quickly as a razor sharp sword. His mind, still working for a few seconds, was confused as his head rolled on the pavement and for about twenty feet the motorcycle continued on a straight path. It then fell to it's side, throwing sparks in the air, even from the wet surface of the road. His now lifeless body rolled from the bike and finally came to a stop in a muddy ditch, where it quivered and jerked violently for a few seconds and then was still.

Belonev saw the bike go down and screamed, "Go, go, go!"

An explosion. from a GM-94 grenade on the highway in front of Aptekar, causing him to swerve violently to avoid the blast and he over-corrected, placing the vehicle in a skid on the wet surface. He pushed down on the brakes hard, but they continued to slide toward a ditch on the side of the road. The car hit the ditch straight on, the front wheels in the trench, and the ass of the vehicle high in the air.

Small arms fire was heard, a few bullets striking the car, as Belonev picked up the radio and said, "I need helicopters on the highway now! We are under attack about half way to Jackson."

"Understand you are under attack about half way to Jackson on the east bound lane."

"Correct, and it is a large force."

"Choppers on the way!"

"Tell them to hurry, or they will only find Russian bodies when they get here." Belonev replied, and then stuck the radio in his pocket.

A bullet struck the car and gave a loud *zing* as it ricocheted off into space. Aptekar opened his door, stood, and a bullet from Esom's sniper rifle struck his head, spraying the inside of the car with blood, bone, and chunks of brain. His lifeless body fell into the ditch, with his shattered head near the front tire.

"Sniper on the drivers side! Exit the car on my side, now!" Belonev yelled to be heard over the gunfire. As the three were leaving the car, the last motorcycle pulled up and the driver was dismounting when he was struck by a hail of bullets. His body danced wildly as the hot lead struck him and he gave a loud scream. He fell to the wet pavement and his screams died with him.

Vetrov was scared as he moved over the wet concrete with Galkin behind him, but had the presence of mind to pick up the dead motorcyclist's Bison and ammo as he crawled past the bloody body. Major Galkin pulled the dead man's pistol and two grenades and then rolled into the wet ditch. Belonev pulled the dead man in front of them, so his body offered some cover, but knew it would not stop a bullet.

"When will the helicopters be here?" Vetrov asked.

"Sir, they are coming as fast as they can, but it will take some time." The Master Sergeant replied, and then spotted a target in the brush of the median. He fired a short burst and saw his target fall unnaturally to the ground.

"If they flank us, we are dead." Major Galkin said.

"Sir, you watch our left and Colonel, I would suggest you watch our right side. I will try to keep the front clear, but there must be a hundred guns out there. When either of you get a chance, glance behind us, because we have four areas to cover and there are just three of us."

A bullet struck the ground behind them and all three ducked as it struck.

"I can see nothing in the darkness." Galkin complained.

"Let me get the cyclist's NVG's, perhaps they still work." The Master Sergeant crawled to the dead man's head, removed the goggles and then jerked his hand back quickly when two bullets struck the body. "Try these, Major." He handed the bloody goggles to the officer.

I have movement on my side, but I cannot see anything." Vetrov said, his voice quivering in fear.

Belonev glanced in the direction and said, "They come." He pulled a grenade, removed the tape holding the spoon, and pulled the pin.

His grenade landed in the middle of the group and while the explosion was loud, the screams following were louder. Belonev quickly stood, squeezed a short burst toward the figures on the ground and then dropped back to the ditch.

From the median, a machine-gun opened up, stitching the dirt in front of the ditch as the gunner walked the bullets to the shallow trench. The Major screamed, fell to the water and began to jerk. The Master Sergeant, who was in the middle, grabbed the man and pulled him erect. From his NVG's he saw where a bullet had burned the Majors left arm slightly.

"Sir, your wound is tenuous and if you want to still be alive when the helicopters arrive, use your weapon. Both of you, be sure of a target before you fire. We need to conserve our ammunition or we will be dead before the aircraft get here."

"Contact the helicopters now, Sergeant, and find out where in the hell they are." Vetrov ordered as he fired off toward the left side.

The GM-94 in the hands of Tom fired once again and the car burst into flames.

"Get down, now!" Belonev screamed and then ducked low in the ditch.

"Where are the aircraft!" The Colonel yelled to no one in particular, but the Master Sergeant picked up the radio and asked, "Calling any aircraft."

"Go, I'm one of three helicopters near the ambush site." The pilot could hear guns firing over the radio and assumed it was the Colonel calling.

"What type of helicopters are responding and how soon until you arrive my area?"

"I am one of two Black Sharks, Kamov Ka-50's, and I have a Ka-60 along to pick up the survivors. We should be at the ambush site in about three minutes, sir."

"This is Master Sergeant Belonev, sir, send the two faster aircraft ahead now, because we're taking heavy fire." He knew the Black Sharks were almost a 100 KPH faster than the Ka-60.

"Understand, Sergeant, and will do. Where are you located and where is the fire coming from?"

After giving the pilot their location, as well as the location of unfriendly fire, the gas tank in the car suddenly exploded, throwing flames high into the air and all three men ducked low in the ditch.

"What was that? Are you still there?" The radio came alive.

"The staff car just blew, hurry! The Americans are advancing on our position."

The burning car lighted the area as bright as day, and the partisans heard a whistle and all moved forward. Belonev raised his head slightly and said, "Keep low and fire. The helicopters will be here in a minute or two!" Tracers of green and red were seen crisscrossing in the air overhead.

Vetrov raised his Bison in his hand and squeezed off a long spurt without even looking over the edge of the ditch for a target. The Major raised his head slightly, fired three rounds, and then was knocked back to the ground behind him. Two more bullets struck him at the same time, one in the chest, the other low and in his stomach. He fell to the bottom of the water-filled ditch and screamed.

Belonev suddenly yelled, "Behind us!"

Again, Vetrov raised his weapon and squeezed off a burst. Out of the blue, his Bison flew through the air away from him, and he pulled a bloody hand down screaming. Glancing at his commander, the Master Sergeant saw three or four fingers missing on the hand.

"Sir, you must pull your pistol with your left hand and help me, or we will be dead in a minute or two."

The radio relayed one short sentence, "We have a target rich environment all around you, so lower your heads."

The area around the two live men became alive with 30 mm cannon fire and horrific screams were heard over the sounds of a helicopter firing. Belonev raised his head to help direct the aircraft and saw bodies flying apart as the cannon struck home. Dust filled the air as he picked up the radio and said, "Clear the median, almost center on us, and do it now."

"On the way."

The second helicopter released two missiles, which struck the target dead on, and huge explosions were heard. Belonev scanned the area around him and spotted no movement at all. *Maybe the Americans have withdrawn?* The Sergeant thought.

The cannons in a chopper coughed once more and anything in the median was instantly turned into hamburger meat. No screams were heard, but the attack had been fast and furious, so it was unlikely any victims realized they were in danger, until hit.

"Down the road from us, perhaps a hundred meters, is a sniper; take him out now."

"Will do."

Missiles were fired and the detonations lighted the area well. It was then the light rain turned hard. His NVG's were useless now, so Belonev removed them and seeing the darkness surrounding him, he shuddered in fear. The only light came from the still burning staff car, but it was almost out.

"You will have to inform me of where to place any strikes now, because my on-board thermal gear does not work well in this rain." The pilot said over the radio.

Vetrov snatched the radio from Belonev's hand and asked, "How far out is the rescue helicopter?"

"Less than two minutes. Leave the bodies, but the two of you need to be prepared to run to the helicopter when it lands on the highway. We will be making passes to the sides of you as the rescue aircraft lands."

"When do we move?"

"When I tell you, and then move to the open door on the side of the aircraft. Watch for the gunner, because he may have to fire to cover your approach. Do not rush forward until I give the word, understand?"

"We will wait for your word."

A bullet struck the dead man in front of them, so both Russians knew the Americans were waiting.

"Sir, get lower in the ditch. We don't want to get struck now, not when rescue is on the way."

One helicopter made a dive toward the ground, which the two men in the ditch, as well as the Americans could hear. Cannon fire was heard, but the Americans realized the aircraft had no specific target in mind, because it fired between their position and the Russians. Then it dawned on Willy, *The aircraft was firing to keep any approaches cleared of partisans.*

John, nearest to the highway, saw the inbound rescue aircraft and pulled the LAW from his pack. He carried two, but suspected one would work just fine. He doubted he'd be able to hit one of the faster Black Sharks, so he held his fire and waited for the rescue aircraft to touch down. He extended the tube and waited.

"We are landing straight in front of the burning car, so wait until we order you to move. All communications will be with us from this point forward." The rescue aircraft suddenly said on the radio Vetrov held.

The second Black Shark went into a dive. Belonev watched in fascination as it never pulled up and struck the ground going full speed. The resulting explosion and blast made the rescue chopper wobble violently as the pilot fought the stick to maintain control. The two Russians on the ground were surprised to see the aircraft was only about fifty feet in the air. The area behind the two survivors was as bright as day, and then came the secondary explosions from the crashed Black Shark. With each explosion there came a bright flash of light and then a loud boom.

When the skids touched the highway, the radio blared, "Now, move!"

Colonel Vetrov tossed his weapon, along with the radio, aside and made a mad dash for the aircraft. Master Sergeant Belonev ran toward the aircraft as well, but was in much better shape than the Colonel. He was about to enter the aircraft when Vetrov grabbed him from behind and spun him around, causing him to fall to the ground. The Colonel then screamed as bullets struck the helicopter, "Go, go, go!"

Master Sergeant Belonev, seeing the aircraft raising cursed, "That damned coward. He only cares about his own ass." The aircraft was ten feet in the air now and Belonev waved frantically at the gunner.

"Gunner to pilot, we still have a man on the ground."

"Black Shark, I'm taking heavy fire from the median." The pilot said, and then ignoring the gunner, continued his upward path.

Belonev, seeing the Black Shark lining up for an attack, realized the Americans could see it as well, so he jumped to his feet and made a mad dash for the ditch, jumped it and moved into the woods to the north. He was surprised he'd not been struck, but understood the enemy was likely moving away from the attack coming by moving at right angles. Their self preservation had saved his life.

Cursing the Colonel, and all officers in general, he moved away from the ambush site as slowly and quietly as he could. He gave thanks to God, for the heavy rain, which masked the noise of his movements. He decided once back at the base, he'd file formal charges against Colonel Vetrov and knew the gunner had seen him clearly, because they'd gazed into each others eyes for a few seconds.

Only first, I have to live long enough to return, he thought.

CHAPTER 26

John kneeled, lined up the sights on the LAW and then squeezed the rubber-covered trigger. He watched, intrigued, as the aircraft was struck right behind the pilots door. With the explosion, a man fell free of the chopper to land on the pavement, his body *smacking* as it struck hard. The pilots door and a body fell a split-second later, landing near the burning staff car. The aircraft began to rotate 360 degrees as someone, most likely the man in the right seat, fought a losing battle for control.

The other Black Shark, on an approach for the median, began to spit 23mm bullets at trees and grass between the two highways. People screamed and John was knocked to his ass when something struck him on the side of the head. Sandra screamed and ran for him. The aircraft flew over the median and then banked sharply to repeat his run.

The rescue chopper suddenly dropped like a rock and fell into the trees just north of the highway, where it burst into an immense fireball. Huge flames rolled inside of each other as they moved for the sky. Come dawn, all that would remain would be the tail and the badly burned remains of the co-pilot and two gunners.

Seeing the rescue bird crash and burn, the last Black Shark aborted his approach and turned for home. The rain was coming down in buckets now as Willy stood from the grasses nearest the road and yelled, "Make sure the dead Russians stay that way! Then, collect our wounded and let's get out of here."

He walked to the dead man who'd fallen from the aircraft, turned on his flashlight and grinned when he saw it was a full Colonel. The large three stars on the yellow board, with the two red stripes, confirmed his rank. Vetrov's head was severely injured on impact with the concrete, but Willy pushed the man's mouth open with his right boot and then leaning forward, placed an ace of spades in the dead man's mouth. *May you rot in hell, you murdering sonofabitch*, he thought.

Esom appeared from the darkness and said, "One man escaped north, moving toward the base. It was raining so hard, even using the night vision sight I couldn't get a clear shot. He was a Master Sergeant."

"Small change for what we were after, so let him go. His getting away may just spread the fear of us a bit, which can only help."

Tom neared and said, "We have over twenty dead and about a bakers dozen injured, including John, who took a rock to the side of his head. Sandra thinks a round knocked the rock in the air, striking him."

"Will he live?"

"She swears he'll recover in a few days. But, my experience tells me a head injury can go either way."

"He's a brave man and has twice downed a chopper, so prepare a litter and bring him out with us. Are any of our injured unable to move under their own power?"

"All can walk, even the one with a sucking chest wound claimed he'd walk out under his own power."

"Take any gear we can find in this weather, herd the troops in close, and let's go home. We've had a busy night. I'm sure this rain will remove all traces of our tracks so make a beeline straight to our encampment."

Back at camp, Sandra placed John beside Dolly, who moved to him and put her head on his thigh. She then squatted by the big dog, petted her a few times to let her know all was well, and then said, "He'll be fine, girl. He took a glancing blow from a rock to his noggin. He should be up and around by tomorrow at some point, which is more than I can say about you."

Top entered the room and asked, "Did John come around? I thought I heard you talking to someone."

Sandra gave a tired laugh and said, "Dolly. She's worried about him, because she can smell the blood."

"Don't laugh, critters have more sense than most people I know. She knows he's hurt and she's scared for him. He's like a father to her, always fussing over her food, water, and comfort. I'll bet you she keeps her head there until he comes around."

Sandra nodded in the dim light of a small candle.

Top said, "You need to eat something and then get some sleep. We may have to move in the morning."

"I figured as much. But how will the Russians react to the fact we killed an important Colonel and they lost two choppers, a staff car and had at least eight or nine dead?"

"How do I think they'll react? They'll be pissed, and I'm sure they'll murder some more of our people to show us just how damned mad they really are. They're a brutal bunch, but you know that by now. This is enough talk. I want you to drink some water, eat, wash up, and then get some sleep."

Morning dawned with more rain, and it was heavy at times. The old house leaked and a number of containers were positioned around the floors to collect the leaking water. John was awake, but wasn't his old self, complaining of a headache and blurred vision, which Sandra knew was normal for a head injury. She gave him a Lortab 10-500, which would kill his pain, but not put him to sleep as fast as morphine would. If they needed to move, she wanted him alert and ready.

Dolly had spent a good five minutes licking his face and hands when he'd sat up, and the love between the two filled Sandra's heart with warmth. It was such a cold and horrible time to be alive, so any affection was rare. She loved John with all her soul and knew he loved her as well, but they hadn't had the place to show their love for each other in some time.

Once the medication was working, John smiled and asked, "Could you bring Willy to me? I'm afraid if I try to stand I'll fall on my ass."

Ten minutes later, Willy was sitting on the floor beside John and they were talking about a possible move, which both knew would have to happen now. Sooner or later, the Russians would learn where they were located.

"So," Willy asked, "this place in the swamp is okay, you think?"

"Better than most. They might blow the place up with rockets, missiles or bombs, but ground troops will never find it. There must be a thousand turns leading to the place and if you take the wrong one, you'll never find it. See, none of the trails are on maps and the top of the house is covered with moss and grasses from over the years. It wouldn't even show on a satellite photo. "

Mollie, who'd been sitting across the room walked to them and then asked, "Are you talkin' 'bout the old Parkerman place?"

"Yep, I am." John said.

Margie, who was sitting up against the wall said, "I spent a week there one night. Heard and saw all kinds of strange shit, but nothing I could identify."

"Bullshit, Margie." John said, chuckled, and then asked, "How well do you know the place, Mollie?"

"I know a good dozen trails leadin' to it, because my man used to hunt gators back in there. I heard tell the place has haunts in it, so I ain't never been inside the place, no sir, not me. I heard that over fifty slaves were kilt there durin' the war of Union Aggression and they still move around that old house at night, lookin' fer revenge is what I heard."

"What kind of shape is the roof and basic structure in?" Willy asked.

"About like this place. It'll leak, but only when it rains pretty hard. I'd guess over half the windows are out, due to folk shooting at them before the fall. I think it's the safest place for us, only we'll have to mine the trails, mark the trails leading to the place, and educate our people about both. If not, the first patrol we send out will never get back."

"The question I really have is this; Do you think our people can mark the trails in some manner so only our folks will know which way to turn? Hell, we can't send a guide with them on every mission and even if we did, if the guide died they'd be screwed."

"We can figure that all out later, if you want to give the place a try."

"I like the idea, myself, but let me run it by Top first and see what he thinks."

"Well," Mollie said, "I don't like the idea worth a tinkers damn. Only I guess I ain't got much say in the move, huh?"

"Nope." Willy said, and then grinned.

John asked, "Mollie, do you really believe in ghosts and such?"

Her eyes grew large as she said, "Yes, suh, I surely do, don't ya?"

"No, I guess I don't, but you're entitled to your thoughts and feelings, so I won't laugh at you like some will if they hear you talk about it."

"I don't give a damn, and I mean that. Folks have been laughin' at me since I was a little kid and it don't bother me no more. First, I ain't pretty like most women and second, I don't talk good. See, I never got much education, because my daddy didn't think a woman was made for anything other than havin' a passel of kids. So my brothers got to go to school, while I stayed home and took care of the little ones. Then, as soon as I could, I got married up and out of that place. I loved my daddy, but his thinkin' was bass ackwards at times."

"I'm going to call a meeting and we'll discuss your swamp house. I'm sure most will like the idea, because I damned sure do. If it'll be hard for us to find the place, it'll be pure hell on the Russians."

Belonev realized after he'd covered less than a mile, he'd taken a wound to his back, but it was minor. The rains soaked him and he had no idea if the injury was bleeding or not, but he felt no weakness, so he kept moving. Each time he thought of Vetrov pushing him out of the way and then leaving him behind, the more he felt the man deserved his horrible death. *That sonofabitch thought only of himself, but he did not know that by pushing me to the ground, he was saving my life. Thank you, Lord, for saving me*, he thought as he moved.

The rains were less now, so he could see better, but mud was ankle deep. *I need to look for tripwires or mines as I move, or I can still end up dead. All others in the car dead but me, and is not that strange? Folks used to laugh at my prayers, telling me there was no God, well, I am proof today that there is a God. I am coming Alena, my wife, and we'll soon make that old farm work. I want to work hard on my farm, make enough money to live on, and sip vodka as I sit in my rocking chair. I am too old to be a soldier now. I must survive.*

As the sun came up, Belonev saw the road to the camp off his left side, so he changed direction. "This is the road from the town of Edwards, so I am close."

He stepped from the brush, frowned at the muddy road, and then started moving toward the base. His back was hurting him now; the slight throbbing he'd initially experienced was replaced with a deep pain. He had morphine in his first aid kit, but knew if he used the drug he'd be unable to travel. His uniform was filthy, covered in mud, blood, grease from the guns, and even scorched from the car fire. He looked down at his filthy hands and suspected his face was no cleaner. *It is hard to be clean, when you have to fight in a pigsty, with two pigs.*

His vision was blurred and he felt weak, as if his body had no power or energy. *It is the blood loss*, he thought, but he couldn't reach the injured position alone. Suddenly, he fell to his knees in the mud and his world grew black. He never felt his body fall to the muddy road.

"Master Sergeant Belonev, can you hear me?" An unknown voice asked.

He opened his eyes and discovered he was in the hospital.

"I hear you," he replied.

"I am your doctor, and you have been injured in battle with the Americans. Your back took a bullet, from side to side, and a vertebrae has been seriously damaged. You have a burn on the right side of your face and numerous small cuts and bruises."

"How long will I be here?"

"Do you mean here at this base or in the army?"

"I do not understand, Doctor."

"Your days in the army are finished, due to your back injury. I doubt, once healed, you would be able to carry a pack over fifty meters before you would have to stop. You will suffer from back pain the remainder of your life, but you have enough years on active duty to retire. Along with your retirement pension, you will receive a slight disability payment each month. I hope to have you on the next aircraft out of here and on your way back to Moscow. It will not be a straight flight, I am afraid, but a series of hops on different aircraft, until you get to the east coast of this Godforsaken country."

"What will my retirement rank be, sir? I need another six months of active duty before I have enough time in grade to retire as a master sergeant."

"Well, I cannot be sure, but the word I had earlier this morning is your rank will be Junior Lieutenant, and you have been submitted for the Order of Saint George, 4th class, for your personal bravery, courage and valor, which allowed us to defeat a strong partisan force. Major Usov, the pilot in the lone surviving Black Shark, recommended your immediate promotion, which was approved, and did the paperwork for the medal. However, the medal will take some time before it is approved, I am sorry to say."

"Sir, I have no education and cannot be a Lieutenant. As for the military action, I do not think we won the fight; after all, Colonel Vetrov died. How do they figure I deserve a medal for just doing my job? Or, do you think Moscow is desperate for heroes here?"

Moving his hand, as if swatting a fly, the Doctor said, "You will be medically discharged, so do not worry about your battlefield promotion, regardless of the reason it happened. It will mean your retirement pension and disability payment will almost double. As a retired Lieutenant, you will only wear the uniform at odd times, so an education is not needed. Major Usov said when you were on the radio to him, you did all the coordination for ground action with the two attack helicopters. He also saw you leading the two officers while defending a ditch. He stated that once the Colonel came on the radio, he could hear the man's fear and confusion. You are now a Russian hero, Lieutenant."

"I will be damned."

The doctor laughed and said, "Now, let me give you some morphine to kill the pain and you need to get some more sleep. Later today, you will be moved into a single room, which as you know is a benefit of the officer class. Congratulations on both the promotion and submission for the medal. I think you deserve both."

"Thank you, sir."

"Now, I have to make my other rounds." the Doctor said and then walked from the room.

A Senior Sergeant, in a bed near the window, with his leg in a cast and in traction said, "Well done, sir."

"Sir? Now that is going to take some getting used to, I think. What is your name?"

"I am Senior Sergeant Tikhokhod, sir, and was injured by a booby-trap. As senior non-commissioned officers, we both know how the game is played. It is more than likely you deserve both the promotion and medal, but then again, Moscow may be looking for a hero. I left Russia just a little over a month ago and from what I could tell, this war is not going well for us. I suspect they will wine and dine you for a year and then put you out to pasture for the remainder of your life."

Belonev grunted and asked, "What do you mean, wine and dine me?"

"Sir, they need a real hero and you are it, I think. Your story will be in all the newspapers, both in print and online, you will be on the television, and they will have you doing public speaking. They will milk all the propaganda they can from your bravery and then send you home all used up."

"Well, I do not give a shit what they do. I survived, while many others did not, and they can give me a medal and promotion if they want. Just surviving this hellhole is enough for me. I will do what I am told and then return to my wife and take up life as a civilian."

Senior Sergeant Tikhokhod reached under his pillow and pulled out a pint of Vodka. He tossed the almost full bottle to Belonev, grinned and said, "I was teasing you with the sir, Master Sergeant, so have a drink."

Belonev took a long drink of the clear alcohol and then tossed the bottle back to the Senior Sergeant. He gave his new promotion some thought; *The base pay for a lieutenant is 20,000 rubles a month, at which I can retire with 40 percent of that as income. I will draw an additional 10 percent because I worked with classified information so, before my disability payment, I will make close to 10,000 rubles a month. As a Master Sergeant, my base retirement would have been around 3,250 rubles a month. That's a pay increase of almost three times as much as a master sergeant and that is a big deal. Of course, I will not know how much my disability will pay until I meet a medical board.*

"What are you thinking on over there?" the Sergeant asked.

"Not much. I am getting sleepy and think the morphine is starting to work, or the vodka."

"Best of luck to you, Master Sergeant Belonev, in the future, and thank you for your service. I suspect they will move you to a private room shortly. They do not like having officers in rooms with enlisted swine." The Sergeant chuckled at his own humor.

CHAPTER 27

At the swamp house, Willy was grinning from ear to ear, and shaking his head. "By God, this place is perfect for our headquarters. It'd take the Russians fifty years to find this place on foot."

"Choppers can see tracks on the trails and smoke from fires, so we'll still have to be careful." Tom said.

"Lawdy," Willy said as he walked to the large window in the living room, "I walked here with you, John, but ain't no way in hell I could walk out on my own. More twists and turns than a rattlesnake. You're right, Tom, we need to sweep our trails clean and watch for smoke from our fires."

John said, "I have teams out now laying mines and making booby-traps. They're also marking any intersections along the trails so we will know which trail to follow. Out here, and this is no joke, if you get lost, you have a better than average chance of experiencing a poisonous snakebite or having a gator eat your ass alive."

Willy sat on the floor, near the window and said, "I've a team upstairs now placing a heavy machine-gun and turning the place into an observation post for us. It's the highest place around and while the floor is weak, it'll do the job. I don't want more than three men up there at a time, because much of the flooring has rotted. I want a sniper, machine-gunner, and an ammo man. No others."

"What kind of machine-gun do you have?"

"We have an M-60, but I've placed a Kord upstairs. It's a belt fed- "

"It's the latest heavy duty machine-gun the Russians use. I'm aware of it and have captured a few, too." John replied.

Sandra, who'd been quiet, suddenly said, "I'm concerned about malaria, West Nile, or other mosquito borne viruses or illnesses. This may be a good place to hide, but I suspect we'll have some fevers after being here a week or so."

"Do we have any malaria tablets?" Willy asked.

"I have a few, but not enough to treat everyone that will likely come down with a fever. West Nile might just kill their ass, too, if they get it, because it's rough to treat even in a hospital."

"Tom, put the word out to all cells that anyone that finds or has any malaria medications to turn it over to Sandra. When we hit Russian convoys, look for malaria medications or even quinine. I can write the few different words out in Russian, so our people know what to look for on the markings on the boxes. I never thought of malaria, but your point is well taken."

Tom grinned and said, "The menu just went up, too, because gator and snake are good eating. Hell, I saw enough gators on the way here to feed us for a year."

"There are some big fish in this place too, but you'd think the gators would have eaten all of them by now, huh?"

Willy chuckled and then said, "All gear, supplies, and ammunition will need to be stored on the ground floor, for quick use. We buried a great deal of stuff near the house we just left, in the floor under the barn, dead center, too. I don't want to risk losing it all if we have to run from here one day. Now, I saw some big trees on the way to this location, so let's place some snipers in them and get them as close to the mines as we can. That way if a man is seriously injured by a mine, maybe we can shoot two or three of the others coming to give him first aid. And don't just place the snipers on the actual trail that leads here, or they'll figure that out eventually. Place them on dead-end trails or those that meander all over the place as well."

"Who in the hell wants to spend all day in a tree?" Margie asked.

"They'll spend three days out and then two days here, so they'll not get bored. We'll also alternate trees, so they'll get a different view on each trip out to the bush."

"Willy," John said, "I hate to bring this up, because I know you dislike the subject, but when are some additional people arriving? We lost a lot of people killing that Russian Colonel."

Shaking his head, Willy replied, "I've sent the word out for some of the cells to come in and report to me. The problem seems to be, well, with the increase in Russian patrols and resulting fights, some of the units aren't where they used to be located. They've been forced to relocate for survival."

"Any idea when we'll have more folks join us?"

"Week to two weeks at best, but maybe as long as a month."

John nodded and then closed his eyes. He was tired and felt as if he hadn't slept well in years. He knew they were as safe as it ever got in occupied America, but he had a nagging feeling of doom, and while he could see no reason for it, it was there all the same.

Finally, he spoke of his feelings to Willy and expected laughter, but it didn't come.

"John, I ain't sure, but you've family ties to this old place and it's possible, since you know what happened to your ancestor, you feel it can happen to you, too. Well, it damned sure could happen to you, but then again, maybe nothing will happen. I respect the feelings a man gets and more than once my feelings have kept me alive."

Esom ran into the house, looked around and spotting Willy he said, "Reports indicate a large group of Russians, maybe five hundred men, fixin' to enter the swamps from the South side."

"Return, Esom, and tell our men to fall back to within a mile of this place. How many booby-traps or mines been placed?"

"Nigh on half, but that's a wild ass guess."

"Return and spread the word."

As soon as Esom left, Willy met John's eyes and asked, "Do you know what this means?"

"Of course I know what it means, and it's not good. There is absolutely no way the Russians can know we're here, except one way."

"What does it mean?" Sandra asked.

Willy's eyes narrowed as he slowly looked at each person and then said, "It means we have a traitor among us, but who?"

The End of Book 2

Coming Fall 2014

THE FALL OF AMERICA

Book 3
Renegade American

- EBOOKS -

The Fall of America: Book 1
*Kindle, Nook, iBooks, Kobo
& Smashwords*

The Fall of America: Book 2
Available for the Kindle

ABOUT THE AUTHOR

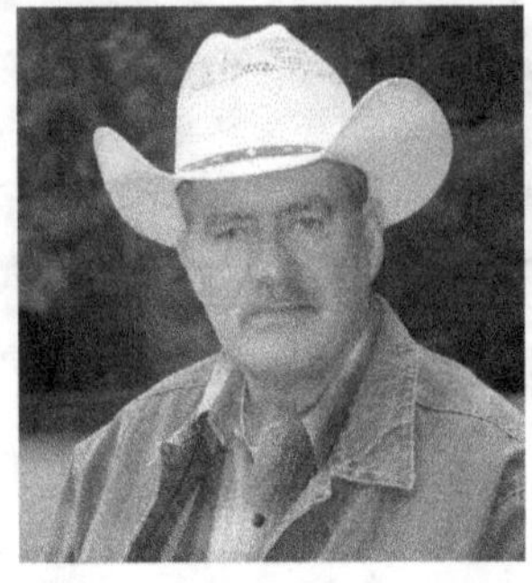 **W.R Benton**, a pen name, is a retired U.S. military senior Non-commissioned Officer with over twenty-six years of active duty service. He grew up in the Missouri Ozark Mtns., where hunting, trapping, camping, and other outdoor activities were the norm. Additionally, he spent more than twelve years teaching survival and parachuting procedures to U.S. Air Force personnel as a Life Support instructor. Mister Benton has an Associate's Degree in Search and Rescue, Survival Operations, a Bachelors Degree in Occupational Safety and Health, and a Masters Degree in Psychology near completion.

Mister Benton is a member of the America Authors Association (AAA). You can visit W.R. Benton online http://www.wrbenton.net or his War Paint Site at http://www.warpaint.info.

Visit him on Facebook at
www.facebook.com/wrbenton01

On a trip to the Lake Clark area of the Alaskan bush, a sudden arctic weather system forces down the small plane of Dr. Jim Wade, and his son David. Both have survived the crash, but not unscathed. Food, fire and shelter are all a priority. Following the death of his father, now it is up to David to figure out what to do next, and how to survive, on a remote Alaskan mountain—in winter!

This is a fictional story of survival, resilience and of the spirit to live. It is both authentic and accurate, having been written by a former Air Force life support survival instructor. For ages 10 and up

Both are available at Amazon and other online bookstores

Set adrift, a family of three are cast out to sea in a rubber raft, where they must find a way to conquer one terrifying tragedy after another or die in the process.

In this gripping story of survival everyone will be tested to their limits. Christian faith and hope are hallmarks of this tale that will touch your heart..